KATHY SWAAR

Sophie

For Bill,

who saw in me things I did not,

and never stopped encouraging me to

"quit my day job and write."

Sophie by Kathy Swaar

Published by Kathy Swaar

Visit the author's website at www.kathyswaar.com

Cover designed by MiblArt www.miblart.com

Interior design by Susi Clark www.creativeblueprintdesign.com

Editorial services by:
Hannah Bauman www.btleditorial.com
Carly Catt www.cattediting.com
Ellen Polk www.ellenedits.com

ISBN Paperback 978-1-7358079-2-8
ISBN Ebook 978-1-7358079-3-5

First Edition

Prologue

t was a clear day in April 1824 when Charlotte Sophia Kraemler made her entrance into the world. The mid-morning sun shone brightly in the cloudless azure sky, illuminating the countryside in golden light. To her parents, Joseph and Margarethe, that blue patch of sky was one of the few things in their lives that was clear. The decade preceding Sophie's birth had been one of upheaval, and with those shifting political sands came new alliances, allegiances, and governments. Founded by Napoleon Bonaparte, the Kingdom of Westphalia was part of the first French Empire from 1807–1813. While it was almost impossible to be part of the French Empire without absorbing some French sensibilities, their families had inhabited this region for generations before Napoleon arrived, and Margarethe never felt French. The 1815 Congress of Vienna changed everything all over again, creating the *Province* of Westphalia from at least five other territories, none of which she felt any affinity for or kinship to. Who were they, really? Were they French? Were they Prussian? Were they simply Westphalians, whoever and whatever that was? Margarethe didn't know. What she did know was that radical change had become a way of life for them, and she detested it.

Propped on a sea of pillows in the bedroom she shared with Joseph and grateful for some solitude and silence following the exertion and cacophony of childbirth, Margarethe carefully studied the features of her newborn daughter, just two hours old. Unlike Margarethe's own mother, she did not hold the opinion that every baby was beautiful. She believed without question that each child was a miracle, a gift from the Creator, but personal experience had taught her that not every infant was attractive in the conventional sense, particularly in the first few days of life. Her firstborn, Carl, had been scrawny, red faced, and lumpy headed for weeks. But Sophie—Sophie was stunningly beautiful. She had inquisitive cornflower-blue eyes, flawless skin, cherubic and perfectly proportioned features. On first sight, Margarethe abandoned the thought of using her daughter's forename, instead choosing a form of her middle name that, to her, seemed much more elegant and fitting for this bright-eyed beauty. "Charlotte" and its familiar form "Lottie" seemed too staid and stodgy, "Sophia" much too formal and strait laced. Regardless of what was written in the baptismal record in the Gutersloh Evangelical Church register, to Margarethe, this child was always and forever Sophie.

Ach, my sweet girl! What kind of a world have we brought you into?

Margarethe was worried, as any mother with young children would be in the face of such uncertain times. There was a gnawing sense of fear and foreboding in the air that had crept into her heart and lodged there, growing by the day. How long would it be before the government changed again, before another king or general or emperor or prince decided he knew better how to rule them than the one currently in power? A year? Or, God forbid, only a few weeks or months? And when it happened again, would there be any hope of a peaceful transition, or would they be thrust into armed conflict, with every town and berg a war zone, every farm and vale a battleground? Would her children have any chance at all at a normal life, or was her son destined to wear a uniform, stand a post, and shoot to kill? Would her daughter—her darling Sophie—have any chance of being anything but a war widow? And what would be left if and when the fighting finally stopped? Crops did not grow well in scorched earth, Margarethe knew, and the thought of not having enough food to feed her family terrified her.

Maggie, Maggie! she chided herself. *Where is your faith?* It dawned on her that at the root of all this angst and worry were those nagging questions of identity and belonging—of who they were and where they fit (or didn't, as the case may be). The longer she gazed into her newborn daughter's angelic face, the more compelling those questions became. Keenly aware of how her mood and demeanor affected those closest to her, Margarethe was concerned her fears might be imprinted on young Sophie's psyche. That would never do. *I can fret myself into an early grave, or I can choose to trust. Who I am does not matter so much so long as I remember Whose I am.*

She pulled Sophie close. "It will be all right, sweet girl," Margarethe whispered. "Somehow, some way, everything will be all right."

Years later, when asked what she remembered most about her mother, Sophie answered without hesitation: "her fierce optimism." It was on display daily as Sophie grew from childhood into a young adult in their large, boisterous household. She and older brother Carl were followed in quick succession by siblings Carl Friedrich in 1826, Wilhelmina in 1828, twins Christian Heinrich and Heinrich Wilhelm in 1831, August Friedrich in 1836, Catharine in 1839, and Friedrich Georg in 1842. And yet, no matter the circumstance, Margarethe was even tempered and soft spoken, always focused on what could be, rather than what was not. She was generous and kind, preferring to instruct rather than criticize, and was the very soul of fairness, no small feat in a household of nine children. When sorrow did strike—when Catharine died in 1843 just four months shy of her fourth birthday and Friedrich Georg died just over a year later at only eighteen months of age—she faced it with grace. Even while acknowledging that her heart was broken beyond mending, she would yet insist that "somehow, some way, everything will be all right." Sophie marveled at that fortitude, that faith, that level of acceptance, that defiant hope, that sheer strength of will every time she saw it.

Chapter One

How can she be so calm? Not a sob—not even a tear! I could never be like that if one of my children died. Never!" Sophie confided to her sister Wilhelmina as they waited for Pastor Schilling to arrive on the day of Catharine's death. Now nearly twenty, Sophie had her mother's well-defined sense of fairness and justice, but none of Margarethe's reticence or equanimity. When presented with circumstances that smacked of being unfair, Sophie took it as her personal responsibility to bring them to the attention of anyone she thought could address and correct them. It was admirable, but not always prudent. The pastor was nonplussed (and her parents mortified) when he arrived at the door and was greeted by Sophie demanding to know how God could have allowed such a horrible thing to happen, pressing him for an explanation for "why my baby sister had to die." To his credit, the poor man tried, but neither the church's doctrine of original sin nor the words of Job in Scripture proved satisfactory to Sophie.

"It isn't fair!" she railed. "My parents' hearts are broken, and my sister is gone before she ever had a chance to have a life! Original sin? How dare you! She was just a baby—not even four years old! She had not lived long enough to do anything sinful! 'The Lord gaveth and the Lord hath taken away; blessed be the Name of the Lord?' I thought God was supposed to be good all the time. There is nothing good about taking Catharine away. It is just plain mean!"

"Sophie!" There was an uncharacteristically sharp edge to her mother's voice. "Pastor Schilling is here to help. It is not polite to speak to him that way. Please apologize, then take Mina and go to your room. Papa and I need to make arrangements for Catharine's funeral."

"I am sorry, pastor," Sophie muttered through gritted teeth. "Please, forgive me. If you will excuse me, my sister and I must go upstairs." She fixed Pastor Schilling with one more withering glare before grabbing thirteen-year-old Mina by the hand and trudging up the stairs. Once in their room, she flung herself on the bed and dissolved in a fit of weeping.

"Do not worry, Sophie." Mina sat down beside Sophie, wrapping her in a hug. "This will never happen to you." Mina had no idea what Sophie's future held, or her own, or anyone else's for that matter. What she did know was that emotional outbursts and conflict of any kind unnerved her; she was willing to try anything to quiet Sophie's weeping and stem the tide of her wrath. "Mama is right," Mina said, calm certainty and authority in her voice. "It will be all right."

"No, it will not!" Sophie stubbornly insisted. "How can things be all right when your baby sister is dead and no one will tell you why?"

"I do not know, Sophie. I just know what Mama says. Maybe sometimes things just happen."

"You sound like that stupid pastor! According to him, God is in charge of everything. But if that is true, then why did Catharine not get well? We prayed hard enough! And it was not just us. The whole town and half the countryside prayed for Catharine, too. Was God just not listening? Did He not care? If the Almighty loves us so much, why does He just let people die?"

"Maybe it is not that He 'just lets people die.' Maybe there are reasons why these things happen, but it is not for us to know or understand them right now."

"Well, I cannot think of a single good reason for this."

"Why does it bother you so much? You were not this upset when Grandpapa and Grandmama died."

"They were old. Old people are supposed to die. Not babies like Catharine."

Mina knew that look: the set of Sophie's jaw, the icy glint in those blue eyes. Her sister was as stubborn as their mother was longsuffering. It was obvious Sophie was not going to change her mind about this. Time to change the subject and move on.

"So, did you talk to Friedrich today? Papa said he was in the shop."

"What if I did?" Sophie snapped.

Mina sighed. This was not going well. Sophie could be light, airy, funny, and warm; she could also be outspoken, intense, moody, and prone to lashing out. "Headstrong and high-strung" was how Papa described her, and Papa would know. He worked with horses every day. Mina had hoped bringing up Friedrich would distract her sister from her anger at the pastor and her sorrow over Catharine's death. Instead, it made things worse. Her sister's love life—or more accurately the lack thereof—was a sore subject.

Sophie wanted more than anything to find her very own prince charming, someone who would sweep her off her feet in a whirlwind fairytale-style romance. Friedrich Rieple, she was sure, could be that charming prince. He was handsome and well-groomed, with raven hair and piercing blue eyes as deep as the ocean. Solicitous and attentive, he showered her with kindness and compliments each time they spoke but, to her great dismay, had done nothing else. Even though he seemed to be genuinely interested in her, he had not spoken to Papa about formally calling on her, which Sophie found infuriating. She saw him as often as she could find an excuse to, but it was never often enough. Papa and Mama thought otherwise, of course. In their minds she was still much too young to even think about suitors or being in a serious relationship.

"I am sorry, Sophie." Mina sighed again. "I did not mean to upset you. It will be all right. Things with Friedrich will work out. You will see."

"If you say 'it will be all right' one more time, I am going to scream. Now leave me alone!"

Sophie had, in fact, spoken to Friedrich, but after everything else that had happened that afternoon, she doubted it mattered. She had gone to the livery stable over the noon hour to keep an eye on things so Papa could go home for his midday meal and check on Catharine and Mama. Catharine had been sick for days, and everyone was becoming alarmed. When Friedrich walked in and saw Sophie at the counter instead of Joseph, he asked at once about Catharine's condition.

"She is no worse today, I don't think," Sophie had told him. "But she is not better either. I am very concerned about her. And about Mama and Papa, too."

She hadn't meant to cry; she wanted more than anything to appear level headed and capable in front of this man she cared so much about, but she couldn't stop the tears that welled up in her eyes as she described the fever that wouldn't break, the painful ulcers in Catharine's mouth that kept her from eating and drinking, the endless wheezing and coughing, and the blotchy red spots that covered her small body. To her surprise, Friedrich reached up, cupped her chin, tipped her face toward his, and gazed into her eyes for several seconds.

"My poor, dear Sophie," he said, offering her his handkerchief. "How sad it is for all of you that Catharine is so ill. My family and I are, of course, praying for her complete recovery, but in the meantime, I will speak to your father and see if there is anything I can do to be of help to you." Friedrich tipped his hat and bowed and was out of the shop in an instant.

He is going to speak to Papa and see if there is anything he can do to help us? He is not a doctor! What could he possibly do? Unless . . . Unless he was not going to speak to Papa about Catharine . . .

Sophie was lost in delicious thoughts of what else Friedrich might have in mind to speak to Papa about when their neighbor Mrs. Schmidt burst into the shop.

"Go home, Sophie! Catharine is getting worse by the second. She is barely breathing. Hurry, as fast as you can! I will look after things here."

Sophie bolted out the front door, not even taking time to close it behind her. But even before she reached the front steps of their home, just down the block, Catharine had slipped away.

Chapter Two

Sophie was a whirlwind of emotions: distraught beyond consolation, weepy and morose, frightened and angry. In spite of what she'd said to Mina earlier, she was well aware of the fact that infants and children died all the time both in their neighborhood and in the surrounding countryside. The prevalence of diseases like measles, cholera, and pneumonia combined with limited medical knowledge and few effective treatments made this a grim reality. But up until now, it had always been someone else's brother or sister. She'd never had to deal with the loss of a sibling personally, and she found it terrifying. Who was next? Was it her? One of the twins? Baby Friedrich? God forbid, Mina? *Dear God in Heaven, not Mina, please*, she begged. *How would I ever survive without the one person in the whole world I can confide in?* She hated having this gut-wrenching grief visited upon her family, hated seeing her mother and even her father cry, and hated above all else the prospect of having to wear black for an entire year. How in the world could she ever hope to secure Friedrich's affections dressed like someone's aged grandmother?

She heard the door to Catharine's room close and counted the steps as Papa walked across the hallway and stopped at the foot of the stairs.

"Sophie," he called, "please come down and help your mother."

She'd been dreading those words. She knew what her mother needed help with—preparing her sister's body for her funeral and burial tomorrow. Steeling herself as best she could, she drug herself off the bed and went downstairs. She helped her mother spread a sheet on the dining room table, then backed away as Papa carried Catharine's lifeless form from her sickbed down the hall and gently laid her down. Tears streamed silently down Sophie's face as she helped her mother carefully remove Catharine's nightgown and undergarments and bathe her, the steaming water a cold comfort in the face of this heartbreaking loss. They worked methodically, without speaking, tenderly drying and dressing Catharine in her best Sunday frock, then combing her platinum curls and meticulously arranging them halo-like around her pale, cherubic face.

Finished at last, Sophie watched her mother gently caress Catharine's cheek, then bend to kiss her forehead one last time. "I will miss you, my angel," Margarethe murmured. "May you rest peacefully in the arms of our Savior, until I see you again."

Overcome by her own grief plus the sadness she felt for her mother, Sophie buried her head in her hands and sobbed. Margarethe pulled her close. Hugging her tightly, she promised once again, "It will be all right, sweet girl. We are all heartbroken, but we will find a way to get through this. Somehow, some way, everything will be all right." She wiped Sophie's tears with her apron. "Come, now. Help me get things cleaned up and the table set. Mr. Schmidt is on his way to help Papa take Catharine to the church and we need to have supper ready for them when they get back."

Sophie nodded wordlessly and began clearing away the basins and cloths.

Moments later, the Schmidts let themselves in the back door. Papa and Mr. Schmidt left to complete their sad errand while Mrs. Schmidt bustled about the kitchen helping Margarethe, slicing strudel and rye bread, laying out bratwurst, and mixing up a vinegar dressing for the roasted beet salad. Sophie busied herself putting a fresh tablecloth on the dining room table, setting plates, silverware, and napkins at each place, and trying not to think. That proved to be impossible. Tomorrow was going to be the worst day of her life, followed by an entire year of worst days, each one draped in black from top to bottom, from beginning to end. She could not even imagine how she was going to manage to sit through Catharine's funeral. *Perhaps the service will not last too long,* she told herself. But of course, that was wishful thinking. Just getting everyone into and out of the church would take nearly forever. Papa was a prominent businessman in the area, and Catharine was young and innocent, beloved by everyone who knew her. The entire population of Rheda and the surrounding countryside, plus half of Weidenbruck would be there.

Yes, she thought, a sudden burst of joy lightening her heart and bringing a smile to her face. *Everyone will be there. Including Friedrich.*

Low, steel-gray clouds threatened rain as Sophie and her family made their way to the church the next morning. It was late April 1843, the week after Easter, yet spring had not fully arrived in Rheda. The tiniest of buds were swelling on the branches of trees and shrubs, and the flowering bulbs were beginning to peek out of the ground, but the air was still raw and chilly. Sophie shivered as she waited to take her seat in the pews reserved for the family in the front of the sanctuary, reluctant to remove her heavy woolen wrap. *We will freeze to death at the cemetery,* she thought miserably, *if we have not already frozen before we even leave the church!*

Pastor Schilling droned on and on—in no particular order—about eternity and faith, original sin, the wrath of God, the hope of Resurrection, how important it was to have been baptized and have secured one's salvation, to be an active part of the church and to be faithful in all things, because, as Catharine's circumstance so aptly illustrated, one did not know just how soon one might be called to one's heavenly home. Exhausted by the level of concentration it took to follow his meandering words, Sophie slumped in her seat. Just when she thought she could not possibly sit still for one more second, Pastor Schilling intoned the closing prayer. As the last *amen* echoed through the sanctuary, they rose and filed out behind the small wooden coffin borne by the elders of the church, accompanying Catharine's body to her final resting place.

After a few brief remarks at the gravesite, Pastor Schilling pronounced the benediction. Teeth chattering, frozen fingers clutching her shawl tightly around her shoulders, Sophie waited her turn to throw a handful of earth onto Catharine's casket. When at last they were done, she turned to leave. Blinded by tears and anxious to get in out of the cold, she stumbled over a tree root, plunging headlong into someone's—she presumed another mourner's—arms.

"Oh, my! I am so sorry!" She looked up to see Friedrich had caught her.

"Sophie! Are you all right?" he asked, gripping her shoulders to steady her. "I was hoping I would have a chance to speak to you. Please, forgive me if this is an inappropriate time. I just wanted to personally convey to you how very sorry I am that it was not possible for Catharine to recover."

"Of course," she said, straightening her shawl and smoothing her skirt. "Thank you so much." She intended to meet Friedrich's gaze with a warm and gracious smile, but the second her eyes met his, the tears started again and would not stop. The more she fought to regain her composure, the more uncontrollably she wept. *What am I going to do? Papa and Mama would be furious with me for making a public spectacle of myself, and I am sure Friedrich finds my weeping repulsive as well.*

"Forgive me!" she begged, barely able to choke out the words.

"My dear Sophie, there is nothing to forgive," Friedrich assured her, his voice gentle and comforting, compassion in his eyes. "To be overcome with grief on the loss of your beloved baby sister is completely understandable. And I am sure losing your footing just now frightened you as well. Please, let me help you."

Taking her arm, Friedrich carefully led her away from the other mourners. When they were out of sight and earshot, sheltered under the massive branches of an ancient oak, he stopped and wrapped his arms around her, pulling her close. His concern for her well-being and the tenderness with which he bore witness to her grief was an instant balm to Sophie's aching, shattered heart. For the first time in days, she felt comforted and safe. Her tension ebbing away, she sank into Friedrich's embrace, her grief pouring out in a torrent of racking sobs. Friedrich cradled her against his chest, gently stroking her hair. When her weeping at last subsided, he pulled out his handkerchief and wiped away her tears.

When the full import of what had just happened sunk in, Sophie was filled with shame and horror. She had allowed Friedrich to escort her away from her family without first seeking her father's permission, and they were alone, with no chaperone in sight. Even worse, he was holding her in his arms while she openly wept in public. If anyone saw them and brought this to Papa's attention, she would not be allowed to leave the house for a thousand years!

She hurriedly backed away, her cheeks burning in embarrassment. "I beg your pardon," she stammered apologetically. "I should not have let my emotions overtake me like this. I do very much appreciate your assistance. You have been most kind, but I must get back to my family. Papa and Mama will be cross with me for wandering away."

"Again, there is no need to apologize." Friedrich's voice was warm and soothing. "You are upset and overwrought, yes, but with good reason. I am concerned that in your present state you may swoon or fall, as you so nearly did a few moments ago. I will walk with you to make sure you are safe and explain to your parents that I was merely offering my support in your grief. It will be all right. Come."

Friedrich once again took her elbow, guiding her carefully back through the maze of trees and tombstones until they reached the gathering of immediate family members still standing by Catharine's grave.

"Charlotte Sophia! Where have you been and what have you been doing?" Papa demanded, both concern and accusation in his tone. "Your mother and I were worried about you."

While she was trying to think of how to explain what had happened without raising her father's suspicions—or ire—any further, Friedrich spoke up.

"I understand your distress, sir. Please, allow me to explain. When I saw that Sophie was weeping and overwhelmed with grief, I simply escorted her a few feet away so that she did not disturb those of you still gathered at Catharine's graveside, and could have a few private moments to compose herself."

"Ah, dear Friedrich," said Margarethe, sighing audibly in relief. "Your kindness is most appreciated. Thank you so much for looking after our sweet girl. Now, please, come join us. We are going home to share a meal, and it would be our pleasure to welcome you to our table."

"You are most kind, madame. It would be my honor to join you. Sir," he said, turning to Joseph. "May I have your permission to personally escort Sophie back to your home? It has been a sad and sorrowful day, and I fear she is extremely weary. I would not want her to fall and injure herself on the walk back."

"You may," Joseph responded, "with my thanks."

Sophie—at once incredulous, elated, and deeply grateful—could barely believe her ears. She had been hoping for months Friedrich would formally ask for—and receive—permission to call on her. It was what she had always wanted, but she had not, in her wildest dreams, expected it to happen today of all days.

Friedrich bowed and stepped back to allow Joseph and Margarethe and the rest of the family to precede them out of the cemetery, then took Sophie's arm and leisurely walked her home. She was physically and emotionally exhausted, weary to the point of collapse, yet ecstatic and giddy with joy at the same time. Her pulse was racing, and her skin tingled where Friedrich's hand gently, but firmly, cupped her elbow. *Is this what true love feels like?* she wondered.

She didn't wonder long. Now that he had Papa's permission, Friedrich called on her regularly, and it was soon clear to Sophie—and everyone else—that she and Friedrich were deeply in love with one another. They were inseparable, spending every spare moment together either at his family's home or at hers, which led to no end of arguments with Papa and Mama. They were adamant that she and Friedrich wait until they were older to marry, for two important reasons. They were reluctant to act outside the social norms of their time and place, and they wanted to be sure Sophie and

Friedrich had both the maturity and financial wherewithal necessary for raising a family.

"We are not trying to punish you, Sophie," Papa insisted. "We love Friedrich and know he will make a fine husband for you, but you do not need to be in such a rush. It is not customary for girls to marry so young."

"Customary? What difference does that make? I love him and he loves me. Why should we have to wait?"

"Stop and think, sweet girl," Margarethe interjected.

"Think about what?" Sophie could tell by the tone of her mother's voice and the imploring look in her eyes Margarethe was attempting to insert some calm into the conversation before Sophie's—and Joseph's—emotions escalated and angry, hurtful words were spoken, but Sophie wasn't ready to drop the issue and give in.

"Are any of your friends or the neighbor girls your age married?"

"Well, no," Sophie grudgingly admitted. None of her contemporaries even had suitors, let alone fiancés or husbands.

"And there are good reasons for that," Margarethe reminded her. "Friedrich will need more than just a few months to establish a solid financial foundation for your family. The war has not been over that long, and the economy is still recovering. Papa and I will need ample time to plan for your marriage as well."

Joseph and Margarethe did not make the rules that governed how church and society functioned at that time, nor did they have the power to change them. All they could do was follow them to the best of their ability. The blessing of the church and the services of the pastor would have to be secured. Pastor Schilling had several parishes in his charge, and while of great importance to the families involved, weddings were not fraught with the same life-and-death theological urgency as baptisms and funerals, so much advance planning was needed to incorporate them into his schedule. The financial considerations alone would require many months, if not years, of saving. And Margarethe had a deeply compelling personal reason for wanting Sophie to wait, one she hesitated to voice.

"But I hate waiting!" Sophie protested, stamping her foot in exasperation.

Joseph and Margarethe exchanged a knowing look. "We know, sweet child. But it is not yet time," her mother said. "Besides, I need you."

"Need me? For what?"

"These last few weeks have been very difficult with Catharine being so sick, and Friedrich Georg just a baby still. I do not mean to burden you, Sophie, but I am getting older. I need help caring for your brothers and sister and keeping the household in order."

"Mama is right," Joseph said. "When it is time for you to marry, I promise you will have our blessing. For now, be patient. Can you do that?"

Now that she had finally stopped to look, Sophie could see the sadness and worry etched on her parents' faces and hear the weariness in her mother's voice. That, she understood. "I will do my best," she promised.

Her courtship went on for what felt, to her, like an eternity, but finally, on another crystal-clear day—this time a sunny winter one where the snow shone like diamonds—Sophie and Friedrich were joined in holy matrimony.

Chapter Three

Always a creature of ethereal beauty, when Joseph escorted her down the aisle of the Evangelical and Catholic Church in Rheda on the day after Christmas, 1851, Sophie was a vision of elegance and grace. Transfixed by the sight of her daughter's slight, willowy frame in her elegantly tailored wedding gown, and the way her eyes danced in the candlelight, to Margarethe, Sophie looked like an angel come to Earth. As they stood at the altar repeating vows and exchanging rings, her sister Mina and Friedrich's brother Caspar at their sides, Sophie radiated pure joy. Shoulders touching, hands clasped, her platinum curls spilling down her back beneath her handmade lace veil made a sharp contrast to Friedrich's raven hair and dark suit. Margarethe's eyes filled with tears as Pastor Schilling spoke the official words that sealed their marriage covenant and pronounced them husband and wife, adding her own silent prayers to the liturgy of the day.

Have mercy on them, Holy One. May theirs be a home of peace and welcome, filled with laughter and joy. Bless them with many happy, loving children and long, long life.

Despite her deep faith and her conscious choice to trust in the wisdom and provision of the Almighty regardless of the circumstances, she was a mother through and through, and in her heart of hearts, Margarethe still worried about her children. The effects of the Three Years' War with Denmark and the revolution of 1848 were still being felt, and the agricultural crisis that had begun in the late 1840s wore on with no end in sight. Things were not as dire in Rheda as they were in places like Baden-Wurttemberg; Rheda was a river town with more ready access to food and supplies than other areas. But when crops were not good, everyone felt the pinch sooner or later and the farmers in their area and to the south had not had a good year since 1846. She feared for Sophie and Friedrich, just starting out, and whatever grandchildren might come along; there was no doubt they would be living in difficult times.

Sophie, on the other hand, was oblivious to anything that was not directly related to the day-to-day life she shared with Friedrich. She threw herself into creating a warm and intimate living space for the two of them, paying little or no attention to anything outside the environs of her own home and immediate family. Her days were filled with all the tasks required to run a household: cleaning, laundry, and making sure Friedrich's favorite dishes graced their table as often as possible. When she wasn't in the kitchen, Sophie could often be found in the parlor of their small but cozy home knitting sweaters and gloves, embroidering pillowcases and dresser scarves, crocheting doilies and tablecloths, crafting comforters and quilts. She loved all of her life, but her favorite time of day was when Friedrich returned home from work. They would have dinner, spend hours in deep conversation, and, when weather permitted, take a stroll through the neighborhood before bed.

While Sophie was content to focus solely on their life together, Friedrich was forced to take a wider world view. Tasked with making a living and providing for his family, economic conditions and world events were something he had to consider daily. Times were challenging, and industrialization and the economic development that accompanies it were still several years away for their part of the world.

He did have regular work, thankfully. As Sophie's father Joseph got older, he was less and less able to work long days in the tack shop or keep up with the many tasks involved in running a livery stable. Friedrich had joined Sophie's brothers soon after their marriage, learning the ins and outs of the livery business, waiting on customers who came to the shop, and assisting with the accounts and bookkeeping. In addition to being able to read and write and work with numbers, Friedrich came from a long line of skilled craftsmen and enjoyed working with his hands. Trained as a shoemaker in his father's shop, if he had any time to spare away from the counter and the ledgers, he could be found in the back, tooling leather for the saddles while Sophie's brothers shoed horses, ran the livery routes, and built and repaired wagons and carriages.

It was early March 1852 now. After finishing the day's round of housekeeping chores, Sophie headed for the parlor and picked up her needlework. Glancing at the mantel clock, she saw that she had two hours to sew before she would need to get supper ready for Friedrich and herself. Taught well by her mother, Sophie was a frugal and efficient homemaker. She saved every scrap of fabric no matter how small and had begun, when she thought Friedrich wasn't looking, to make quilts for the babies she hoped would soon arrive. In fact, that very afternoon, as she pieced a coverlet for that (to her knowledge) unconceived infant, she daydreamed about what it would feel like to nuzzle her very own child to her breast. *I cannot wait until our first baby arrives! How I wish he or she were already here.* She sighed. She wanted children immediately, of course; it was all she thought about. She was stunned when Friedrich had told her, the first time she mentioned how much she longed to be a mother, that it would be better if they did not have children right away.

The memory of that conversation was burned into her brain—as clear as if it had just happened yesterday. Friedrich had become quite cross with her, and, truth be told, she had been equally as cross with him. With neither one of them willing to change their point of view—or even compromise—the atmosphere between them had become quite chilly. There were no lingering goodnight kisses, no intimate caresses before they went to sleep on that particular evening, or for many evenings afterward.

The very thought of not having children until later—or possibly at all—incensed her. She had already, in her estimation, come dangerously close to being an old maid. She could not bear the thought of being childless as well.

Waiting, pah! she thought bitterly. *Always it is the waiting. It is not fair!* She knew Papa and Mama were only doing what they thought was best when they insisted Sophie and Friedrich wait to marry. They wanted to be sure Sophie was considering things carefully; that she and Friedrich truly loved one another. Mama was also trying to protect her; to be sure she would not be the subject of gossip and wagging tongues. Had she married when she wanted to—at not even twenty—she surely would have been. But Margarethe was not concerned for Sophie alone. She was worried about Papa and the livery stable too. Perceived as someone who could not manage his own affairs—someone whose children did not behave appropriately and according to social norms—some may have assumed Papa ran his business in a slip-shod manner as well, and refused to do business with him. *Mama was always reminding us to "stop and think!"—to consider how our words and actions would affect and be perceived by others. She said it almost as often as she said, "somehow, some way everything will be all right." And she did need my help at home after Catharine's death— especially when Friedrich Georg died the very next summer. But is using prudence and logic the only acceptable means to make choices? Is there not a time and place for pursuing one's hopes and dreams? Most of my friends have children already; if we do not have a baby soon, Papa and Mama may not be alive to see their grandchildren. That would be heartbreaking to me!*

Friedrich thinks I am being selfish; concerned only with my wants. That is not true at all! I have such wonderful memories of my own Grandmama and Grandpapa. I want so much for my children to know that same joy. And I want my parents to experience the blessing of grandchildren. It is not about me at all—this is for them.

As Sophie reached the end of the seam she was working on, the clock chimed five. Knotting and clipping the thread, she slid the needle through a scrap of fabric, then placed it in the tapestry case with her thimble and scissors. Folding the small quilt with care, she tucked it out of sight in her sewing basket under a pair of pillowcases she planned to trim with hand-tatted lace borders. She went into the dining room and added logs to the fire, set the table for supper, then went to the kitchen and began laying out their evening meal. Carrots from the root cellar and Friedrich's favorite sausages were sliced into an iron skillet and placed over the fire to roast. The scent of cinnamon, cloves, and allspice filled the room as she opened a jar of pickled beets and spooned them into a serving dish. She filled a platter with red onions, rye bread, and generous slices from a wheel of local cheese. For dessert, there was apple strudel, golden brown underneath its dusting of confectioners' sugar.

Everyone knew that Dorothea Schmidt made the best apple strudel in Rheda. Attempts were regularly undertaken, but no one yet had been able to duplicate her glorious concoction. No one, that is, except Sophie. Her mother and Mrs. Schmidt were best friends, in and out of each other's homes a dozen times a day. Having no children of her own, Mrs. Schmidt had embraced Sophie and her siblings as if she had given birth to them herself. She secretly bestowed the strudel recipe on Sophie as a wedding gift, with strict orders to tell no one where she had gotten it, to never share it, and to refrain from taking it to any social gathering at which Mrs. Schmidt would likely be in attendance. Sophie was happy to oblige, making the strudel exclusively for Friedrich until after Mrs. Schmidt's death.

Hearing the front door close, Sophie marked Friedrich's footsteps from the hallway where he hung his hat and scarf on the hand-carved walnut hall tree, through the dining room, and to the kitchen.

"Ah, my sweet prince!" She threw her arms around his neck and covered his face with kisses, then laid her head on his shoulder, reveling in the earthy aromas of leather, saddle soap, and fresh straw clinging to his clothing. "I have missed you so much! How was your day? Was Papa able to come to the shop?"

"Hello, my love." Friedrich warmly returned her embrace and kissed her cheek. "Yes, Joseph came over after his midday meal and greeted customers for an hour or so. He looked tired, though, Sophie. I hope it was not too taxing for him. Christian took him home in the wagon on the way to make a delivery, so he did not have to walk."

Sophie frowned in dismay. For the past three winters, Papa had struggled to stay well, and his failing health was one of the few things that could take her mind away from her own hearth and home and her burning desire to have children.

"He was able to be out for a little while, though, and that is good," she said, trying to dispel her apprehension and avoid casting a pall on their evening. "Supper is ready, my love. Sit down, and we will eat."

Sophie filled a plate and served Friedrich, then joined him at the dining room table with her own. While they ate, Friedrich talked about who had been in the shop that day, what deliveries had been made, and enchanted her with a description of the new saddle he was working on.

"I am sure it is beautiful," she said, pride filling her voice. "I cannot wait to see it. I was going to go to Mama's tomorrow and help her hem a dress she is making. Perhaps I will walk over to the livery stable and take a look on my way home. Would you like more sausage? Another slice of bread?"

"I am quite content. It was perfect. Just enough."

"Then how about dessert? I made strudel."

"I cannot turn down my favorite thing in all the world—besides you, of course. You take such good care of me, Sophie!" As she reached over to pick up his dinner plate, Friedrich caught her hand and brought it to his lips, smothering her palm and the inside of her wrist with lingering kisses.

Cheeks flaming and pulse pounding, she quickly took the plates to the kitchen. Friedrich wasn't usually so demonstrative outside of the privacy of their bedroom, but she had to admit she enjoyed his attentions. Her wrist tingled deliciously where his lips had been, and a wave of warmth washed over her as she imagined more kissing and caressing later that night.

"Would you like a glass of sherry as well?" she asked as she served the strudel.

"Oh, my dear, that would be lovely."

When they finished their strudel, Friedrich retired to the parlor with his sherry and the evening paper while

Sophie washed the dishes and straightened the kitchen and dining room. When she was finished, she joined Friedrich in the parlor.

"Come, talk to me, my sweet." Friedrich put down the paper and motioned for her to join him on the settee. "You have heard all about my day. Tell me about yours."

"It was just a regular day. I made the strudel, cleaned up the kitchen, swept the floor, dusted the parlor and dining room, then spent the afternoon sewing until it was time to get our supper ready."

"What are you making? Let me see!"

Sophie took a deep breath, then got the small quilt out of her sewing basket, holding it up for Friedrich to inspect. A patchwork of tiny postage-stamp sized blocks, Sophie had arranged them so that the shades and patterns of the fabric formed an elaborate star in the center of the quilt. When she finished layering it with wool padding and added her stitched embellishments and binding, it would be fit for a princess—or a prince.

"It is beautiful, my love!" Friedrich exclaimed. "You are exquisitely talented! But," he said, his smile of admiration fading and his brow knitting in concern, "I have to ask. Are you making this as a gift for one of your friends, or is this a hint for me?"

Watching his expression change, a flash of anger shot through her. "I am making it because I want to," she snapped. "Is that such a terrible thing?"

"Of course not, my sweet. I am sorry. I did not mean to upset you. But I have explained how I feel about having children—at least I have tried to—many times."

"I know what you said, that it would be better to wait. But the panicked frown on your face when you thought I made the quilt for *our* baby makes me doubt you were telling the truth. Admit it," she prodded in an accusatory tone. "You do not want children at all!"

"That is not true." He sighed wearily. "I am not opposed to having children. Of course, I want a houseful of sons to carry on our family name and beautiful daughters who look just like their mother. I just believe it is better that we do not have children *now.*"

"But, Friedrich!" she wailed in protest. "You know how important this is to me!"

"Yes, I do." He took her hand and held it, entwining his fingers with hers. "It is also of the utmost importance to *me* that you and our family are safe and happy, and ours is not a safe and happy world at present."

"But the war with Denmark is over!"

"The fighting may have stopped, but there is no formal treaty in place and no way of telling how long it may take for all sides to agree. If negotiations are not successful, we will be at war again. I cannot bear the thought of you and our children having to endure that kind of hardship—or of having to leave you and go fight."

"The thought of you having to go to war terrifies me, too," Sophie said, shuddering as she spoke. "And I know you are worried about the economy and how unsettled everything is. But this is not about just us," she reminded him.

"I want to wait for a while, Sophie. Not forever. In a few months, there may well be a treaty in place; everything will be better after that," he promised with a reassuring smile, bringing her hand to his lips and kissing it gently.

"I am sorry to be cross with you, my prince. I do not want to argue. But I loved my grandparents so much, and when you talked about how tired Papa looked today, it frightened me." Her voice caught, and tears welled in her eyes and spilled down her cheeks. "I want so much for my parents—especially Papa—and your parents, too, of course, to see and hold their grandchildren before they die." Her words trailed off into sobs.

"Ach, Sophie!" Friedrich cupped her face in his hands, then pulled her close. "Forgive me for upsetting you so."

Regaining her composure, Sophie brushed her tears away with the back of her hand. "This is a gift for our parents only we can give them. And you know what Mama always says," she reminded him. "It will be all right. You will see, Friedrich. Somehow, some way, everything will be all right."

"Of course, my sweet. I am sure you and your dear mother are correct."

What Sophie and Friedrich did not know—could not know—was that new life was already, at that moment, stirring inside her. By April, she was suspicious, and by June, her slight figure was full enough for everyone to notice. Sophie had been happy before; now she was deliriously so. With every look in Friedrich's direction, her blue eyes twinkled merrily; every word she spoke was uttered with lilting pleasure; every task was done with joyful abandon, even on those days when exhaustion dogged her steps and sickness kept her from eating regular meals.

For Friedrich, those months were a constant emotional seesaw. In his heart of hearts, he was bursting with pride and looking forward to the birth of their first child. He almost had no choice; Sophie's joy was contagious. But he was also deeply concerned about her well-being and that of their child, and could not shake his apprehension over the economy and the uncertain political climate. He worked hard to keep his uneasiness hidden when he was at home, doting on Sophie at every turn, doing his best to honor her every request, helping whenever and wherever he could, but the days spent at his desk and the tack room of the livery stable were filled with anxiety and worry.

By mid-November, Sophie awoke each morning wondering if today was the day their baby would arrive. As always, she was tired of waiting, and utterly and completely tired of being tired. She longed to hold her son or daughter in her arms, to count perfectly formed fingers and toes, to swaddle him—or her!—in that exquisite handcrafted quilt, to feel the babe suckling hungrily at her breast. She wanted to experience it all, and she wanted it all now.

On the evening of November 22, weary beyond words, she went to bed far earlier than her usual time. Friedrich kissed her goodnight, smiled, and said, "Rest well, my sweet. And maybe our little one will be here tomorrow!" Two hours later, Sophie awoke in the grip of intense pain. "Friedrich!" she cried, "Go get Mama and Mina! I do not think our little one is going to wait until tomorrow!"

In the end, it took many hours for the baby to make her appearance. The longer Sophie labored through the night and into the next day, the more worried Friedrich became, but early in the afternoon of November 23, 1852, Sophie Elise Rieple made her entrance. She was stunningly beautiful, a perfect blend of her parents' features. She had Sophie's flashing blue eyes, delicate bone structure, and flawless complexion, and Friedrich's raven hair.

Two weeks later, on December 5, yet another crystal-clear day much like the one on which Sophie and Friedrich were married, their families gathered at the Evangelical Catholic Church in Rheda to celebrate Sophie Elise's baptism. Although it took the help of both of the twins and August and Mina to get Papa and Mama into the church and seated in their pew, everyone was there—Papa, Mama, and Friedrich's parents, too. Following the worship service, everyone gathered at Friedrich and Sophie's for a celebratory meal. The sight of their parents, her siblings and their families, along with the Schmidts crowded around her dining table, and later filling the parlor, dining room, and kitchen with laughter and conversation, overjoyed her.

Later that night, as she rocked her daughter to sleep, Sophie found herself musing over the past and how her life had unfolded. Always one to live in the moment, with little patience for those who did not do the same, this was unusual. She was not sure why these thoughts came to mind at this particular time; still she indulged herself in what turned out to be a warm and pleasant reverie. She had been convinced the day of Catharine's funeral was going to be the worst day of her life, and that the whole year following would be equally as bad. It was a sad day, the saddest she had ever faced, but it turned out to be one of the best days of her life. That was the day she found her prince charming. He had indeed swept her off her feet, and now here they were with their very own little princess. The war was finally officially over; the London Protocol had been signed in May. Everyone was breathing a collective sigh of relief and looking forward to better days ahead.

Mama was right all along, she mused. "Things will be all right, Sophie Elise," she whispered to her firstborn, kissing each of Sophie Elise's perfectly formed fingers one by one. "Somehow, some way, everything will be all right."

Chapter Four

The rest of December was equally as joyous as those first two weeks after Sophie Elise's birth. In fact, to Sophie, life was perfect.

The Christmas season was her favorite time of the year. She loved the holiday traditions and celebrations, and now that she had a daughter of her own, she threw herself into celebrating each one with unbridled zeal. Although Sophie Elise was just two weeks old, Sophie had already crafted an intricately embellished stocking to hang by the fireplace for her on St. Nicholas Day, December 6. In the weeks that followed, she and Mina were often at Mama's, helping her ready the house and make cookies and confections for the many holiday gatherings and feasts that would take place between Christmas Eve and the New Year. Sophie especially enjoyed the intimate conversations about married life she and Mina shared during that time. Heinrich had recently asked for Mina's hand in marriage, and a wedding was being planned for the spring of 1854. The girls took full advantage of seeing each other almost every day to make plans for Mina's wedding—what her bridal gown would look like and the style of dress Sophie would wear as matron of honor. It also gave them the chance to learn all the secrets and special touches Mama used in making the Christmas treats that always graced her holiday table, including her famous Stollen.

On that particular morning, Sophie had risen early to get her own household chores done quickly, anxious to get to Mama's and start on the baking.

Margarethe was waiting for them on the porch, arms out in anticipation of holding Sophie Elise even before Sophie reached the gate. Sunlight peeked through the clouds, dappling the sidewalk and the front steps with patches of light, and the delicious aroma of cinnamon, ginger, and baking bread wafted out through the open front door.

"There's my darling girl!" Margarethe cradled Sophie Elise in her arms, her eyes shining with joy. "Come in, Sophie." Shifting Sophie Elise to her right hip, she motioned Sophie into the house, and gave her a one-armed hug. "Mina just got here. As soon as we get Sophie Elise settled, we can start on the Stollen."

Under Margarethe's watchful eye, Mina scalded milk and set it aside to cool, then measured yeast, flour, and sugar into a bowl. Sophie got out the large stoneware crock her mother always used for bread making, then gathered the ingredients for the main dough: more flour and sugar, lard, butter, salt, and lemon rind.

"What about the fruit and nuts, Mama?" she asked.

"There they are—in that small crock covered with a tea towel." Margarethe pointed to a saltware bowl sitting on the cabinet behind Mina. "I got them ready yesterday. The flavor is so much richer if they steep in the brandy overnight. Check the milk, Mina. If it is cool, stir it into the flour, sugar, and yeast you measured out."

Sophie pulled a wooden spoon out of the cabinet drawer. "Should I get the rest of the dough ready now?"

"The yeast mixture needs to sit for a while," Margarethe explained. "We can polish the silver while we wait."

Seated around the ample dining room table, Sophie and Mina chatted about the details of Mina's wedding while their hands made the silver shine. When they were finished with the silver, Margarethe checked the yeast mixture.

"It's perfect," she pronounced. "Go ahead and mix the ingredients for the main dough," she told Sophie, "then add that to the yeast mixture."

After several minutes of mixing and stirring, Sophie had everything combined. She turned to Margarethe with a questioning look. "Should I add the fruit and nuts now, Mama?"

"Not yet. Turn the dough out on the board and knead it until it is completely smooth, and let it rise again. Then you add the fruit. One more rest after that, and it will be ready to bake."

"No wonder mine never turns out as light as yours! I just mix everything together, let it rise once and bake it."

"Ever the impatient one!" Margarethe said with a chuckle. "There are times when waiting is necessary; sometimes it is best. And not just for Stollen."

While she loved every minute of the holiday season, Sophie's favorite memory of that year was decorating the Christmas tree on Christmas Eve. She delighted in watching Sophie Elise's wide-eyed fascination as branch after branch of the tree was filled with shiny, colorful ornaments and twinkling candlelight. Later that evening, the whole family gathered at the church for Christmas Eve worship. Sophie cradled Sophie Elise in her arms as she listened to the familiar words of the Christmas story and seasonal hymns, wondering if Mary's heart had been as full of love, contentment, and hope as hers was.

To her great dismay, those joy-filled, perfect days were short-lived. On New Year's Eve, Papa was stricken with pneumonia and did not live out the week. They once again gathered at the church, Margarethe, Mina, and Sophie quietly weeping through the service, the boys stoic and somber. Even more time was spent with Mama, helping her with household tasks, sharing memories and tears.

Sophie was ecstatic, one midsummer day, to share the news that she and Friedrich were once again expecting a baby. Margarethe was overjoyed at the prospect of another grandchild and began knitting sweaters and booties and sewing blankets and gowns in anticipation.

But as summer slipped into fall, Margarethe's health began failing. Plagued by shortness of breath, a fever that would not abate, and a racking cough, she took to her bed in late September. Sophie and Mina tended her day and night, but recovery was not possible. Yet again they gathered at the church—this time to say goodbye to Margarethe—on a wet, dark October day where the driving rain outside and black-shrouded sanctuary and mourners mirrored Sophie and Mina's unrelenting tears and broken hearts as they walked the valley of the shadow once again.

Ushered to the front of the church just before the service started, Sophie took her place in the pew behind Carl, Heinrich, and Christian, struggling to keep her composure.

I am beginning to hate this place. For every happy occasion we celebrate here, there are twice as many sad ones. It has not even been a year since Sophie Elise's baptism, and this is the second funeral. Oh, Mama! I am going to miss you so much.

When another beautiful baby girl was born in February of 1854, Sophie was both overjoyed and yet haunted by sorrow that her parents weren't there to welcome her into the family. Blond and blue-eyed, Friedrich and Sophie named her Margarethe Marie Louise, after the grandmother she so closely resembled. Sophie did her best to make sure her girls knew the story of their grandparents' lives, regaling them often with tales of Joseph and Margarethe—how Grandpapa worked every day with horses, Grandmama made the best sauerbraten and Stollen in the world, and how much they loved their children and grandchildren.

A welcome antidote for her grief, Sophie was also consumed with putting the finishing touches on Mina's wedding gown, and the dress she would wear as matron of honor for Mina's March 10, 1854, wedding. It turned out to be a perfect day—an occasion just as joyous as Sophie and Friedrich's marriage celebration had been.

Chapter Five

In the midst of all the happiness surrounding Marie Louise's birth and Mina and Heinrich's marriage, Friedrich remained restless and morose. Sophie could see it in him daily, particularly when he arrived home from work in the evening. Moody and cross, he spoke curtly to her, if he spoke at all, and he rarely held or played with their daughters. Where they once filled their evenings with discussions about his work at the livery stable, lately he had had little to say about how the day had gone or who had come to the shop. As winter dissolved into spring, Friedrich became increasingly more withdrawn. He never mentioned the saddles he so loved to craft in his spare time, and he no longer read the evening paper. By mid-March, Sophie could stand it no longer. As soon as supper was over that Sunday night, she put the girls to bed and confronted Friedrich as he sat staring out the parlor window into the twilight.

"What is wrong?" she demanded. "You used to be happy, Friedrich. Every day you would tell me all about what happened at the shop. When you were not sharing the details of your work with me, you were spoiling our daughters with stories and treats. You have barely said three words to me this entire day, and you have not played with the girls at all. Tell me! What is the matter?"

Instead of answering her question, Friedrich asked one of his own.

"How would you feel about taking a trip?"

"A trip? What do you mean? The only reason people take trips is to visit relatives. We have no reason to travel; our families both live right here."

"Have you never wanted to see new places, do new things?"

"No. Everything I have ever dreamed of—everything I love—is right here. Besides, who would take care of the accounts at the livery stable and work on the saddles if you were not there?"

"Things are different at the shop, Sophie." Friedrich sighed. "I did not want to worry you, so I kept my concerns to myself, but everything has changed since Joseph died."

"What do you mean 'everything has changed'? How have things changed?"

"Your father always treated me as an equal of Christian and Heinrich's and invited me to take part in all the discussions pertaining to the business. Your brothers are in charge now, and they make all of the decisions without consulting me. I am just an employee, not one of the owners, and I have no say in what happens. I do not know how much longer I will be able to work there."

"That is rubbish!" she protested. "My brothers would never let you go. I will speak to Christian and Heinrich myself, and make certain you will always have employment. You will see. It will be fine."

"You do not understand, Sophie." Friedrich briefly closed his eyes and took a deep breath. "I am at the livery every day. I see and hear things you do not. Christian is speaking of selling and leaving."

"How could he do such a thing? *Why* would he do such a thing?" She shook her head in disbelief. "Everyone knew it was Papa's intention that the twins would keep the livery stable going after he was gone."

"That was your father's dream. And it is not a bad thing to want your sons to follow in your footsteps. But Christian's desires are quite different. He is not interested in running a livery stable. He wants to pursue his own dream—owning a cigar shop. Truth be told, he wants the same thing I do, Sophie. It is not just about having a job."

"Then what is it about?" she demanded, her voice rising in anger. "You are right, Friedrich. I do not understand!"

"It is about being able to build a future for our family," he said, his shoulders sagging in weariness and frustration. "It is my responsibility to provide for you and the girls. I do not feel it is possible for me to adequately do that when someone else is making the decisions that affect my ability to earn a living. The way things are, if I stay on at the livery, I am abandoning you to the care of others, and what kind of a man does that make me? And yes, before you remind me, I know the war is over, but things are not improving as quickly as everyone expected them to, and I truly do not see a future for us here."

Sophie collapsed onto the settee in stunned silence. Immersed in running her own household and caring for her precious baby girls, she had no idea things were different at the shop since her father's death, and she had assumed, since Friedrich had not said anything to the contrary, that the economy was improving just as everyone had been told it would. She found it hard to believe that Christian and Heinrich would ignore Friedrich's concerns and ideas; she could not imagine her brothers, her own flesh and blood, treating him that way—nor could she, in her wildest dreams ever envision Christian leaving the livery—but Friedrich had never given her any reason to doubt his word. She did not know what to think.

"How long of a trip are you talking about?" she asked hesitantly. "Going to Gutersloh? To Frankfurt? Hanover? Berlin?" When Friedrich did not answer, she paused, eyes widening in disbelief. "You are not thinking of going all the way to Switzerland, are you?"

His answer froze her heart.

"No. I think our best chance for a future is in America."

Struggling to comprehend how Friedrich could even suggest such a thing, her shock and confusion gave way to desperation. *Dear God, he is serious. But why go all the way to America? Could we not find a place to build a future here? I need roots. Connection. And so do our girls. I cannot imagine leaving everything I have ever known and raising them in a strange and unfamiliar place. And I cannot leave Mina! I would never survive without her.*

"America? We do not know anyone in America! We do not know the language or the customs. We know nothing about *anything* in America! How will you find work? Where will we live? Friedrich, this is madness!"

"No," he insisted, shaking his head. "Not madness—opportunity. A chance for me to make my own way in the world and provide for my family the way I am supposed to." Rising from the settee, he held his hands out in front of her. "Look at me, Sophie. I am an artist, not an accountant. Crafting things with my hands is what brings me joy, but there is no time for that at the livery stable these days." He paced in front of her, gesturing as he spoke. "Without your father there, there is no one to wait on customers and manage the accounts but me. I have time for only occasional small repairs, not the real leatherwork I enjoy so much.

I have not talked about any of the saddles I have been work-ing on, because I have not made one in weeks. Even if I had time for saddle-making, there is no demand for them, your brothers tell me. So, I sit at my desk, day after day, making entries in ledgers, a rigid, finite task in which there is no creativity involved whatsoever. Doing those same things— and nothing else!—over and over and over blunts my senses and drains my spirit in ways I cannot even describe to you." He walked over to where she sat and knelt in front of her, taking her hands in his.

"I cannot live this way, Sophie," he pleaded. "I am ready to start over in a new place where I have the opportunity to make my own decisions and my own way in the world— where I can make things with my hands. You asked me how I was going to find work? There are many things I can do besides what I do at the livery stable. Yes, I can read and write and keep accounts and make saddles. I can also make shoes and roll cigars. I can paint and do carpentry. If I have to, I can do stonework and lay bricks. America is the new world—everything is being built from the ground up there. I will be able to find work doing any of those things. I might even try something new and different like farming. And, you forget, we do know people there. Some of my family went to America years ago—in the late forties when the revolution started. There will be relatives ready to welcome us when we arrive, and we will not be making the voyage alone. My cousin Christian and his family are going as well. We will travel with them."

She jerked her hands away. Like her mother, Sophie found change and upheaval loathsome and detestable; the more sudden the change, the more she despised and resisted it. Overwhelmed by Friedrich's words, panicked and full of fear, at that moment she was unable—and unwilling—to consider any viewpoint but her own. "I have no desire to travel halfway around the world with complete strangers," she retorted, crossing her arms tightly across her chest. "I have no desire to travel anywhere at all. I do not know your cousin, or his wife. I have not seen them since our wedding day. I barely know any of your family, for that matter, and I do not believe they even like me!"

"Sophie, that is ridiculous!" Again, Friedrich shook his head in disbelief. "I worked in your father's place of business, so of course we saw your family more often than we did mine, but they all adore you. The thought of leaving the people I am closest to and the only home I have ever known saddens me also, but I have been thinking about this since your father died and your brothers took over the business; I can see no other way."

"Does that mean, then, that we are through discussing this? That the decision has been made, regardless of how I feel about it?" she asked, her voice cold and brittle.

"Did you ever see your mother question your father's judgment or decisions about what was best for the family?" he asked, rising from the floor and sitting back down beside her.

While Sophie had no idea what her parents discussed behind the closed door of their bedroom, she had to admit her mother had never taken issue with what Papa said in front of the rest of the family. What Papa said, went.

"No. She did not. But we are not Papa and Mama. Can we not talk about this more? It just feels so unfair!"

"I understand how you feel, Sophie. Please, believe me when I say that. But that does not change our circumstances, or my decision. We are going to America. The ship leaves two weeks before May Day and is expected to arrive in New Orleans on or around the first of June. We will take what we can and sell the rest of our belongings to pay for our passage."

"That is only a month! That hardly gives me time to pack. When were you planning on telling me?" she asked accusingly. "The night before we left?"

"I was going to tell you later this evening, after the girls were asleep and you and I were settled in our room." He reached up and gently caressed her cheek. "I am not doing this to hurt you or intentionally cause you hardship; I am doing it because I believe it is the best way to be sure I can provide for you and our daughters. I am doing it because I love you, Sophie." He wrapped his arms around her in a comforting embrace. She stiffened at his touch, and he pulled away. "You are fond of reminding me of your mother's words, God rest her soul. You would do well to remember them as well. It will be all right. Somehow, some way, everything *will* be all right, my sweet. You will see."

But Sophie did not see. Outside, the weather was glorious, one of the most beautiful springtimes the region had ever seen. Inside Friedrich and Sophie's home, the atmosphere could not have been colder. They spoke little; in fact, they barely saw each other. Friedrich was occupied from dawn till dusk every day seeing to the selling of their furniture and making arrangements for traveling to Bremen. Sophie alternated between fits of weeping and fuming about the house throwing clothes and bedding into trunks and slamming cupboard doors, as the home she had so lovingly created was dismantled piece by piece in front of her eyes.

On the night before they left for Bremen, they joined Mina and her husband Heinrich for one last meal together. Friedrich and Heinrich sat in the parlor discussing the finer points of tobacco varieties and cigar rolling while Sophie Elise played with her favorite doll and Marie Louise napped in Friedrich's arms. In the kitchen, Mina and Sophie laid out the evening meal. Try as she might, Sophie could not stop the tears that fell unbidden into the sauerkraut as she spooned it into the serving dish, and splashed on the plates as she helped Mina set the table.

"Mina, what am I going to do without you?" Sophie said, her voice cracking with emotion. "I have never traveled further from my home and the people I love than a carriage ride across the river to Weidenbruck. I will know no one on that ship, and I know no one in America. What am I going to do?"

"But Friedrich has family there already. Christian and Louise and their children are traveling with you." Mina put her arm around Sophie and gave her shoulder a reassuring pat. "And you will have Friedrich and the girls. You will not be alone, Sophie; you will have family all around you."

"I barely remember Christian from our wedding day; I do not recall being introduced to their children, and I do not know Louise from Eve. I think she hates me."

"Sophie! What a terrible thing to say! How could you even think such a thing?"

"Friedrich and I made a point of seeking out and speaking personally with each of our wedding guests. We wanted everyone to feel welcome. But when we greeted Christian and Louise, she acted like I was not even there. No hello, no offer of congratulations. She would not even look me in the eye. It was my wedding day, Mina," Sophie complained. "And she ignored me!"

"I am sure it was nothing personal," Mina insisted, trying to soothe Sophie's discontent. "Was she not expecting Anna Catharine at the time?" Mina asked in a hopeful tone. "Perhaps she was just tired, or not feeling well."

"Perhaps," Sophie grudgingly admitted. "But even if I were well acquainted with her, it is not going to be the same as having you to talk to. I am going to miss you so much, Mina!" she wailed. "What if I never see you again?"

Mina wrapped her arms around her sister and held her while she wept. "Shhh! Do not speak that way, Sophie. I am going to miss you, too. But who knows, if Friedrich is right, and things really are better in America, maybe Heinrich and I will come, too. Maybe someday we will all live together there, just like we have here. Remember what Mama always said—"

"No, Mina!" Sophie pulled away from her sister in anger and frustration, shaking her finger in Mina's face. "Do not utter those words. That is all Friedrich has said to me for the past month, and I do not ever want to hear it again. But I do hope you're right about America. If I have to go, I hope you can come, too, before many months pass. I do not know how I will survive without you."

"If we can come, we will," Mina promised, wrapping Sophie in another hug. "Now, go call Heinrich and Friedrich, and we will eat."

Focused on the conversation around the table, on helping feed Sophie Elise, and nursing Marie Louise, Sophie was able to keep her emotions in check through dinner and dessert. But as soon as the meal was over, that control started to unravel once again. Wanting to hang onto every single moment she could with Mina, she started to clear the table, but Mina shooed her away.

"You have a long trip ahead of you tomorrow, Sophie. You need your rest. Take your little ones home and get some sleep," Mina advised. "Write to me as soon as you can. I want to know everything. And here, give me one more hug before you go."

Despite Mina's soothing words and constant attempts to reassure her, there was no rest for Sophie. She wept all the way home, and long into the night.

Chapter Six

The trip to Bremen was bone-jarring and, to Sophie, seemingly endless. Friedrich tried to make it all seem like a grand adventure, alternating between making up silly verses that he sang to the girls, pointing out landmarks, and offering historical commentary on each new region they traveled through. It was all lost on Sophie. Already tired and irritable after a sleepless night, she became more disheartened and despondent with each passing mile. The closer they got to Bremen, the busier the road became. By the time they arrived in the city, Sophie was in a state of shock.

She had never seen so many people, horses, wagons, and carriages in her life; the unfamiliar sights were a blur, and as they got closer to the harbor, the buzz of activity became mind-numbing. She retreated even further into herself, speaking only when Friedrich or Sophie Elise demanded her attention, nursing Marie Louise in silence. Knowing they would need to rise early the next day, Friedrich found lodging for them at an inn near the waterfront. Sophie stumbled through getting the girls to sleep and collapsed on her bed in exhaustion.

Friedrich made plans for the next day. Once they arrived at the ship and unloaded their belongings, he would take the horse and wagon to the closest livery stable and sell them, hoping to receive enough money to allow them to book a cabin.

Well before sunrise, Friedrich and Sophie rose and dressed. In a strange place, stiff and sore from long days of riding in the wagon, paralyzed with fear over what the future may hold, even though she had slept, she did not feel rested. They got tea and toast in the common room of the inn, loaded the trunks onto the wagon, then made their way to the ship. It took what seemed like forever to get the trunks unloaded, and Friedrich was much later than he wanted to be arriving at the livery stable. Sophie huddled on deck, shivering in the morning chill while impatiently awaiting his return, baby Marie Louise in her arms, Sophie Elise clinging to her skirts. At last, he reappeared and went to talk to the steward. This time, he was back in minutes. Sophie sighed in relief, then noticed his frowning countenance.

"I am afraid we will have to go to the lower deck," he apologized. "I got a more than fair price for the horse and wagon, but by the time I returned, all the cabins were taken.

I will take you and the children to our berth, then find someone to help me with the trunks."

Sophie sniffed in distaste as they made their way below. The farther down they went, the stuffier the air became. The smell of musty straw mingled with human perspiration, rancid lard, and rotting potatoes and made her gag. The windowless space and the sheer number of bunks squeezed into it further dampened her mood. She studied the area carefully, committing the location of their berths and the path to the stairway to memory. When Friedrich and the steward returned with their possessions, she set about getting their beds made and her little ones settled. She was surprised when Friedrich immediately turned to leave again.

"Where are you going?" she asked.

"I need to find Christian and Louise."

Exasperated, Sophie turned without answering and finished arranging pillows on the bed so baby Marie could safely sleep. As she had been for most of the past month, Sophie was both seething with rage and gripped with terror. The very idea of traveling so far away from her home to a strange place where she knew no one unnerved her, and that lack of familiarity caused her to imagine the worst of everyone and everything that crossed their path. She feared for her own safety and, above all, for the safety of her baby girls. Marshaling what was left of her patience, she turned her attention to Sophie Elise and Marie Louise.

"Come, Sophie Elise. Stay close to Mama. I will tell you a story while sissy naps." The girls were unhappy, too. Marie Louise had fussed off and on all morning long, and she could not get Sophie Elise moving at more than a snail's pace. She prayed that Christian and Louise would arrive soon so Friedrich could return to her side once again. Minutes that seemed like hours went by. Still people filed in and filled up cots and bunks, hundreds of them by now. With a growing sense of alarm, Sophie began adding up in her head just how many people would be crowded together in the cramped, windowless space. *Lord, have mercy. How will we ever survive?*

"Hungry, Mama," Sophie Elise whined.

"Yes, sweet girl, I know you are. We will see if we can get something to eat as soon as Papa comes." They had set out on the three-day trip to Bremen with what she was sure would be plenty of food, but by the time they arrived at the inn last night, there was nothing left. She thought back to the meager ration of tea and toast they had at the inn that morning; Friedrich wanted to be sure they had enough money for a cabin, so they did not order a full breakfast. *Pah!* Sophie snorted to herself. *A lot of good that did us. We should have eaten like kings and bought bread and cheese and fruit to bring with us onto the ship.*

"Mama! Hungry!"

"Yes, I know, princess. Lay down with your sister. We have to wait for Papa."

"No! No wait for Papa! Eat!" the toddler shouted.

Sophie could feel the other passengers staring, and as she turned to offer her apologies, she noticed the raised eyebrows of many of the women. One of them quickly left, only to return a short time later with a member of the crew. He stomped over to Sophie, stopping just inches away from her.

"See here, now, we've already had a complaint about yer squalling brats," he snarled. "Keep 'em quiet," he threatened, poking her shoulder, "or it won't be pleasant for you—ner them neither."

The man's gravelly voice—his accent one Sophie was unfamiliar with—grated on her nerves. His lined and pock-marked face was framed by greasy strings of gray hair, his clothing worn and frayed. He smelled as if he hadn't bathed in months, which was bad enough, but the worst part of the encounter was the way he fixed his eyes on Sophie. It felt like he was looking not just at her but *through* her, into her very soul, exposing all her fears and mocking them in turn.

"What's a pretty little thing like you doin' here all by yerself, anyway?" he asked with a leer, leaning forward and reaching up to touch her hair.

Sophie felt the blood drain from her face. She recoiled and prayed she would not swoon.

"I beg your pardon, sir." She heard Friedrich's voice from behind the sailor, a razor-sharp edge to his otherwise polite words. "My wife's appearance and her circumstances are none of your concern. She and I will see to our children, and I would ask that you immediately return to your duties, whatever they might be, and leave her in peace."

"You done been warned," the crewman growled as he turned to leave. "Keep 'em quiet or you'll wish you had."

"Oh, Friedrich!" Sophie collapsed into Friedrich's arms, clutching him in relief. "I was terrified! I am so glad you are back. Did you find Christian and Louise?"

"Yes, they are on board, but they could not get berths near us. They are at the other end of the ship."

"Well, I am sorry to hear that," Sophie replied. "You and Christian have much to talk about. And I was hopeful the voyage would give Louise and me and the children a chance to become better acquainted. Their youngest is close in age to Sophie Elise, is she not?"

"Yes, Anna is almost three, Carl is five, Johanna is seven, and Friedrich is nine."

"Hungry, Papa! Eat!" Sophie Elise shrieked.

"Is there anything to eat? Your daughter is hungry, in case you had not heard."

Friedrich glanced at Sophie Elise with a wry smile. "I think everyone onboard has heard, and perhaps the entire port as well. Unfortunately, there will not be anything until tomorrow morning, according to the steward I talked to while I was waiting for Christian and Louise to come aboard. I can go see if they brought any extra food with them, but it will take a long while for me to make my way to their berths in this crowd of people."

"No. Do not bother them. I am sure they are busy trying to get themselves and their children settled before we sail. I would rather you did not leave just now anyway. I need to feed Marie Louise, and it would help if you were here to keep an eye on Sophie Elise."

The ship got underway shortly after that. Thankfully, many of those berthed on the lower deck went up to watch the ship put out to sea and bid one last goodbye to those still on shore, so Sophie had a few moments of relative privacy in which to nurse her youngest child. Even though she had asked him to stay, Friedrich insisted on going up to watch as well.

"I have never seen or done anything like this, Sophie," he said wistfully, his eyes shining in wonder. "I want to experience it, at least once."

Marie Louise finished nursing and drifted off to sleep, and after positioning her on the bunk and barricading her with pillows, Sophie picked up her oldest daughter and settled her on her lap. "Here, Sophie Elise. You can have Mama's milk just like Marie had."

"No Mama's milk! Cookies!"

"Mama does not have any cookies. Mama's milk is all I have right now." Sophie Elise squirmed out of her mother's grasp and collapsed wailing in a heap on the floor. She cried long enough and loud enough to wake Marie Louise, who began crying as well.

Dear God. Sophie sighed, wearily leaning her head against the frame of the bunk. *Help us all.*

Chapter Seven

Had you asked the ship's master, Mr. Brandorff, or any of the members of the *John Schmidt*'s crew, they would have told you, to a man, the spring 1854 voyage from Bremen to New Orleans had been completely uneventful. Fantastic, even. There were a handful of minor squalls, but no severe storms or gale force winds to blow them off course, nor had they run aground on any sand bars or reefs. No other ships had been seen, no pirates or marauders were encountered, and there had been no major disturbances among the passengers or crew. To this point, there had not been a single death, an amazing feat considering the fact that they were traveling with three hundred seventeen passengers on board, fifty-five under ten years of age, and sixteen of which were infants. With no weather incidents to contend with, they were making excellent time, and Mr. Brandorff had every expectation they would dock in New Orleans on or around June 1, as scheduled.

For Sophie, it was the worst six weeks of her life. Desperately lonely, she made repeated overtures to Louise, inviting her to meet for an afternoon of sewing and conversation, or to bring Johanna and Anna and Carl and Friedrich to play with Sophie Elise. Each time she was rebuffed, and soon stopped asking.

The days were a blur of wailing children, surly crew members and fellow passengers, and little that was fit to eat or drink. Even if there had been an abundance of delicious food, Sophie would not have been able to consume much. The weather was good, but she was not accustomed to sea travel, and her stomach churned and rolled with every movement of the ship. Always small and delicate, after two pregnancies in quick succession, and now nursing an infant without adequate food and drink, Sophie was dangerously thin. She said nothing to Friedrich, but she began to have serious concerns about whether she had the physical strength and stamina to survive the voyage. She was emotionally exhausted as well. Fears of strangers, pestilence, and shipwreck haunted her waking hours, and nightmares of losing her precious babies interrupted her sleep multiple times each night. Her angelic face was drawn and lined, and pounds melted weekly from her slight frame. While the fresh air would have been invigorating, she rarely left her berth to go above deck; she was too tired to climb the stairs while carrying Marie Louise.

Friedrich was not well either. Tired, wan, and thin, he often left her alone with the children, purportedly to find Christian and discuss what they were going to do and where they were going to go when they arrived in New Orleans. Instead, she found out later, he spent his days alone at the rail, staring off into the horizon. As time went on, he spent more time below decks on his bunk, dozing off and on and occasionally making notes in a journal.

By the end of the second week at sea, her children were visibly suffering as well. Sophie Elise was constantly hungry and cross. Marie Louise fared even worse. Unable to keep anything down, she became dehydrated and grew weaker with each passing day. Soon she no longer had strength enough to cry, and instead wheezed and whimpered throughout the day and into the evening. Each time Sophie woke in the night (if she managed to sleep), the first thing she did was make sure her babies were still breathing.

As the days wore on, Marie Louise's respiration became increasingly irregular and shallow. Inquiries about a doctor and overtures to the crew for assistance had produced no response. None of their fellow passengers offered any help, and she never saw Christian and Louise.

The night of May 11, Sophie slept fitfully, tossing and turning. When she was jolted awake just after midnight by another of her ghoulish dreams, her hands immediately flew to Marie Louise's chest. This time there was no rise and fall, nothing but silence and cold, cold skin. She reached for Friedrich and frantically shook him awake.

"She is not breathing, Friedrich! She is dead! She is dead!"

Friedrich jumped down from the top bunk to Marie Louise's side, and in an instant knew Sophie was right. He sighed heavily, tears filling his eyes. Pulling Sophie into his arms, he held her close. "You know how sick she has been. At least she is not suffering anymore. It will be all right," he whispered as he stroked her hair. "It will be difficult—the hardest thing we have ever done—but we will get through this. Somehow, some way, everything will be all right."

"No!" she screamed, tearing herself from his embrace and shoving him away. "Do not *ever* say that to me again, Friedrich! Never! It will *not* be all right. Nothing will ever be all right ever again!"

The sides of the windowless deck seemed to be closing in around her. Her head was swimming, her heart was pounding, and it felt as if the weight of the entire world was pressing on her chest. She had to get out of that sea of humanity and find somewhere where she could breathe. Oblivious to the stirring and whispering of those around her, Sophie lifted Marie Louise's lifeless form from the lower berth and stumbled through the maze of cots, half walking, half crawling up the stairs to the upper deck of the ship.

Gulping in the cold night air, shaking uncontrollably, she collapsed near the rail, cradling Marie Louise and rocking back and forth, sobbing until she had no tears left. Had you asked her, she could not have told you how long she sat there. It could have been minutes or hours, days or weeks, perhaps even years. When Marie Louise stopped breathing, time stood still for Sophie. As she gradually became aware of her surroundings again, the first thing that registered was the rancid stench of the surly crew member who had threatened her earlier on. Her eyes widened in horror as she saw him, clearly outlined in the moonlight. He was close enough to touch her, a wanton, feral look in his rheumy gray eyes.

Pointing at Marie Louise, he made a noise that was somewhere between a snarl and a laugh. "Well, now. Looks like that one hain't goin' be making no noise no more." Brandishing a filthy rag in Sophie's direction, he licked his cracked and blistered lips. "And I'm here to make sure you stop yer noise-makin' as well. You was warned about the squalling." Sophie huddled against the rail, frozen in fear, too numb and exhausted to respond. The crewman bent over and reached for her arm but froze in his tracks when a stern voice addressed him from behind.

"Your assistance in this matter is not required, Mr. Wilson. If you are on duty, please return to your station. If not, please make your way back to your berth."

Spitting in Sophie's direction, the crewman shuffled off and went below.

"My apologies, madame. I am Mr. Brandorff, the ship's master. I will see that Mr. Wilson does not bother you again. May I ask what the trouble is?"

Sophie looked up. Blond, with a silver-streaked beard, Mr. Brandorff was tall and thin, yet exuded a wiry strength. His face was creased and weathered from many years at sea, but there was a calmness about him and kindness in his eyes.

"My daughter," Sophie said, her voice barely above a whisper. "She is dead."

"My sympathies, madame. We must, of course, immediately give her a sea burial, but I can offer a few appropriate words if you would like. My uncle was a parish priest, and I am familiar with the liturgy."

Sophie stared numbly for several moments, trying to gather her thoughts. *This cannot be happening. Sea burial? I cannot. Oh—Friedrich. I need Friedrich.* "My husband. He is below with our other daughter. He will want to be here."

"I doubt that, madame. No one ever *wants* to attend to matters such as this, but I understand your wish for his presence." Turning aside, Mr. Brandorff shouted toward the wheelhouse. "Mr. Fischer. Please, go below and bring the lady's husband and child. And pick up a length of sailcloth."

A short time later, Friedrich and Sophie Elise were on the deck beside her. Mr. Fischer handed Mr. Brandorff a bundle of frayed fabric, then returned to his post. Tears welled in Friedrich's eyes, then rolled silently down his face. Sophie Elise ran to her mother, still sitting on the deck, and, when she saw Marie Louise, shook her shoulder. When Marie did not stir, Sophie Elise began wailing at the top of her lungs.

"Sissy! Sissy! Wake up, sissy! Why won't she wake up, Mama?"

Mr. Brandorff lifted Marie Louise from Sophie's arms and gently wrapped her small form in the sailcloth. Sophie struggled to her feet, clinging to the rail with one hand, the other holding Sophie Elise close.

"Her name, please, madame?" Mr. Brandorff asked.

"Margarethe Marie Louise Rieple," Sophie whispered. "We called her Marie Louise."

"You are dust, Marie Louise Rieple, and to dust you shall return. In the sure and certain hope of Resurrection to Eternal Life in Jesus Christ our Lord, we commit your body to the sea. Blessed are those who die in the Lord, says the Spirit. Amen." Mr. Brandorff crossed himself, lowered Marie Louise over the rail and released her. Her tiny, frail body hit the water with a muffled splash that barely registered above the sound of the waves lapping the side of the ship. To Sophie—who felt as well as heard it—it was as though the entire universe had imploded. Limbs shaking, head pounding, her body convulsed with sobs, she crumpled to the deck, pulling Sophie Elise even closer.

Friedrich remained at the rail, staring into the inky waves, saying nothing.

A commotion near the stairway drew their attention. "Please, wait!" someone shouted. Sophie saw Christian and his wife, Louise, hurry toward them. Even through the haze of her grief, there was no mistaking the family resemblance. Raven-haired and blue-eyed, with the same height and build, Christian and Friedrich looked more like brothers than cousins. Louise hung back, clinging to Christian's arm, both sadness and uncertain wariness on her face.

Realizing Marie Louise's sea burial had already taken place, Louise began weeping quietly. Christian confronted Mr. Brandorff. "This was a family member of ours, my cousin's beautiful daughter. We just heard about her death and wanted the opportunity to kiss her goodbye. Would it have been too much to ask for you to wait just a few more moments until we arrived?"

"I was completely unaware you were on your way, sir. Please understand, I did not mean to intentionally exclude you. I am trying to save lives," Mr. Brandorff explained. "I am not a doctor and do not know exactly what the cause of the child's death was, but if perchance it was some sort of contagion, by doing this now, as quickly as possible, there is every hope that we may be able to halt the spread of disease. I am trying to make sure, to the best of my ability, that you and your family, along with the rest of the passengers, all live long enough to reach your destinations. My apologies, sir, and my deepest sympathies to all of you on your loss. Please, try to get some rest."

Mr. Brandorff bowed in Sophie's direction, then vanished into the night, leaving them in silence. Louise dabbed her eyes with her handkerchief. Sophie—still sitting on the deck—did her best to soothe Sophie Elise. At last, Christian spoke. "We are so sorry, Friedrich. I only wish we had known sooner how sick Marie Louise was. We came as soon as we heard she had died. Your hearts are broken, I am sure. Is there something we can do to help you? Perhaps you would like us to take Sophie Elise with us for a while. She and our Anna are close in age. They can play together, and Johanna will help keep an eye on her. You and Sophie should have a bit of time alone to grieve this terrible loss." Before Friedrich could respond, Sophie spoke.

"Thank you, Christian," she said, her tone icy and stiff. "But that will not be necessary. Losing one of my daughters is almost more than I can bear; I do not intend to let the other one out of my sight. Come, Sophie Elise. Mama will take you downstairs so you can go back to sleep."

"No sleep!" Sophie Elise screamed. "Sissy!"

Christian and Louise bade Friedrich goodnight as well and retired to their berth.

In his cabin at the stern of the ship, Mr. Brandorff opened the liquor cabinet and poured himself a drink, then sat down to log the events of the day. When he finished making a record of the day's sail, he pulled out the passenger list. He drew a line through Marie Louise's name, adding a cross beside the entry. In the far-right column marked "Number That Have Died on the Passage," he wrote the date, May 12, 1854. He didn't include any further explanation, but he had seen enough to know the likely cause of Marie Louise's death. The most common shipborne illnesses at that time—at least in his experience—were cholera and typhus. What he hoped, more than anything, was that his insistence on immediately burying her at sea had indeed halted the spread of whatever it was that had taken Marie Louise's life. He put away his pen and papers, downed the contents of his glass in one gulp, and retired for the night.

Friedrich stayed on deck, overcome with regret. All his pronouncements about their future being brighter in America came back to haunt him one by one. They were barely halfway there, and their family had been ripped apart. Sophie had not taken the decision to move well to begin with, and the voyage had already been extremely hard on her physically. This tragic turn of events might mean the death of their marriage, and possibly of the end of Sophie's life as well.

I kept assuring her things would be all right, but at this moment nothing is further from the truth. In addition to being heartsick over the loss of his baby girl and the grief this was causing both Sophie and himself, Friedrich was physically ill as well. As an adult, he had more physical reserves to fight off illness than Marie Louise had, but his health was declining with each passing day. He was trying his best to hold on, for Sophie's sake, and for his children, but he was not sure how long he would be able to do so. He buried his head in his hands and leaned on the rail, trying to figure out what to do, but in his extreme weariness and raw grief, he simply could not think.

Sleep, he told himself. *What I need first is sleep. I will go down and rest, and I will sort things out tomorrow.*

Below deck, Sophie was at her breaking point, her heart shattered, her spirit crushed. Mimicking her mother's mood, Sophie Elise sat on her lap, sobbing uncontrollably. *This entire trip has been one long series of nightmares, each one worse than the last.*

She thought back to the conversation she and Mina had the day their sister Catharine died. "Do not worry, Sophie,"

Mina had assured her. "This will never happen to you." *How I wish you had been right, Mina! But it has happened to me, and I do not know how I will survive. I would give anything to have you here to comfort me!* Her gaze fell on the trunk at the foot of her cot, full of all those things from home she'd insisted to Friedrich she could not live without: the brass candlestick that sat on the hall table, the linen napkins accented with hand-tatted lace, the silver samovar her mother so lovingly served coffee from in the dining room of her family home. She would gladly throw them all overboard in an instant if doing so would bring Marie Louise back. *How foolish you have been, Charlotte Sophia,* she told herself bitterly. *Things do not matter. Life and love are what matter.*

Still Sophie Elise wailed on, drawing ragged, shaky breaths irregularly between heaving sobs. Desperate to quiet her remaining child and her own jangled nerves, Sophie unbuttoned the bodice of her dress, loosened the laces of her petticoat, and pulled Sophie Elise close.

"Here, sweet princess," she whispered. "Have some Mama's milk."

That simple, desperate act calmed them both. Sophie Elise's sobs quieted, and as she nursed, Sophie's thoughts turned to her own mother. *Oh, Mama! How did you ever survive? You buried two babies! How were you able to live with that much grief and still insist that things would be all right? Whatever in the world made you say such a thing?*

Sophie recalled the very last conversation she had had with her mother. Margarethe had been seriously ill with pneumonia. Her condition deteriorated daily, to the point where she was barely able to breathe. Sophie had been there helping Mina tend her when Margarethe called them to her side. Clasping their hands in hers, she spoke.

"Do not worry about me," she had insisted between shallow, wheezing breaths. "Things did not always turn out the way I wanted them to, but still, my life has been a good one. Always remember: the choice is yours. You can be angry and miserable when disappointments come, or you can choose to live with faith and trust. It will be all right, my sweet, sweet girls. Somehow, some way, everything will be all right." She had smiled faintly, given their hands a firm squeeze, and drifted into blessed, peaceful, eternal rest.

Even when life seems out of control, we still have choices about how we respond. That was what was behind her mother's strength and optimism, Sophie realized. *Ach, Mama! How wise you were and how fortunate I am to have been born your child! Forgive me for ever doubting your words. I did not understand then, but now I see. And you were right all along. I am not in control of every event in my life. I cannot change what has already happened; much as I would love to turn back time and have my daughter back, it is not within my power, or anyone else's, to do so. But I can choose—from this moment forward—what I do with what life has handed me. Wallowing in my grief will serve no* one—not me, not Friedrich, and especially not Sophie Elise. They need me. So, I will choose as you chose. I will choose life. Even though my heart is broken, I will choose to believe and trust. The Lord giveth, the Lord taketh away. Blessed be the name of the Lord.

Looking down, she saw that Sophie Elise was finally asleep. She gently eased her child onto the bed. Buttoning her dress, she lay down as well and was lost in quiet slumber when Friedrich returned.

My sweet girls, he thought. *How grateful I am to see you resting after such a difficult and tragic night!*

From that moment forward, even as Friedrich seemed to fade away in front of her very eyes, Sophie's strength grew with each passing day. She showered affection on Friedrich and Sophie Elise with reckless abandon. She consumed as much as she could whenever there was food and drink available; she laughed, she talked, she slept. Though she fell asleep each night with tears staining her pillow, she woke each morning with an unshakable resolve that defied description. The other women pointed and whispered, not sure what to make of her. Those in close proximity stared when they heard her break into peals of laughter or regale Sophie Elise with fairy tales, all of which were filled with charming princes, beautiful princesses, great heroics, and had the happiest of endings. The crew members gaped in disbelief as she and Sophie Elise scampered and played on the upper deck each afternoon, their laughter echoing across the ship. Even cold, distant Louise, who usually ignored Sophie completely, noticed and commented.

"Sophie! This is not natural!" she insisted, her voice full of reproach. "Your baby daughter is dead. You should be overcome with grief."

"I *am* overcome with grief, Louise. My heart is well and truly broken. I miss Marie Louise every minute, and I grieve for her every single day. But grief is not the only thing in my life. It is as Solomon said in scripture: 'There is joy and sorrow.' I will embrace both. I can spend the rest of my days shrouded in misery and grief, or I can live with faith. Marie Louise's life ended when she took her last breath, but the rest of the world did not, and Friedrich and Sophie Elise need me. Life goes on, Louise, and I choose life. All of it."

Chapter Eight

The next afternoon, while playing with Sophie Elise on the upper deck, Sophie heard, in brief snippets of conversation between members of the crew, that they would be arriving in New Orleans in a matter of days. With great excitement, she shared the news with Friedrich that evening.

"We will be in New Orleans soon, my prince. We have many things to attend to. We will need to find a place to stay, and you and Christian will need to look for work. We should make arrangements to talk with those members of the crew, or perhaps Mr. Brandorff, and see what they know about the city. Sophie Elise is already asleep. You stay here, and I will go find Christian and bring him so you can make plans together."

"Work, Sophie?" Friedrich said, his voice full of both bitterness and disgust. "Look at me. I can barely walk. My hands are too weak and unsteady to write more than a few words at a time, and most days I'm too weary to concentrate. Work is impossible. There are no plans to make."

"Then I will speak with Christian. When we get to New Orleans, I will have him help me find a place for us to stay, and I will look for work."

"Doing what?"

"You always tell me what a talented seamstress I am. From everything I have heard, New Orleans is a large city and everyone needs clothes. I will make the rounds of the tailors' and dressmakers' shops and find work there. You can look after Sophie Elise and recuperate."

"I do not like the idea of you working, Sophie."

"Nor do I, but I like the idea of starving even less. If you are unable to work, then at the moment there is no other choice. Rest, sweet prince, and watch over our princess while she sleeps. I will go and speak with Christian." She patted his arm, then turned on her heel. Pulling a handkerchief out of her dress pocket and covering her nose and mouth, she made her way toward Christian and Louise's berth at the opposite end of the ship.

More than two hundred fifty men, women, and children were crowded into the rows of double-decker bunks that filled the steerage section. It was a space so dark and dismal, accomplishing even the simplest of daily activities—eating, sleeping, hygiene—was burdensome. The sheer number of people overwhelmed the few toilets at the bow of the ship;

many passengers, out of necessity, kept buckets by their berths for human waste and seasickness. That, along with a lack of clean water and a place for bathing, resulted in an overwhelming stench.

Knowing they would be at sea for several weeks, Sophie had carefully packed their linens with herbal sachets to keep them as fresh as possible, yet even with her lavender-soaked handkerchief held tightly to her face, she could barely keep from gagging and retching as she traversed the length of the vessel.

The sounds of human suffering were everywhere. She passed berth after berth of fellow passengers—obviously ill—huddled on their bunks coughing, wheezing, and moaning. Infants whimpered and wailed, youths bickered amongst themselves over anything and everything, and exhausted and exasperated parents screamed like shrews—both at their children and at each other.

Sophie was anxious and uncertain as she approached Christian and Louise's berth; all her previous attempts to become better acquainted with them had been fruitless. She still barely knew them and had no way of knowing how the news about Friedrich's ill health would be received. Hoping to settle both her stomach and her nerves, she stopped several feet away and took three deep breaths.

At one end of their bottom bunk, Louise sat reading to Anna and keeping a watchful eye on seven-year-old Johanna's sewing. At the other end, Christian was showing their boys

Friedrich and Carl, nine and five, how to tie various types of knots. Louise saw her approach and motioned to Christian, who called out a greeting. "Sophie! How are you? Is there something you need?"

"Hello, Christian. Hello, Louise. I am well, thank you. I need to speak with you about our plans. When I was on the main deck playing with Sophie Elise this afternoon, I overheard some of the crew members talking. It seems we will be in New Orleans soon. Just a few more days, at most."

Louise sighed audibly in relief. "Oh, I am so glad to hear that! I am more than ready to be on dry land once again!"

"As am I!" Sophie agreed. "I was hopeful you would accompany me to speak to Mr. Brandorff tomorrow, Christian, and see what he can tell us about the city and where we might find lodging and work."

"I had expected Friedrich and I would do that together."

"As did I. But that is not possible now."

"Not possible? Why not?" Eyebrows raised, Christian put down the rope he was tying and rose from the bunk.

"Friedrich is not well," Sophie said, nervously fidgeting with her handkerchief. "He has spent most of the time since Marie Louise's death in his berth. Until today, I assumed he was using the time to make notes in his journal about all the things we would need to do on our arrival. I was wrong."

"I had thought it was time to begin making plans, but not wanting to impose on you in your grief, I decided to wait and let Friedrich seek me out when he was ready," Christian said, worry on his face. "I am sorry to hear of his illness."

"I appreciate your concern. And while I, too, do not wish to impose, I have no choice but to ask for your assistance. With Friedrich unwell, it is now up to me to make arrangements for leaving the ship and finding lodging and employment in New Orleans. You will help me, won't you?" she asked, hoping she didn't sound too desperate.

"Of course. We will speak to Mr. Brandorff at his earliest convenience tomorrow morning, and then you and I can discuss what is best for us to do."

"Hmmph," Louise muttered. Glancing over, Sophie watched Louise's expression change from one of concern to an angry glare. Choosing to ignore it, she turned her attention back to Christian.

"Thank you so much," she said, masking her irritation over Louise's reaction with what she hoped was an appreciative smile. "I am anxious to hear what Mr. Brandorff can tell us, and to continue to make plans for our future. Until tomorrow then." She raised her handkerchief to her mouth again and turned to leave.

Mr. Brandorff was more helpful than she had ever dared to hope. Unbeknownst to her, there was already a large population of Germans in New Orleans, including a group Mr. Brandorff referred to as The German Society of New Orleans, whose sole reason for existence was to help immigrants like herself and her family get settled in the New World. Greatly relieved by the information they'd received, Sophie chattered nonstop as she and Christian walked back to their below-decks berths.

"I am so grateful to know there will be people to help us! People who speak our language, are familiar with the city, and can help us find a place to live . . ."

"Sophie—"

Wrapped up in her own thoughts and heedless of Christian's attempt to join the conversation, she prattled on. "As soon as you and I get Friedrich settled at the hotel, we will go to the German Society office and . . ."

"Sophie! There are other things we need to discuss."

"Oh, of course there are—many other things. You and I will need to secure employment. And I will also need to find a physician to treat Friedrich as quickly as possible, but according to what Mr. Brandorff said, that should not be difficult. There are many doctors and a hospital in New Orleans. With proper care, I am sure he will be well and able to work in no time. Then when we have saved up ample funds, we can travel to Illinois together!"

"Sophie!" Christian grabbed her wrist and pulled her around to face him. "Listen to me. We are not staying."

Sophie flinched and stumbled backward. Had Christian not still been holding her arm, she would have fallen overboard. "What do you mean 'we are not staying'?"

"Louise and I talked late into the night last night. As we conversed, it became clear to me that she and I must travel north immediately."

"But you promised you would help us!" She jerked her hand away, her shock and disbelief evaporating into a cold rage.

"I agreed that we would go together to talk to Mr. Brandorff, then discuss what was best for us—for *all* of us. Yours are not the only considerations here."

Sophie's eyes narrowed in an icy glare. "I did not say—nor did I intend to suggest—that Friedrich's and my concerns were more important than yours," she retorted. "There must be some way to address both your family's needs and ours in a way that is equitable. Could you not stay for a few weeks—just until we get settled and I find work?"

"No. I do not believe that is wise. The whole point of coming to America was to build a future for ourselves. I am afraid if we stay in New Orleans—even for a short time—we will lose the opportunity to purchase farmland in Illinois. I cannot bear the thought of having come all this way—caused my family to endure all of this hardship—for nothing. If Louise and I go now, we can find suitable property and start building immediately. When Friedrich is well enough to travel, you can join us. We will do everything we can to help you once you arrive."

"He cannot walk, Christian! Will you at least help me get him and our trunks from the ship to an inn or hotel?" she begged.

"I am sorry, Sophie. I cannot. This is indeed a cruel turn of events for Friedrich and places a terrible burden on you, but there is no time. I must get Louise and the children off the *John Schmidt* and secure passage to St. Louis as soon as we dock."

"If that is what you deem best for your family," she said, her voice hard and brittle, "then that is, of course, what you must do. Rest assured I will not trouble you any further—for anything."

Without waiting for a reply, she turned and walked back down the main deck in the opposite direction. Stopping amidships, she leaned against the rail, wrapped her arms tightly around herself and stared out across the waves. Livid with Christian and Louise for abandoning them when they most needed help, she was also fighting back panic.

I do not understand how Christian and Louise could be so heartless. How will I ever manage to get Friedrich and Sophie Elise and our belongings off the ship by myself? Had it been Christian who was ill, Friedrich would have done anything and everything—moved heaven and earth to assist. But I cannot let Friedrich see how upset I am or speak unkindly about Christian—this cousin he loves like a brother. Friedrich is frail and distraught enough as it is. I must not add to his misery.

Lord, have mercy. Have mercy on us all, and help me, please. I cannot do this alone.

As she walked back down the length of the deck and down the stairs to her family, she made a conscious effort with each step to breathe deeply, release her anxiety and panic, slow her pounding heart, and soften her expression.

By the time she reached their berth, she was almost calm. She kissed Friedrich's cheek and swept Sophie Elise into her arms in a bear hug.

"What did you find out, my sweet?" Friedrich asked.

"Mr. Brandorff was very helpful," she said, sitting down on the bunk beside him and taking his hands in hers. "There is, what did he call it? A German Society, a group that helps people like us who are just arriving in America get settled. He will give me specific instructions on how to get in touch with them when we arrive, and they will help us find a place to live, a place for me to work, and a doctor for you, my prince." She did not mention her conversation with Christian and hoped Friedrich would not think to ask.

"Ah, that is good. You have done well, my darling. I am so sorry you have to do this on your own and I am not able to help. Are Christian and Louise going to be nearby?"

Sophie groaned inwardly, wondering how to answer his question without causing him distress or sounding bitter and angry. After a moment, she simply said, "Christian and Louise have made other plans."

"Ah." She could hear the sadness and resignation in his voice. "I am sure Christian is doing what he deems best for his family, just as you are working so hard to take care of us. It will be all right, Sophie. Somehow, some way, everything will be all right."

"I'm sure it will, my prince," she said, struggling to swallow her ire and keep from lashing out. "I think I will take

Sophie Elise to the upper deck where she can play in the fresh air. Would you like to come with us? I can find Mr. Fischer and ask him to come and help you up the stairs."

"No, my sweet. I thank you, but I think I will stay here. You are right; we have many important decisions to make. I need to collect my thoughts."

Anxious to move on with their lives, for Sophie, those last few days on the ship seemed to drag by. While she and Sophie Elise played on deck each afternoon, Friedrich remained in his bunk, making notes in his journal as he was able.

At last, at midmorning on a brilliant, sunny day under a cloudless azure sky, she heard Mr. Brandorff calling out orders for the crew to make ready to dock. He graciously sent Mr. Fischer to help her get Friedrich and their trunks off the ship and find them transport to the closest hotel, and had given her the location of the German Society's office so she could begin getting them settled as quickly as possible. She had listened carefully as he described the city and what they would find there the morning she and Christian met with him, but nothing he said prepared her for the sights that greeted her when she stepped off the deck of the *John Schmidt* and onto the pier.

Chapter Nine

A sprawling, raucous melting pot, Antebellum New Orleans was unlike anything Sophie had ever experienced. The harbor in Bremen seemed calm in comparison. As the wagon slowly made its way through the crowded streets from the waterfront to the hotel, her senses were assaulted by what seemed like a thousand things she had never seen, heard, or experienced before.

Accustomed to enjoying the fresh sea breeze on the deck of the ship for the past few weeks, she was ill prepared for the stench that hung in the humid Louisiana air. The smell of human excrement combined with rotting fish, the sweat of fishermen and dock workers, and the piles of trash that lined the harbor boardwalk left her coughing and gagging. Slave markets lined the streets near the pier where dark-skinned people—most naked, or nearly so—were penned like animals, waiting to be bought and sold. A large crowd milled around inside the first enclosure they passed, punctuating the auctioneer's calls with shouted bids. An even larger crowd watched from outside the fence, roaring in either approval or dismay every time the rap of the gavel signified a sale had been made. A short distance from the crowd outside the fence, a lone man in a black suit stood waving a Bible and decrying the buying and selling with moral judgments and threats of eternal damnation.

The wagon ground to a momentary halt as several people hurried across the street in front of them. Sophie gaped in horror as one of the auctioneer's assistants shoved a young African girl into the center of the ring, then, in response to the auctioneer's insistence to show the crowd her "attributes," ripped her thin, ragged shift open. Shamed and embarrassed, the girl tried to cover herself, only to have her hands smacked away by the ring man's whip. Shuddering in disgust and outraged by such cruelty, Sophie turned away. She was familiar with servitude—indentures, apprenticeships, "hiring out." In tumultuous times with harsh economic realities—like those in her homeland during the war with Denmark—that was the only means of survival for some. But she had never witnessed human beings being bought and sold—and beaten—in public and regarded as a means of entertainment by the local citizenry.

People of every culture and nationality under the sun crowded the busy thoroughfares. The shop windows were filled with unusual objects and foods, and exotic aromas filled the streets. There were clusters of women on every corner wearing heavy makeup and little else. They shouted at male passersby in a variety of different languages, none of which Sophie understood, although the wads of currency stuffed in their bosoms and the straps of their garter belts made it clear some sort of commerce was involved.

"What in the world are they selling, Friedrich?" she whispered. She saw no carts or baskets nearby, no bread or linens or vegetables or flowers.

"They are selling themselves, Sophie," he sighed wearily.

Shocked into silence, she put her hands over Sophie Elise's ears and diverted her gaze to the other side of the street. A bustling port city, New Orleans seldom slept, but the summer of 1854 was particularly boisterous. The previous year had been one of the worst in the Crescent City's history as a Yellow Fever epidemic ravaged the population from May through October. Nearly eight thousand people had perished, and in the wake of such catastrophic suffering and death, the city had nearly ground to a halt. Ships stopped arriving, trade dried up, and chaos ensued. But now, with the epidemic over, ships sailed in and out of the harbor daily, and the city's pulse was pounding once again. This was good news for Sophie, had she realized what it meant. It would be much easier for her to find work now that economic recovery was in full swing. Instead, her mind was occupied with the unfamiliar and unnerving scenes she'd witnessed as the wagon slowly rumbled through the crowds toward the hotel.

This is a terrible place. I cannot imagine raising a child in such an environment. Christian was right. We should be on the next boat north, too.

By the time they reached the hotel, she was on sensory overload and Friedrich was completely exhausted. Thankfully, the proprietor, Mr. Kruger, spoke German, and she had no trouble at all planning for their stay. He assured her that the bellman would assist her in getting Friedrich upstairs and their trunks to their room. He was even kind enough to confirm the directions to the German Society office Mr. Brandorff had given her, and she was relieved to learn it was just a few blocks from the hotel.

Too weak to grip the stair rail and support himself, it took both Sophie and the bellman nearly twenty minutes to get Friedrich up the staircase and settled in their room. Checking the time, she found it was after one o'clock.

"It is past time for our midday meal. I will go get you something to eat, my prince. What would you like?"

"I am not hungry, Sophie. Some water is all I need."

"Cookies, Mama!" shouted Sophie Elise.

"I will bring you a proper meal, princess. We will see about cookies later, I promise."

She went downstairs to the front desk and inquired of Mr. Kruger about food for her family.

"It is past our usual luncheon service. There is a market across the street and at the end of the block, but just having come from the dock, I am sure madame has not had a chance to obtain any local currency. I can arrange for some bread, cheese, and fruit to be sent to your room," Mr. Kruger promised.

"Oh, thank you so much." Sophie breathed a sigh of relief. "Is there a bank or exchange office close by where I can change our currency for what is used locally?"

"Yes, madame. The bank in this district will be able to help you and is not far away. I can provide you with directions."

"I have plans to visit the German Society office this afternoon as well. Is the bank perhaps close by?"

"Ah, the clerks at the German Society will be able to offer you all the assistance you need," he assured her.

"Thank you again, Herr Kruger. I am deeply grateful for your assistance."

Sophie went back upstairs to their room, and within moments, a member of the hotel staff came bearing a tray filled with bread, cheese, and bananas, water for Friedrich, and a glass of milk for Sophie Elise.

"There is supposed to be someone at the German Society office until five o'clock, Friedrich," Sophie said, after she and Sophie Elise finished eating. "If you will be all right, I will go and see what I can do to find us a place to live and inquire about work. And according to Herr Kruger,

I will also need to see about exchanging our currency. Do you feel strong enough to keep an eye on Sophie Elise, or should I take her with me?"

"I am sorry, my sweet, but the carriage ride from the ship has seemed to sap every ounce of my strength," Friedrich apologized. "I know it will be inconvenient, but I think it would be best if she went with you."

"Rest well then, my prince. There is a glass of water for you on the table next to the bed. I will return as quickly as I can." She kissed Friedrich's forehead, picked up her handbag, then called Sophie Elise. "Come, princess. You and Mama are going for a walk." Sophie Elise clapped her hands gleefully and skipped ahead of Sophie as they walked through the hotel hallway and down the stairs. "Take my hand, please," Sophie said as they reached the front door. "There are many people outside, and I do not want you to get lost."

In a matter of minutes, they had walked the few blocks to the German Society office. Much to Sophie's relief, even though the streets were busy, everyone seemed intent on their own affairs; no one bothered her in any way. Just inside the door, a man sat at a large table covered with stacks of forms, a large ledger, pens, and pencils. After being asked for their names, they were shown to a crowded waiting area filled with row after row of straight wooden chairs. Sophie recognized many of the people waiting as fellow passengers from the *John Schmidt*. She found a single empty seat in the row farthest away from the door and pulled Sophie Elise onto her lap. "We must sit and wait quietly until it is our turn, princess. If you are tired, you can sleep in Mama's lap while we wait."

"No sleep, Mama. Play!" Sophie Elise giggled, but it was very warm in the waiting room, and she soon became drowsy and fell asleep in Sophie's arms. People were regularly escorted back into a different part of the building, but there was a steady stream of new arrivals all afternoon; the waiting room remained full. After an hour's time, a gentleman approached her.

"Madame Rieple? Good afternoon. I am Herr Franke, and it is my pleasure to assist you today. Please, follow me." They wound their way through the crowded waiting room and down a narrow hallway to a cramped windowless office in the back of the building. "Please, have a seat, madame. What can we help you with?"

Sophie explained that they had just arrived on the *John Schmidt* and had been directed to the society by the ship's master, Mr. Brandorff. "We need a place to stay," she continued, "and I will need to find work. Although my husband is highly skilled in several different trades, the voyage was very difficult for him, and he is not well enough to work at present. We had planned to travel north with his cousin's family and had thought they would be able to assist us, but their plans have changed."

"It will take a day or two to arrange, but we should be able to find lodging for you. There are several rooming houses in the city. How many in your family, madame?"

"Just my husband, myself, and our daughter."

"Three. Very good." Herr Franke nodded. "Now, you mentioned employment for yourself. Might I inquire what skills you have?"

Sophie shifted nervously in her chair, unsure how to answer.

Would it be considered lying if I say I am a seamstress even though I have never been formally employed? What will I say if Herr Franke asks for the names of employers or dress shops I have worked at? I do not want to be untruthful, but I have to have a job, and I do not know any other way I can find one.

"I am a seamstress," she said, hoping she sounded more competent and certain than she felt. "Back home in Rheda, I made all of our clothing, pieced quilts, knitted scarves, hats, gloves, and socks, crocheted and tatted, and embroidered linens. I also designed and crafted both my and my sister's wedding gowns. I was hoping I would be able to secure employment in one of the dressmaker's or tailor's shops."

"Very good, madame." Herr Franke nodded his approval. "And do you speak other languages besides German?"

"I am fluent in French."

"Excellent. If you would be so kind as to tell me where you are staying at the moment, I will make note of that. As soon as we have located lodging for you and your family, I will send word to you."

Sophie gave him the name of the hotel and the number of the room they had been assigned.

"You will hear from us as quickly as arrangements can be made, Mrs. Rieple, hopefully in just a few days. You mentioned your husband is unwell. I will also send word to Dr. Foster and request that he call on your husband at his earliest convenience. Is there anything else we can help you with today?"

"Just one more thing," she said. "I will need directions to the local bank."

"If madame needs local currency, we can change a few thalers for you," Herr Franke assured her. "And I will also write down the address and directions to the nearest bank."

Sophie shifted Sophie Elise's sleeping form and reached inside her handbag, then handed Herr Franke a handful of coins.

"I shall be back momentarily, madame."

Herr Franke returned shortly with several bills and a card with directions to the bank.

Sophie thanked him profusely and rose to leave. Sophie Elise stirred and stretched in her arms. "Ah," Sophie exclaimed. "My sweet princess is awake. Come, Mama is finished here. Time to go back to the hotel and see Papa."

They found Friedrich sleeping when they returned, his journal beside him. Sophie was relieved he was able to rest. She settled Sophie Elise with one of her dolls and set about unpacking the things they would need for the evening. She laid Friedrich's comb, straight razor, shaving cream, brush, and mug on the dresser, along with her own hairbrush and nightcap. Out of the other trunk, she got nightgowns for herself and Sophie Elise, pajamas for Friedrich, and robes for each of them.

As she unpacked, she marveled at how helpful the staff at the German Society had been. *I have no idea how I would have managed to make all of the necessary arrangements by myself.*

A short while later, Friedrich stirred and opened his eyes.

"Papa!" Sophie Elise squealed in delight, running to the bed and hugging him.

"Ah, my sweet, you have returned. What did you find out?"

"It may be a day or two, but the man at the German Society said he should be able to find us lodging. They will send word to us here as soon as arrangements can be made, and they will also have a doctor come as well."

"Ah. That is good. You have done well, my sweet. And how was our little princess?" Friedrich asked, patting Sophie Elise gently on the head. "Not too much trouble, I hope."

"Not at all. She napped quietly while we were waiting and did not wake up until I was ready to return. It will be suppertime soon, Friedrich. I will go downstairs and get something for you to eat. Just tell me what it is you would like."

"Nothing for me, Sophie. I have no appetite."

"You must eat, Friedrich. You are wasting away."

"Perhaps tomorrow, my sweet, when I have had a bit more rest. I will surely be hungry by then. You and Sophie Elise should go to the dining room and get some supper. I am sure our little princess is ready for a cookie," he added, smiling and winking at Sophie Elise.

"We will be back soon, my sweet." Kissing him lightly on the forehead, she gathered Sophie Elise and headed downstairs to the elegantly appointed dining room. Compared to her experience on the ship, the hotel felt like Eden. After six weeks of gruel, boiled potatoes, and stale bread, Sophie had almost forgotten what good food tasted like. It was not the cheese, cold cuts, and vegetables she was accustomed to having for the evening meal, but the dishes were well prepared and delicious. She and Sophie Elise shared a plate of roasted beef served with mashed potatoes smothered in rich brown gravy, butter-and-brown-sugar glazed carrots, and a freshly baked baguette. The hot tea was divine—a luxury she hadn't enjoyed since the morning they'd left Bremen.

"Are you finished, my princess? Shall we go back upstairs and see Papa?"

"No Papa! Cookies!" Sophie Elise insisted.

"That's right." Sophie smiled. "We talked about cookies. Mama will ask." When the waiter returned to the table, Sophie inquired if there were any cookies available.

"I am sorry, madame, not here. There is a bakery at the end of the block that sells various kinds: tea cakes, Madeleines, molasses cookies, and meringues. They will be open first thing in the morning. For now, might I suggest some beignets?"

"Ben— what? What sort of dish is that?"

"A local specialty, madame. A small, fried pastry, topped with fine sugar. I would be happy to bring some for you and the little one to try. They are quite delicious."

The waiter returned shortly with another cup of tea for Sophie and a plate of pastries buried under a mountain of confectioner's sugar. She had never seen anything like them, but she tried one and found that the waiter was correct. They were indeed one of the most delicious things she had ever tasted. She handed one to Sophie Elise, who gobbled it up instantly, clapping her hands in delight and engulfing them both in a blizzard of powdered sugar.

"Look, Mama! Snow!" Sophie Elise dipped her hands in the sugar and clapped again, giggling as the fine white powder once again filled the air around them.

"Yes, princess, you are right," Sophie agreed with a chuckle. "It does look like snow. One more, then we must go."

Sophie sipped her tea pensively while Sophie Elise finished the last beignet, caught between joy and concern.

Their evening meal in the hotel dining room had been a heavenly—but momentary—respite; she relished savoring the delicious food and seeing her daughter's unbridled joy, but she could not shut her worry over Friedrich and his condition out of her mind.

"Come, princess," Sophie said, wiping Sophie Elise's face and hands with her napkin. "Time to go see Papa."

Chapter Ten

True to their word, within two days' time, the miracle workers at the German Society of New Orleans had secured lodging for Sophie and her family in a modest rooming house in one of the predominantly German neighborhoods near the business district. Sophie had been able to secure employment at Madame DuVall's dress shop just a few blocks away the very afternoon they moved in, and the older couple in the room next to theirs, the Mullers, had volunteered to look after Sophie Elise while Sophie worked each day.

Recent arrivals from Bavaria, Franz and Elisabeth Muller—who, the moment she saw them, reminded Sophie both of her parents and Mr. and Mrs. Schmidt—had come to New Orleans for the same reason most German immigrants made the trip: to escape the upheaval and hardship in their homeland. Mr. Muller—formerly a mason but at nearly sixty unable to work long hours laying bricks and setting stone in the Louisiana heat—did odd jobs and repairs and ran errands for the boardinghouse and other nearby businesses. Mrs. Muller, in her late forties, helped the proprietress with the laundry at the rooming house each week and did alterations and mending. Many of the other rooming house residents were regular customers of hers.

A devout Christian who took seriously the gospel mandates to "love thy neighbor" and "do unto others," Mrs. Muller bustled over with a bowl of fruit and a laundry list of helpful hints about the rhythms of life in the rooming house as soon as Friedrich and Sophie arrived and was instantly taken with Sophie's plight—a small child and a sick husband to care and provide for. She fell in love with Sophie Elise and doted on her in the same manner Dorothea Schmidt doted on Sophie and her siblings back in Rheda.

Everything had fallen into place except for Friedrich's health. The doctor had come the day after her visit to the German Society and had tried many treatments over the course of the week, but Friedrich's condition continued to worsen. He could eat nothing, and soon he was no longer able to leave his bed. Sophie worked from eight o'clock in the morning until six o'clock each evening, and then spent most of each night attending to Friedrich's needs, cleaning him up, applying cold compresses to his face and neck to cool him off, turning him to try to make him more comfortable. Nothing helped.

"I am so, so sorry, my sweet prince. I wish there was more I could do to comfort you." She stroked his hair and wiped his feverish brow with a cool cloth.

"Do not worry, Sophie. You are doing your best, and I appreciate your care for me. Try to get some rest, my love. I know you have work tomorrow."

Miraculously, both of them slept for several hours that night. At six o'clock the next morning, Sophie rose and dressed. Friedrich awoke soon after that. She bathed him and dressed him in clean pajamas and put fresh linens on the bed. By then, Sophie Elise was awake and ready to be fed and dressed.

"Can I get you anything before I leave for work, my prince? Would you like some water?"

"Just bring my pencil and my journal, my sweet, and I will be fine."

She laid the journal and pencil next to him on the bed, kissed his forehead, gathered up Sophie Elise, and went out the door.

Friedrich picked up his pencil and began writing. Even after sleeping the night before, he was bone-tired, and the pain in his midsection was increasing alarmingly. The shortness of breath that accompanied any movement forced him to stop often and rest. Still, he doggedly wrote on.

I had such grand plans, he thought bitterly as he struggled to get words onto the page. *I never expected anything like the horrors we have experienced in the past six weeks. Perhaps that was my biggest fault: clinging to my dream of an idyllic new life in America to the exclusion of all else. There is a part of me that still cannot believe my life is ebbing away with each passing moment, but it is true. I am weary unto death. I do not know if I have enough strength to say everything I need to say, but I must try. I cannot leave this world without making sure Sophie and my darling little princess know how much I love them.*

When all but the last two pages of the journal were filled, he laid it aside and dozed off in fitful sleep. By late afternoon, the pain was too intense to allow him to rest any longer. He tossed and turned, trying to find a comfortable position, but nothing he tried did anything to alleviate the cramping, and his frequent movements only increased his exhaustion.

When Sophie returned from work that evening, she found him wide awake, covered in watery excrement and writhing in agony. She immediately went next door and explained what was happening to Mrs. Muller and asked if she could watch Sophie Elise a little while longer.

"Of course, Sophie dear. I will make certain the babe has a bite of supper, and I will keep her for the evening as well. You tend to your poor dear Friedrich, and do not worry about us. Would you like me to send Mr. Muller to fetch the doctor?"

"Oh, yes, if it would not be too much trouble. I hate to see Friedrich suffering so." While she waited for Dr. Foster to arrive, Sophie busied herself cleaning him up. She put Friedrich's pencil and journal in the dresser, carefully changed the linens, and bathed and dressed him in fresh pajamas, trying to be as gentle as possible in the process.

When he arrived, Dr. Foster examined Friedrich carefully.

"I am sorry, madame," he told Sophie. "I have tried every treatment that is available, but by the time cholera progresses to this point, there is little that can be done besides try to keep the patient as comfortable as possible. I can offer some medication that may help alleviate the pain and allow him to rest." He pulled a small brown bottle out of his bag. "Here, Herr Rieple. Take a small sip." He placed the cap back on the bottle and handed it to Sophie. "Offer him a small amount of this liquid every few hours. Hopefully it will help keep him comfortable."

Stunned and in shock, Sophie stared blankly at the small brown bottle in her hand.

"If the medicine does not help and he is still in pain tomorrow, I will try to make arrangements to have him admitted to the hospital," Dr. Foster said, closing his bag. "More than that, I cannot do. Again, I am sorry."

"Thank you, Dr. Foster. I appreciate your efforts."

After showing Dr. Foster to the door, she collapsed in the chair at Friedrich's bedside. The doctor's pronouncement that there was little that could be done prompted a series of painful memories: first her sister Catharine's death back home in Rheda, then that horrible night on the deck of the *John Schmidt* when she sat and wept over Marie Louise's lifeless body. *This cannot be happening* again. *Have I angered the Almighty in some grievous and unforgiveable way and unleashed this suffering upon us? Is everyone and everything I love going to be taken from me? Oh, sweet prince! I cannot even begin to imagine life without you.*

Sophie curled up beside Friedrich, her left hand in his, her head on his chest monitoring his respiration. Within a short time, his pain eased enough for him to doze off, but he was not able to sleep for long. Soon he was again tossing and turning and moaning in pain. Sophie found it necessary to administer several doses of the medicine during the night. Her fear and worry deepened with each passing hour.

Lord in heaven, please help us. He cannot go on like this. And neither can I.

"I am going to leave early, my sweet," she told Friedrich the next morning. "I will go speak to Dr. Foster before work and ask him to come and take another look at you. Here, take another small sip of the medicine before I go."

Sophie stopped at Mrs. Muller's and told her how the night had gone. "I am going to speak to Dr. Foster and ask him to come by and see Friedrich again today. He said that if the medicine did not help with the pain that he may admit Friedrich to the hospital." She spoke softly, hoping Sophie Elise would not overhear and become upset.

"Ach, the poor dear. I will take care of the little one. Do not fret about a thing."

"Thank you, Mrs. Muller. You are an angel!"

But as Sophie walked the tree-lined streets toward Dr. Foster's residence, Mrs. Muller's words nagged at her.

"Do not fret about a thing," she says. She sounds just like Mama. I know she means well, but my husband is dying. I can do nothing but fret. About everything!

Dr. Foster was just coming down the front steps of his home. She explained that she had used the medicine several times during the night, but Friedrich's pain kept returning.

"Yes, Madame Rieple. I understand. As soon as I have spoken to the hospital staff, I will send a messenger to Madame DuVall's to let you know what arrangements have been made."

"Thank you, Dr. Foster."

Sophie went to the dress shop and began her tasks for the day. There was a wedding gown to finish the beading on, which must be ready by Friday afternoon, and this was already Wednesday. After that, there were several Christening gowns on order that would need her intricate embroidery added to the skirts. Sophie tried her best to concentrate, but her thoughts kept going back to her poor Friedrich. She kept glancing at the clock, wondering how soon Dr. Foster's messenger might arrive, and praying it would be soon. It was midafternoon when the messenger finally came to the shop.

"I have a message for you from Dr. Foster, Madame Rieple. He instructed me to tell you there are no hospital beds available at the moment. He will continue to check on Mr. Rieple daily and will have him transported to the hospital as soon as there is room."

"I understand," Sophie murmured. "Thank you for delivering the message." She spoke quietly, trying not to draw attention to herself or disturb the other workers around her, but on the inside, panic welled up inside her. *How am I going to be able to care for him, and work too?*

Just as Sophie was rising to go speak to her, Madame DuVall strode over to her worktable, her brow knitted in concern. "I heard what the messenger said, Sophie. And I have been observing, throughout the day, how difficult it has been for you to concentrate on your work. If it would lead to you being more productive, I could allow you to leave now and take some of the orders home with you. Sit and sew by Friedrich's side. When he is admitted to the hospital, which I hope happens before the day is out, you can immediately return to the shop and work your regular hours."

Tall, thin, beautiful, yet severe, Jeannette DuVall was a driven woman with exacting standards. Born in one of the poorest neighborhoods of Paris, she struggled throughout her childhood, which was defined by one thing: deprivation. Seeing her mother struggle daily to find work and put food on the table, watching as a steady stream of men came and went—but never stayed—she learned at an early age to take care of herself, to do what she had to do to survive. Work was the god that ordered her days, financial security and self-sufficiency the altar she worshipped at, and she had no time or patience for those who did not share her views.

She fled Paris and came to America in her late twenties and immediately began building a career as a milliner. By 1854, her stock of high-quality fabrics, her keen sense of style, and her insistence on flawless craftsmanship had made her one of the most sought-after dressmakers in the city. She required all work to be done in-house so she could personally supervise both the execution and the quality of the finished product. From her work area, a raised platform spanning the entire rear of the building, she could see all the way to the street, allowing her to monitor everything and everyone in the shop. Instantly recognizing Sophie's creative talents and considerable skills on her first day at work, Madame DuVall knew she would be a tremendous asset to the business. It was for that reason alone—not out of sympathy or charity—that she bent the rules and allowed Sophie to take work home.

"I am so grateful, madame!" Sophie exclaimed in relief. "I will be back in the shop as quickly as possible. The christening gowns are small; I will take those. I should be able to complete several of them this evening." Gathering a stack of the white gowns and her sewing supplies, she rushed out the door, nearly running the eight blocks back to the rooming house.

It was obvious when she walked into their room that Friedrich was markedly worse. He was burning up with fever, moaning in pain but otherwise unresponsive. Although his moaning became louder, he did not open his eyes or make any effort to speak when she bathed and dressed him in clean, dry clothes. She tried to give him another dose of the medicine Dr. Foster left, but he was not able to swallow. Sophie prayed harder than she had ever prayed in her life that Dr. Foster's orderly would be there soon to take Friedrich to the hospital, but minutes turned into hours, and still no one arrived. Consumed with sorrow, Sophie sat by the bed holding Friedrich's hand. She was supposed to be sewing, but she couldn't stop her tears long enough to see to craft the stitches.

At eight o'clock she heard a knock at the door. *Finally!* she thought to herself, as she rushed to answer it. But it was not the orderly, as she had hoped. Instead, it was Dr. Foster.

"I stopped by to check on Mr. Rieple on my way home from the hospital," he said. "I am sorry, madame. There are still no beds available." He examined Friedrich, and then turned to address Sophie, his expression grave. "His condition continues to deteriorate, madame. I must warn you that it is entirely possible that he may not survive long enough to be admitted to the hospital. Paralysis has started to set in, and I fear his vital organs are failing."

Sophie collapsed into her chair and began weeping once again. "What am I going to do?" she wailed. She knew Friedrich was gravely ill; Dr. Foster had told her two days ago that nothing could be done besides try to keep Friedrich comfortable. Still, she was not prepared for his imminent death. Even as his health visibly failed and her concern mounted daily—even though she knew the end was coming—she could not yet fully face it.

While Sophie struggled to come to terms with Dr. Foster's words, there was another knock at the door. When Sophie answered, Mrs. Muller came in carrying Sophie Elise in her arms. "I hate to bring more bad news, Sophie, but I am afraid the little one is ailing as well. She started taking sick last night, but I knew you had your hands full taking care of Friedrich, and I did not want to add to your worry. I kept hoping she would be better after a good night's sleep, but she has only gotten worse as the day has gone on." Sophie Elise whimpered and reached for Sophie.

"Lay her down on the bed, please," Dr. Foster said, "and I will have a look."

After several minutes, he turned to Sophie. "I am afraid, madame, that the little one is suffering with the same malady afflicting Mr. Rieple. Because she is so small, the disease will progress even faster. It will only be a matter of days, and very few days at that. If she is in pain, you may try a drop of the medicine that I left for your husband. If a hospital bed becomes available, I will send my orderly and have her admitted at once."

Chapter Eleven

Sophie spent the night doing her best to comfort her ailing family. For the most part, Friedrich remained unresponsive; the medicine Dr. Foster left quieted Sophie Elise for an hour or two at a time, so Sophie rested when she could. The next morning, Mrs. Muller sat with Friedrich and Sophie Elise so Sophie could go to the dress shop and explain to Madame DuVall that Friedrich had not been admitted to the hospital and she would not be able to come to work. She promised to keep working on the christening gowns at home while she tended Friedrich and Sophie Elise. "As soon as I have them finished, I will have Mr. Muller bring them to the shop. You can send more work back with him."

"I *hope*, for all our sakes, that this is not a prolonged circumstance, Sophie."

Sophie cringed inside seeing the scowl on Madame DuVall's face. The impatience and resentment in her voice struck fear in Sophie's heart.

"I hope not as well, madame. I will be back in the shop as soon as Friedrich and Sophie Elise have been admitted to the hospital, I assure you. I am praying there will be beds available before the day is out."

"Hmmm." Madame DuVall raised one eyebrow, her skepticism evident. "Very well then. Go on. Get as much done as you can, and I will expect you back here at your earliest convenience."

"Of course, madame."

Both enraged by Madame DuVall's lack of compassion and fearful of losing her job, Sophie rushed out of the shop, slamming the door behind her. *I thought when I was allowed to take work home, I would be able to rely on Madame DuVall's understanding and kindness. I was mistaken. It is obvious she cares only about her business and not about the lives of the people in her employ. There must be hospital beds available for my prince and princess today. And I must get those gowns done.*

Hoping both Friedrich and Sophie Elise were sleeping— or at least resting as comfortably as possible—she slipped quietly into their room.

"How are they doing, Mrs. Muller?"

"About the same as when you left, dearie. I promised I would help the proprietress get caught up on the laundry today. Let me help you put clean linens on the beds, and I will take these down and make sure they get washed."

"Oh, thank you!" Sophie hugged Mrs. Muller in gratitude. "You are too kind!"

"I am happy to do what I can. If you need something in the night, just knock."

"I will. Hopefully, I will hear from Dr. Foster soon. Thank you again."

But the orderly did not come that day. There was little time to sew with two seriously ill people to take care of, but Sophie did her best to keep working, and the next morning she was able to send Mr. Muller to the dress shop with three completed christening gowns. He returned with a half dozen more for her to work on. "Just set them on my chair, please, Mr. Muller. I will get started on them after I bathe and dress Friedrich and Sophie Elise. Thank you for all of your help." Tipping his hat, Mr. Muller solemnly bade her goodbye.

She got a pitcher of water and basin and bathed Friedrich, taking care to move him as little as possible. After dressing him in clean night clothes, she gently rolled him onto his left side so she could put fresh linens on the bed. As hard as it was, both physically and emotionally, she was grateful for the opportunity to provide what comfort and care she could for the ones she loved most. Focusing on her family's needs kept her from dwelling on Madame

DuVall's harsh words the day before, and the hurt and anger they'd caused.

On the opposite side of the bed from where Friedrich was facing, engrossed in tucking the sheet in as tightly as possible so the bed was smooth and comfortable, Sophie was startled by a sudden gurgling, choking sound. "Friedrich!" she screamed in alarm. "What is happening?" Rushing to his side, she frantically tried to prop him up, hoping that would help clear his airway enough for him to breathe. Before she could lift him high enough to get a pillow positioned behind his head, he was overcome by a paroxysm of violent coughing. She watched helplessly as blood gushed from his mouth, splattering everywhere. The sight of Friedrich struggling to breathe and the horrible strangling sounds he was making terrified Sophie. She ran next door in panic, pounding on the Mullers' door. "Help me! Please! And send Mr. Muller to get Dr. Foster!"

Mr. Muller left at once. Mrs. Muller followed Sophie back to their room and helped her turn Friedrich over and get his head elevated, then began mopping up the river of blood that covered him, the bed, the chair, and the christening gowns. Friedrich's coughing and wheezing gradually eased once he was on his back; the bleeding decreased as well, slowing to just a trickle at the corner of his mouth, then stopping a few moments later. Mr. Muller returned just then with Dr. Foster; the Mullers slipped out while Sophie—still shaking with fear—recounted what had happened.

He listened carefully to her explanation, then turned his attention to Friedrich, checking his vital signs and examining his extremities. "His respiration continues to decrease. His pulse is getting weaker due to the loss of blood. It will not be long, madame. I am sorry."

All of the emotion pounding in Sophie's veins just moments ago—the adrenaline, the horror, the panic and fear—vanished as Dr. Foster's words sunk in. A dull ache settled in the center of her chest.

"How long?" she asked timidly, fearful of both the answer to that question and of what might happen in the meantime. Watching Friedrich suffer so was heartbreaking; she was not sure she could take any more.

"Moments. An hour, perhaps; two at most. If you would like, I will remain here with you until the end."

"If you would be so kind, sir, I would appreciate it very much. I am exhausted, and still quite afraid; I do not believe I can face this alone."

They passed the next half hour at Friedrich's bedside. Dr. Foster on his right, occasionally checking his pulse and listening to his heart. Sophie on his left, her right hand holding Friedrich's hand to her cheek, her left hand on his chest, silent tears streaming down her face, as she recounted everything this man meant to her.

Oh, my prince. I will never forget the very first time I saw you. I was transfixed by how handsome you were, the sincerity and compassion in your beautiful blue eyes, and the kindness and courtesy with which you treated me—and everyone else. And that never changed. Your love for me and your patience with me—even when I was demanding and impatient, which was far more often than I want to admit—was never-ending. And you treated our darling girls the same way. The joy on your face when you held Sophie Elise for the first time is a memory I will cherish always. The only thing that would add to the wonderful life we shared would be to have you forever.

At 10:30 a.m., Friedrich drew one last, shuddering breath.

"I am sorry, madame," Dr. Foster said. "I will send word to the undertaker at once."

Sophie nodded without speaking. Dr. Foster checked on Sophie Elise, then let himself out, while she continued to sit at Friedrich's side.

I cannot believe you are gone, and all I have left is aching emptiness, dust and ashes. You would still be alive had we stayed in Rheda, I am certain, but there is no point in wasting time thinking about that. You had your heart set on building a new life for us here, and there was nothing that would change your mind.

But you suffered so much for your dream! And I abandoned you in that suffering. From the moment the decision was made to come to America, I became consumed with myself. Early on, with my anger and fear, later with my grief over losing our precious baby girl and my obsession with protecting Sophie Elise.

We should have mourned Marie Louise together. Rather than constantly trying to drag you along with me to where I was, I should have made the effort to be present with you where you were. Instead, I left you behind, alone and lonely in your sorrow. I cannot imagine the depth of your misery and how difficult it must have been to be both physically ill and losing strength every day, while at the same time being lost in the emotional wilderness of raw grief. I am sorry, my prince. You deserved better.

When the undertaker and his assistant arrived over an hour later, she was still holding Friedrich's lifeless hand.

"Forgive me, Madame Rieple. I am sorry for your loss and do not wish to unduly disturb you, but Dr. Foster asked me to come and remove the body. May I ask you to step away, please?"

Sophie stood up, gently smoothed Friedrich's tousled hair, and lightly kissed his forehead. "Goodbye, my prince," she whispered. Sophie Elise tossed and turned but did not wake.

They moved Friedrich onto the stretcher and placed the shroud over his body. Turning back to Sophie, the undertaker asked, "Is there a particular parish we should contact in order to make arrangements for the funeral, madame?"

"N-n-n-no," Sophie stammered, trying to choke back tears. "We just arrived from Prussia on Thursday of last week. I know no one and have not had a chance to contact any of the local congregations.

"There is a German Evangelical Orthodox church not far from here," the undertaker said. "If madame would like, I can contact Pastor Buehler and ask him to call on you."

"That would be most appreciated." Learning that a pastor was available and a proper funeral for Friedrich was at least a possibility, Sophie felt a flush of gratitude. It was immediately tempered by monetary concerns. *Coffins, burial plots, and grave markers cost money. And I do not have much.* "If I might ask, sir, what will the charge for your services be?"

"I have spoken at length with Dr. Foster, and considering the circumstances of your husband's death, madame, there will be none."

"No charge?" she asked in disbelief. "I do not understand."

"It is my practice to assist those in need as I am able, madame."

"I am deeply grateful, sir," Sophie said, placing her hand over her heart in relief, and feeling some of her tension ebb away. "Thank you so much."

After the undertaker left, Sophie's thoughts drifted back to Marie Louise's unceremonious sea burial. She crumpled to the floor. *My poor darling girl! I wish we had been able to say goodbye to you properly!* She wondered what Pastor Buehler was like and whether it would in fact be possible for him to conduct a funeral service for Friedrich given the fact that they weren't members of the parish. After a few moments she regained her composure, checked on Sophie Elise, then went next door to the Muller's.

When Sophie tearfully related that Friedrich had died, Mrs. Muller buried her face in her hands and wept as well. "I am so, so sorry," she said, wiping her tears with her apron. "To lose one of your darling babies before you ever arrived and your husband within the first week of coming to America are cruel blows! And now Sophie Elise is sick as well. You poor dear! I cannot imagine the depth of your sorrow." Ignoring the blood stains on Sophie's dress, Mrs. Muller reached out and wrapped Sophie in a hug.

Safe in Mrs. Muller's comforting embrace, all the emotions that were welling up inside Sophie and crashing into one another—her anguish and heartbreak over Friedrich's death, her guilt and shame over her own selfishness, her concern for Sophie Elise, her anger and disappointment over Madame DuVall's uncaring attitude, and her uncertainty and fear about the future—all came pouring out in heaving, racking sobs. She wept for many minutes, and for many minutes more, she simply lay in Mrs. Muller's arms. When she was finally calm enough to speak, she thanked Mrs. Muller profusely.

"I am so grateful for all of your help, Mrs. Muller. I cannot tell you how much it means to me. I must go check on Sophie Elise now, and Pastor Buehler is supposed to call as well. Thank you again for everything."

While she waited for Pastor Buehler to arrive, Sophie finished cleaning up the room and set the sheets and christening gowns to soak in cold water in hopes of getting the blood stains out. After slipping into a clean dress, she washed her face and combed her hair. Just then, Sophie Elise began to stir and whimper. "I know you are miserable, sweet girl," Sophie said in a low, soothing voice as she wiped the child's feverish brow with a damp cloth. She could not bring herself to tell Sophie Elise that her Papa was gone; she was not at all sure she could hear and understand anyway. "Mama will get you some more medicine," she whispered, "and you can go back to sleep." Placing a drop of the liquid from the small brown bottle on Sophie Elise's tongue, Sophie held and rocked her until her princess began to quiet down. Just as Sophie Elise drifted off to sleep once again, there was a knock at the door.

A tall, thin man in a black suit and clerical collar tipped his hat and bowed slightly when she opened the door. "Good afternoon, Madame Rieple. I am Pastor Buehler. The undertaker brought me word of your misfortune. I am very sorry for your loss. Is there some way that I or the parish can be of assistance to you?"

Sophie motioned for Pastor Buehler to come in and closed the door behind him. "Thank you so much for coming. Please, sit down," she said.

Pastor Buehler thanked Sophie with a smile, removed his hat and gloves, and settled comfortably in the chair. Sophie sat down opposite the pastor, handkerchief in hand.

"My family and I just arrived last week from Prussia. Outside of my employer, the people next door, and Dr. Foster, I know no one." Sophie nervously twisted the handkerchief around her thumb while she spoke.

"With my husband and daughter both ill, we have not had a chance to contact any of the local churches or attend worship and are obviously not members of your parish. I did not know, under the circumstances, whether it would be possible for you to conduct a simple funeral service for my husband." She paused to wipe tears from her eyes, then continued. "Our youngest child died on the voyage over, and we had no way of providing a proper funeral for her, which added to my heartbreak immensely." Sophie once again stopped to wipe her eyes. "It would mean a great deal to me to be able to properly say goodbye to my dear Friedrich. My funds are limited, but I want to do what I can."

"It would be my honor to serve Christ by serving you, madame," Pastor Buehler said, leaning forward and nodding briefly. "I understand the importance of appropriately commending those we love to God's care, and I will be happy to accommodate your request. If you do not have the wherewithal to purchase a burial plot and grave marker, other arrangements can be made."

Sophie leaned back in her chair in relief. "Oh, thank you so much, pastor. I am most grateful."

"Because of the circumstances, Dr. Foster requested that burial take place as soon as possible. I can meet you at the undertaker's place of business and conduct a service for your husband later this afternoon. Would four o'clock be acceptable to madame?"

Sophie paused. She was relieved Friedrich's suffering was over, and relieved that she would now be able to say goodbye to him properly, yet the thought of having to say goodbye to him at all shattered her heart all over again. And she still had Sophie Elise to care for. *But it must be done,* she reminded herself, *and waiting will not make things any easier.*

"Yes," she said finally. "I can meet you at four o'clock."

"Very good, madame." Pastor Buehler handed her a card with his name and the address of the church on one side and the address and directions to the undertaker's on the other.

"Thank you again, pastor, for your kindness."

Pastor Buehler rose and put on his hat and gloves. "Grace and peace to you, Madame Rieple, and my deepest condolences. I will see you later this afternoon."

After showing Pastor Buehler out, Sophie once again knocked on the Muller's door.

"The pastor will perform a funeral service for Friedrich later this afternoon at the undertaker's establishment. I also need to go to the dress shop and speak with Madame

DuVall. There is no way I can take Sophie Elise out; she is much too ill. Would you be able to sit with her, Mrs. Muller?"

"Of course, dearie. Just knock when you get ready to leave, and I will be right there."

"Thank you so much, Mrs. Muller. You are an angel."

In between dosing Sophie Elise with the medicine Dr. Foster had left and comforting her as best she could, Sophie rummaged through their trunks looking for a suitable dress to wear for Friedrich's funeral. She had lost so much weight on the voyage from Bremen, her clothing no longer fit properly, and there was no time now to make alterations. Finally, underneath her winter wrap, she found a black skirt that could be pinned and made to fit. With her white blouse and a black shawl, it would do. White was not appropriate mourning attire, she knew, but she had no other choice. She dressed, knocked on Mrs. Muller's door, and then walked to the dress shop with the christening gowns.

"Sophie!" Madame DuVall exclaimed. "I am delighted to see you have returned to work!"

"I am sorry, madame, but I cannot stay."

Madame DuVall's expression of pleasant surprise immediately faded to dismay. "What do you mean you cannot stay? When we spoke previously, you said you would be back at your earliest convenience, so of course when you walked into the shop, I assumed you were here to work."

"Yes, madame. And again, I am sorry. My husband died this morning." Sophie's voice cracked with emotion, and she had to take several deep breaths in order to keep from losing her composure. "Because he required so much care in his final hours, I did not get the other christening gowns you sent finished. I need to be at the undertaker's soon for his funeral service, but I wanted to apologize in person."

"I had every expectation the gowns would be finished. Do you not understand how important this is? I cannot sell stock I do not have."

"I did as much as I could," Sophie insisted. "You must believe that. And I did get some of the gowns finished."

"There are half a dozen more you did not manage to complete," Madame DuVall retorted harshly, jabbing her finger at the stack of gowns in Sophie's arms. "You will be here first thing in the morning to finish them, I trust?"

"I am afraid not, madame. My daughter is ill as well, and I need to care for her."

"That is unacceptable."

"I understand the difficult position this has put you in, madame. And I deeply regret it." *She is already livid with me. What will she do when I tell her about the stains on the gowns?* Stung by Madame DuVall's harsh words and fearful of her wrath, for the briefest of moments, Sophie flirted with the idea of just leaving—dropping the christening gowns, walking out of the dress shop, and never going back. In the end, her sense of integrity would not allow her to do that. *The gowns were sent home with me, and that makes me responsible for them. I must explain what happened.* "There is one more thing I must tell you. There was a mishap with the gowns. I have soaked them and removed the stains as best I could."

"Let me see!" Madame DuVall snapped, yanking the pile of dresses out of Sophie's arms and inspecting them one by one. Sighing heavily in disgust, she turned to Sophie and shoved one of the damaged garments in her face. "These gowns are completely ruined and cannot be sold. And I can no longer keep paying you for work that does not get done. I gave you every chance, Sophie, but I have to let you go."

Sophie's heart sank. "Madame DuVall, please!" she exclaimed, her voice rising in desperation. "I must have employment! It will not be long, I promise you! Within a day, two at the most, I will be able to return to work!"

"I have no choice. You have cost me far more in the six days I have employed you than you have earned. You are done here, Sophie."

That same dull ache she felt that morning after Friedrich slipped away once again settled in the center of her chest. She left the dress shop without another word, and plodded east down Chartres Street, shoulders slumped and eyes downcast, then north toward the undertaker's storefront at 84 St. Ann. The weight of her grief and disappointment wrapped around her like a chain, making every breath, every step, an effort.

"You are done here, Sophie," she had said. *Yes, I am done. Everyone I love is either dead or dying, and I now no longer*

have employment. It feels as though the entire universe is conspiring against me; everything I touch turns to ashes.

The midafternoon sun was edging to the west as she walked up Bienville Street, shrouding that side of the block in shadows and bathing the east side in a golden glow. Shop windows sparkled, and the brass hardware on doors and lampposts gleamed in the sunlight. It was a perfect June day; the neighborhood was bustling with shoppers, and conversation was buzzing in the outdoor cafés. Sophie saw and heard none of it. Lost in her own thoughts and oblivious to everything around her, she nearly walked past the mortuary. At the last possible moment, she glanced up and saw the proprietor's name on the window, "J. Fernandez. Provider of everything necessary for Burials."

Opening the door, she found Pastor Buehler waiting inside.

"Good afternoon, Madame Rieple. I am sorry we are meeting again under such sad circumstances, but it is my privilege to offer my assistance during this most difficult time. Before I begin, if I may ask, how is your little one?"

"Failing," Sophie said flatly, "just like poor Friedrich. I fear she will not last the night. I was hoping that Dr. Foster could secure a bed in the hospital for her, but there are none available at present."

"I am sorry to hear she is not improving, madame. I am sure you are anxious to get back to her side. Shall we begin?" he asked, gesturing to a doorway in the back of the room.

"If you do not mind, pastor, I have a question. You mentioned that there were other arrangements that could be made if I was not able to purchase a burial plot and stone. May I inquire as to what those arrangements are?"

"Of course, madame. The Charity Hospital Cemetery has an area set aside where the deceased may be buried in unmarked graves. That is where Friedrich will be interred. I will inquire of the undertaker and provide you with the section number and the general location of his burial plot. Come, let us get started now so that you may return home as quickly as possible and continue to keep watch on your little one."

He led Sophie into a small, bare room at the rear of the building where Friedrich's body lay on planks, covered with a clean, white sheet. There was a single chair off to one side, which Pastor Buehler offered to Sophie. "Please, have a seat, madame. And if you are ready, I will begin."

Sophie nodded mutely and bowed her head as Pastor Buehler intoned the invocation. Never straying from the liturgy, he offered no personal remarks about Friedrich's life, until the closing prayer.

"We beseech you, Heavenly Father, to look down with mercy on those who grieve this day. A father and husband in the prime of life has been torn away from his family by terrible affliction with disease. We pray that he would be welcomed into your kingdom, held in your tender embrace, and blessed with peace and rest in your eternal realm.

We pray that those left behind would feel the sweet presence of your tender Spirit, that they would be comforted in their great grief, and given strength to carry on. All of this we ask in Christ's name. Amen."

Following Pastor Buehler's words of commendation and benediction, Sophie slowly raised her head. "I am most grateful, Pastor Buehler. The service was a great comfort to me. May I have a few moments alone to bid my beloved goodbye?"

"Of course, madame. I shall be in the office at the front of the building should you require assistance."

Sophie stared at Friedrich's lifeless form for several minutes. Just as it had when she lost Marie Louise, time seemed to stand still. She had no idea if it was permissible or not, and she hadn't thought to ask Pastor Buehler before he left the room, but she was desperate for one last look at her beloved's face. As she pulled back the shroud, grief rolled over her in waves so intense it felt as though her very bones were being ground to dust. She collapsed on Friedrich's chest, weeping from the very depths of her being. *My sweet prince! I love you so! Whatever will I do without you? How will I ever make my way in the world without you by my side? Sophie Elise will be gone soon as well, and I will be utterly and completely alone. Oh, Friedrich! I do not think I can go on!*

For many long moments, she simply stood vigil in that plain, spare room. Stroking his cheek and smoothing his hair, she mused over their life together, all the things they had spent so many evenings talking about, the dreams Friedrich wanted so much to pursue that would now never be. Thoughts of Sophie Elise brought her back to the present. *Goodbye, my prince. I must go now and see to our firstborn. Please, hug Mama and Papa and our little Marie Louise for me. And may you rest peacefully in Jesus's arms until I see you again.* Placing one last kiss on Friedrich's forehead, she dried her eyes, pulled up the sheet, and made her way back down the hall to the front of the building in search of Pastor Buehler. Had anyone asked her later what the room looked like or how the rest of the mortuary was appointed, she could not have described any of it. All she remembered was that last look at Friedrich's face.

"Thank you again, pastor. It meant a great deal to me for you to be able to provide a funeral service for my dear Friedrich on such short notice. I should have inquired when you called on me earlier, but in my distress, I did not think to do so. Since we are not members of your parish, what is the fee for your services?"

"It was my honor to minister to you in your time of need, Madame Rieple, and I thank you for asking, but the parish sees to my welfare quite adequately. With your husband's unexpected death and an ailing child to care for, you will have need of every resource in the coming days, I am sure. Your gracious offer is most appreciated, I assure you, but there is no need for payment. I have spoken to the undertaker and have secured the location of the plot Friedrich will be placed in." Pastor Buehler handed her a small card.

"My deepest thanks, and God's blessings to you, pastor," Sophie said. "Now, if you will excuse me, I must get back home to my little princess."

Sophie left the undertaker's shop and walked east to Esplanade Street, then turned south and headed toward Decatur Street and the rooming house, the bright late-afternoon sun a sharp contrast to her somber mood. *There are some small graces*, she reminded herself. *Friedrich no longer suffers, and the selfless generosity of the undertaker and Pastor Buehler almost made up for Madame DuVall's hatefulness and lack of compassion.*

In his parlor that night, Bible open on his lap, Pastor Buehler reviewed the events of the day as he prepared for evening prayer. Weighing on his mind and heart were the funeral service he'd conducted for Herr Rieple and his reply to Sophie when she asked about remuneration. There was, in fact, a fee schedule in place for services of baptism, marriages, and funerals for those who were not members of his parish, but Sophie's situation was so tragic, so heartbreaking, he could not bring himself to mention it to her, insisting no payment was required. At the time, given the circumstances, he'd deemed the lie to be little enough and white enough the Almighty would not be unduly offended by it, but now, conviction pierced his heart. He bowed his head and prayed.

I give you thanks, Heavenly Father, for your presence, and for the grace you so freely offer. While I know that in offering my services to Madame Rieple I was undoubtedly doing your will—caring for those in need in whatever way I am able—I am also aware my answer to her question about the fee for my services was not truthful. It seemed a small thing at the time; it would have felt predatory to have taken her money, of which, by her own admission, she has little—especially when she also has an ailing child to care for. But as the Psalmist writes, "thou desirest truth in the inward parts," so I humbly confess to you my sin of lying. Have mercy on me and forgive me, Almighty Father, for this and all my shortcomings this day. Create a new and contrite heart within me, as I commend myself, body, soul, and spirit, into your gracious keeping. All these things I ask, in the name of Jesus Christ my Savior. Amen.

Chapter Twelve

*A*rriving back at the rooming house, Sophie went straight to her room, not bothering to check the hall table for mail or going to the dining room, even though the evening meal was already being served.

Quietly letting herself in, she tiptoed over to Sophie Elise's bed where Mrs. Muller, rosary in hand, kept her prayerful vigil. "How has she been, Mrs. Muller? Not too restless, I hope."

"Sleeping on and off. I just gave her another dose of the medicine Dr. Foster left," Mrs. Muller replied. "It keeps her quiet for a while, but not long."

Sophie nodded, quickly turning away in hopes of hiding the tears that sprang to her eyes when Mrs. Muller described her little darling's condition.

Seeing her tears and the exhaustion etched on her face, Mrs. Muller jumped up and wrapped Sophie in her arms. "Oh, my poor dear. You've had so much suffering in such a short time. I hope the pastor's service for Friedrich was some small comfort to you."

"Pastor Buehler was most kind. And so are you, Mrs. Muller." Sophie sighed wearily. "I do not know what I would do without your help."

"I just wish there was more to be done for her." Mrs. Muller sighed. "Is there anything else I can do for you, Sophie dear?"

"Not right now." Sophie shook her head. "You should go home and see to Mr. Muller. It is nearly suppertime."

"I will, Sophie dear, and when we are finished, I will pop in with a bite for you. Will you need me to watch the little one tomorrow while you work?"

Too ashamed and far too weary to repeat the whole story, Sophie simply said, "No thank you, Mrs. Muller. That will not be necessary. I am not going to the dress shop tomorrow."

"Very well, my dear. I am right next door. Just shout if you need anything. Try to get some rest yourself when the little one naps."

"I will, Mrs. Muller. Thank you again."

While Sophie Elise slept, Sophie changed from the skirt and blouse she had worn to Friedrich's funeral into the plain gray dress she had usually worn to do housework back in

Rheda. She carefully folded the clothes, placed them back in the trunk, and then, out of habit, straightened the rest of the room. Opening the dresser drawer to put away her brush and comb, she noticed Friedrich's journal. He had never talked about or shown her any of the entries. She assumed he was using it to write down his thoughts and plans for what they would do once they arrived in America, but she had no idea exactly what those pages held. Outside of his clothing and a few personal items, it was all she had left of him, and missing him with every fiber of her being, she sat down and started to read.

Her assumptions regarding the contents of the journal were partly correct. The first few pages did contain lists of things that would need to be attended to and decisions that would need to be made when they docked in New Orleans.

There were notes in the margins next to some of the entries, written at various times during the voyage. Some were clear and straightforward; others made no sense to Sophie. She pored over the pages, trying to read between the lines and get some sense of what Friedrich had been thinking. The decisions were all hers now, but in the fog of raw grief, she had no idea whether it would be best to find employment and stay in New Orleans, or to make her way as quickly as possible to Illinois where Christian and Louise and the rest of Friedrich's family were.

Christian and Louise! She had not seen or heard from them since disembarking from the *John Schmidt*. She knew they intended to leave immediately for Illinois but had no idea if they were on their way or if they were still in the city awaiting passage on a riverboat north. Consumed with trying to work while caring for her own ailing family, the welfare of theirs had not crossed her mind. But now, not only were they on her mind, the mere acknowledgment of their existence caused the painful memories of her last conversation with Christian on the *John Schmidt* to come flooding back.

After promising he would help her care for Friedrich, Christian had abruptly changed his mind the next morning. He and Louise left as soon as the ship docked without saying goodbye—without so much as a backward glance. Hot, angry tears spilled down her cheeks as she recalled them hurrying away from the *John Schmidt*, leaving her to rely on Mr. Fischer to load their trunks and help her get Friedrich into the carriage.

I suppose I should make an effort to locate them and apprise them of Friedrich's death. It is my obligation; they are members of his family too. But they are the last people in the world I want to be in contact with. Family? Pah! If this is what Friedrich's family is like, I am better off without them. They did not care enough to help when us when Friedrich was sick and needed it most; I doubt they will care that he is dead. I have no idea how to go about finding them, and even if I did—even if they are still in the city—I am sure all they would do is reprimand me for not waiting for them before holding Friedrich's funeral just as they reprimanded Mr. Brandorff for not waiting until they arrived when we buried Marie Louise at sea. A pox on them both, and on all of their children!

Sophie dissolved in a fit of weeping. She wept for Friedrich, for Marie Louise, for herself, and for Sophie Elise. She wept *in* anger and for *being* angry. She wept in embarrassment—by now ashamed of how critical she felt toward Christian and Louise and sharply aware of how disappointed both her mother and Friedrich would have been in the unkind thoughts she harbored. She wept for all the questions she had no answers for, for the uncertainty that loomed, for the gaping hole in her heart where her life used to be.

In the end, her mother's sense of fairness and rigorous ingraining in Sophie of common courtesy and social graces—and Friedrich's fondness for his cousin—prevailed. *I will go, as soon as it is practical, back to the German Society, inquire if they assisted Christian and Louise, and see if there is a way to reach them.*

That settled in her mind, she turned the page in Friedrich's journal and continued to read.

13 May 1854

My dearest Sophie,

I well remember the joy and brightness of the glorious day when you and I were united in holy matrimony. In my mind's eye I can see you coming down the aisle of the church in Rheda, and the radiant expression on your face is one I never grow tired of recalling. When you and I looked into each other's eyes and made our solemn promises to one another that day, we were not thinking of sleepless nights with sick children or those months when expenses far exceeded income or any of the difficult circumstances with which we have had to contend in our life together. All we saw was the chance to spend all the time we could with one another. Still today, that is one of the most appealing thoughts I have: to spend unlimited time in your company.

To be sure, we have changed in the three years we have been married. Even in such a limited time, there has been much growth, some painful and purchased at great cost, with many tears. But in all the changes we have seen, I have always known that love was there. You have shown me daily, and I have come to believe as well that love is not merely a feeling, but also a decision. Each day there is a choice to live with love and care, or not. The ideal, of course, is that we would always be loving and caring with one another, but for my part, I know there have been days when I was neither. For that, I am so, so sorry.

I will regret to my dying day the decision to wrest you from the home and family you loved and take you across the sea. It has been a time of extreme hardship, in which the most horrible and unthinkable of things has happened. Each and every day has been full of trials no one should ever have to endure. Had I not stubbornly insisted on traveling to America, our beautiful baby girl would likely still live.

Forgive me, my love, for all the undue pain and suffering I have caused you. The fact that you still love me after everything that has happened fills me with one overriding emotion: thankfulness. Thankfulness to you for the love that has so enriched and beautified my life, and thankfulness to God that we were brought together. Your love is a priceless and cherished gift to me, my sweet, one that fills me with confidence and hope for tomorrow.

I had wished to be much stronger by now; alas, this strange debilitation baffles and annoys me. I am doing my very best to improve daily, but should that not be the ultimate outcome, please know how very, very much I love you.

With much gratitude, I remain,
your faithful and loving husband

Friedrich

20 May 1854

My dearest Sophie,

I cannot tell you how much joy it brings me to see you each and every day. When we lost our sweet Marie Louise, I feared for your very life. You were so thin and frail, and I worried the weight of such intense grief would be the death of you as well. Instead, you have risen like a phoenix from the ashes of your broken heart and become even more devoted to Sophie Elise and me.

You have always been beautiful, my sweet, but you have a radiance about you these days that is brighter than the sun. Your calm strength holds me like an anchor. The sheer abandon with which you shower love on me and on our darling daughter is a joy to behold. I love to hear your laughter, and I love overhearing the fairy tales you regale Sophie

Elise with each day. To see you running and playing with our little princess when just a short time ago I feared for your very survival is a priceless treasure to me.

You never cease to amaze me, my love, and I cannot believe the good fortune I enjoy just being your husband. Mine is the most blessed of existences, and my gratitude is unending. I shall be in your debt forever, a burden I will gladly bear so long as it affords me the opportunity to remain always in your presence.

I love and adore you, my sweet, with my whole heart.

Yours forever and always,

Friedrich

27 May 1854

My dearest Sophie,

I think of nothing but you these days. I am so grateful for your love and devotion, both to me and to our Sophie Elise. I rest each day in hopes that my strength will begin to increase and will soon permit me to regain my health. I long to again be actively involved in all those things we used to enjoy so much: an evening stroll, deep conversation, playing with our beloved little princess, and making plans for our future.

I deeply regret this malaise that has taken hold of me and prevented me from doing all those things and more. Christian and I should have been busy for weeks making plans for traveling to Illinois when the ship docks in New Orleans, but I have been too weary to do so. Even when I was regularly able to move about the ship, I rarely had the energy for planning or thinking. Standing at the rail and gazing out over the sea seemed to be all I could manage. Forgive me for these failures, my sweet. I want nothing more than to provide for you, and it shames and disgusts me that I cannot!

And yet, still you love me. You love me without question. You love me without reserve. Truly, every ounce of your attention these days is focused on caring for me and for our darling Sophie Elise, and I am at once both humbled to the core and filled to overflowing with gratitude.

I love you without end, my sweet. You are life itself to me.

With gratitude for all you are and all you do,

Friedrich

30 May 1854

My dearest Sophie,

There are so many things I want you to know, and I fear my time with you is growing shorter and shorter. I should have begun to feel better many days if not weeks ago; I have not, and though it pains me to say it, I am afraid the chances of my recovery are growing ever dimmer. I so wish I was able to attend to our affairs and take care of you and Sophie Elise properly! That was, after all, the entire reason behind this ill-fated trip. I should have been the one to speak to Mr. Brandorff and make plans for our future with Christian. As this day proved again, you have done all the work while I lie here taking advantage of your good nature. Nothing I have done up to this point has been good enough for you, my love.

Nothing is good enough because you are everything to me. Your presence in my life is the very best thing that has ever happened to me. If I could compose poetry, those lines would not be beautiful enough to share with you. I wish I were able to sing and could compose a song to you that would tell you how much you mean to me. These past few weeks it seems that you have almost physically carried me when I have been unable to carry on by myself. I am sure my life would have been an even bigger failure without your love to keep me trying and building me up when I was weak.

There is really nothing in this world that I have seen that compares with your love. I wanted you to know I am still so happy to be yours. Mere words cannot contain the emotions that come over me when I see you. Please know that I think of nothing but you and how much I love you. If we were able to be together forever it would not be enough time.

With all my heart,

your Friedrich

1 June 1854

My dearest Sophie,

I know your day is an extraordinarily busy one. I pray all will go well at the German Society office and that you will be able to secure the assistance we need. I just wanted to tell you that you make my days and nights wonderful in addition to all of the other things you do. Your love and concern for me is deeply appreciated, and I notice each small thing.

I apologize again for my inability to attend to my responsibilities and beg your forgiveness. If there were a way to make it up to you, my darling, I would not hesitate. I love you more than life itself, and I am blessed to be your husband.

Your Friedrich

6 June 1854

My dearest Sophie,

It seems there is never enough time to tell you how I feel or the things I think about. You are so busy trying to keep our little family cared for, and my days are coming to an end. I had so hoped the doctor would be able to help me, as I know you did as well, but I am not improving, and what I was merely suspicious of before has become my sad reality. Much as I wanted it, recovery is not to be for me. So, again, I put pencil to paper in order to ensure that you know how very much I love you.

Everything in my life is better for having met you. The difference you have made in every facet of my existence is incredible. And at the heart of all of that is your love. My greatest joys are great and joyous only because I can share them with you. You not only taught me what love is, you have made it impossible for me to imagine my life without it. I still hate to be separated from you for even a moment; I long for you to return as soon as possible when we have to be apart. I loved you when we first met, but over the years, that love has grown even more. I am more blessed than I deserve to be your husband.

Yet I so easily get bogged down in doubting my acceptability these days: I am too weak, too frail, too needy, too ill. You work all day at Madame DuVall's dress shop, and then come home and work all night caring for me and for our little princess. My inadequacies are many, and I am powerless to improve even one of them. But—but when you return at the end of the day and greet me, I lose myself in your sweet kisses, I lose myself in your endearing embrace, I lose myself in just being with you. When you are by my side, all of those other things fade away, and there is only you and our love. Still today, my greatest desire is to spend unlimited time in your presence, to never be outside your embrace.

By the time you read this, my love, I will have drawn my last breath, and my life will be over. Please, do not grieve excessively for me. I will be at home with God, reunited with our darling Marie

Louise, with Mama and Papa, and all those who have gone before. I will not be weak or tired or sick anymore. You are still young and beautiful, Sophie, and you have a whole lifetime ahead of you. Take Sophie Elise and find somewhere to be happy. Find joy; find love.

I will always love you, Sophie. Goodbye and Godspeed to you, wherever you may go, whatever you may do.

Your prince,

Friedrich

Sophie closed the journal and buried her head in her hands, wailing in anguish. *He knew. He knew for a long, long time he was never going to get well. So he used every last ounce of strength he had to tell me goodbye. All those days when he was exhausted beyond reason, when he should have been resting, when he was getting weaker by the minute, he was struggling to get all these words down on paper.* She could track Friedrich's decline by the appearance of the handwriting as the entries progressed. By the last one, his fine, spidery script had become a broken scrawl. *Oh, my sweet prince! Time was so short, and I had no idea! I should*

never have taken employment at the dress shop. I should have stayed right here by your side and done nothing but care for you every single minute of every single day. How I failed you when you needed me most!

Her thoughts were interrupted by a knock at the door. Mrs. Muller was there with bread, cheese, fruit, and a cup of tea. "Here is the bite of supper I promised. I know you are grief-stricken and exhausted, Sophie, so I did not bring much, but this will keep you until breakfast. How is our little angel?" Instantly regretting her choice of words, Mrs. Muller broke into a string of tearful apologies.

"It is all right, Mrs. Muller. You need not apologize. You are quite correct; she is by far closer to heaven now than she is to Earth. She has been sleeping since you left. Her breathing has slowed, but she does not seem to be in distress or pain. I am praying that continues, and that she quietly slips away sometime soon. Thank you for the food. I shall especially enjoy the tea."

"Is there anything else I can do, Sophie? Will you be all right here with the little one by yourself?"

"You have done so much already, Mrs. Muller, I cannot, in good conscience, ask for more. I will be all right. If I need something, I will knock."

"Try to rest as you can, my dear. I will check on you in the morning."

Sophie nibbled on the cheese and bread and savored each sip of the tea. When she was finished, she moved the chair next to Sophie Elise's bed, where she dozed on and off during the night. Each time she woke, Sophie Elise's breathing was perceptibly slower. Shortly before six o'clock in the morning, Sophie stirred and looked over at Sophie Elise. Her chest rose and fell once, and then stopped.

Her little princess was gone.

By nine o'clock, Sophie had spoken to Dr. Foster, the undertaker, and Pastor Buehler. After washing her face and putting up her hair, she once again removed the black skirt, white blouse, and black shawl from the trunk and dressed for the day.

Chapter Thirteen

A grim resignation seized Sophie. Having wept so often and so much in the two months since that March night when Friedrich told her they were leaving for America, by now she had no tears left. At one o'clock that afternoon, she stood, dry-eyed, in front of the shrouded, lifeless body of her beloved firstborn daughter as Pastor Buehler—for the second time in two days—intoned words of resurrection and benediction. When he finished, Sophie thanked him and went immediately to the German Society office.

"Good afternoon, madame," the man at the door greeted her. "May I have your name, please?"

"Sophie Rieple," she replied.

"Thank you so much. Please, have a seat. We will be with you shortly."

A quarter of an hour later, she was escorted to the same office she'd visited earlier in the week.

"Good afternoon, Madame Rieple. How may we assist you today?"

"Good afternoon, Herr Franke. We arrived from Prussia on Thursday of last week with members of my husband's family. My husband, daughter, and I remained in the city, but my husband's cousin and his wife and children had planned to book passage on one of the packet boats and continue traveling north to Illinois. I need to locate them if possible, and I thought perchance they may have come here for assistance. If so, I was hoping you might know whether they have departed already or if they are still here." She gave the clerk Christian's name, and then waited while he checked the week's assistance lists.

"I am sorry, Madame Rieple. It appears as though they left New Orleans the same day you arrived on the *John Schmidt*."

"Do you know of any way I might be able to contact them?" Sophie started to explain that she needed to let Christian and Louise know Friedrich and Sophie Elise had died but found herself unable to say the words. Instead, she simply told the clerk there was family news she needed to apprise them of.

"According to the notes I have, they were on their way to St. Louis, and then planned to book passage on another boat that would take them further north. Their destination is listed as a town called Havana, Illinois."

"Would it be possible, then, for me to somehow send word to them there?"

"Certainly, madame. Havana has a post office; a letter can be sent. They will be happy to assist you with the necessary arrangements for mailing it from the post office here. It is not far—just a few blocks away on Toulouse Street." The clerk wrote the name of the town and the address of the post office on a small card and handed it to Sophie. "Is there anything else we can assist you with today?"

"Well, I am sorry to have to ask, but I am once again in need of employment. You were kind enough to help me secure a position at Madame DuVall's dress shop when we arrived last week, but when my husband and my daughter became ill, I had to remain at home and tend them, and my employment was terminated yesterday."

"I am sorry, Madame Rieple. Let me check to see what may be available. I will be back momentarily."

While conversing with Herr Franke—providing the necessary answers to his questions—Sophie was able to stay focused. Now, in the silence, while she waited for him to return, her thoughts were racing in every direction. *What will I do? What should I do? What can I do? I do not want to dishonor Friedrich and his wishes; he had his heart set on joining the rest of his family in Illinois, but I cannot abide the thought of being anywhere near Christian and*

Louise. New Orleans is such a strange and unfamiliar place; I am not sure I want to stay here either.

Her only other choice—one she had not even considered until just now—was to go back home to Rheda. She would love to see Mina and her brothers and their families. She had no one in New Orleans except Mr. and Mrs. Muller. But she was not certain whether she could survive another ocean voyage—physically or mentally. Those days on the *John Schmidt* were a living hell on Earth, full of every kind of hardship imaginable. That is where she lost Marie Louise, and where she began—without her even realizing it—to lose Friedrich as well. Things were difficult enough traveling with her husband and family. She was too terrified to even consider what might happen to her traveling alone.

Just then, Herr Franke returned. "There are no openings for seamstresses at the moment. There is, however, a sales position at one of the tobacconists. Does madame have any sales experience?"

Sophie's heart sank. She was counting on being able to find work in another one of the dressmaker's or tailor shops; sewing was what she knew. Sophie had never worked anywhere besides her brief tenure at Madame DuVall's, but she had to have some way of supporting herself. In desperation, she grasped at the opportunity. "I do not have any direct experience in sales," she admitted, "but both my sister's husband and members of my late husband's family operated tobacco shops in Prussia in the town I am from. Having visited my brother-in-law's shop and listened to him converse with my husband through the years, I have come to know a bit about tobacco and cigar varieties."

"Very good, madame," Herr Franke said, nodding encouragingly. "With your permission, then, I will contact the tobacconist and see if he would be willing to offer you an interview. I will be in touch with you as soon as I hear from him."

"Thank you, sir. You have been most helpful."

Sophie left the German Society office. The conversation with Herr Franke—the circumstances that made it necessary, thoughts of Christian and Louise and memories of the *John Schmidt*—had left her emotionally drained. Going back to the rooming house felt impossible. She could not—at that moment—face the empty room, the still-fresh horror of the two deaths that had taken place there, and all the uncertainties and questions now facing her—questions she had no immediate answers for. It was too much. Desperate for some sort of respite, instead of traveling down St. Louis Street and turning west, she turned east. For two solid hours she simply walked, soaking up the sunshine, taking in the beauty of the city, browsing the unique and varied storefront displays and studying the distinctive architecture.

As the afternoon began to wane, she made her way to the rooming house, arriving shortly after five o'clock. After a long walk in the fresh air, her spirits were somewhat revived—enough for her to notice she was hungry, something she could not have comprehended two hours earlier. There was a banana on the table—the remains of what Mrs. Muller had brought the night before. *That will do.* Friedrich's journal was still lying where she'd left it on the dresser. While she slowly savored the banana, she once again went through the lists Friedrich had made in the front of the book item by item.

I should write to Christian and Louise, she remembered, *if I can find some paper. Oh! And Mina. Dear me, I must write to Mina!* She turned to the back of the journal and found there were two blank pages left. She carefully tore them out. Hands trembling, not sure how to convey such devastating loss in mere words, she slipped Friedrich's pencil out of the loop in the journal's binding and began to write, hoping Mina and Christian would be able to read her shaky script.

10 June 1854

Dear Mina,

Well, I survived, and I am here in New Orleans. Yes, I, not we.

What was supposed to be the beginning of a new life in a new world has turned into one heartbreak after another.

Marie Louise became ill on the voyage and died on March 12. There was no choice but to bury her at sea. And although he tried to hide it—and was far more successful than I care to admit—Friedrich was ailing by then as well.

I was able to find a doctor as soon as we arrived, but it was too late; Friedrich was already too sick and frail to have any chance of recovering. Shortly after that Sophie Elise started showing signs of illness. Friedrich's funeral was yesterday afternoon, Sophie Elise slipped away early this morning.

Christian and Louise were no help at all. I begged them to stay until I could find work, but they left for Illinois the same day we docked in New Orleans.

Please come, Mina. Come quickly, I beg you. I am all alone, and I have no idea what to do or how I will survive.

Your beloved sister,

Sophie

10 June 1854

Dear Christian and Louise,

I am in hopes your trip north on the riverboat was uneventful—far less difficult than the voyage on the John Schmidt—and that you and your family have arrived safely and are well.

Although I hate to do so, and hope I am not disturbing you unduly, I write with sad news. Immediately after we arrived in New Orleans, Friedrich's condition deteriorated drastically. Shortly thereafter, Sophie Elise was also stricken with what the doctor surmised was cholera, contracted on the ship, a horrible disease for which, at least in their case, there was no effective treatment. Friedrich died yesterday; our beloved Sophie Elise slipped away this morning. Because of the circumstances, it was necessary to bury them immediately, but I was able to secure the services of the pastor of the German Evangelical Orthodox Church who conducted proper funeral services for each of them.

If there are any of Friedrich's other family members living near you or if any from home are in contact with you, please let them know what happened.

Sophie stopped, unsure of how to end the letter. None of the usual and customary closings felt right, given the way she and Christian had parted. While less angry than she had been, she still could not honestly offer Christian and Louise warm or sincere regard, affection, or respect, nor was there anything about their relationship that evoked in her any feelings of gratitude. After struggling over it for some time, she simply signed her name. Laying the letters aside, she changed from the clothing she had worn to the undertaker's into an everyday dress.

As she crossed the room to pack her skirt, blouse, and shawl in her trunk, the sight of Sophie Elise's favorite doll—still lying on the little one's bed—caught her attention. She stopped and picked up the doll, straightening the yarn hair and smoothing the hem of the dress she had so lovingly fashioned out of the same fabric as the last one she had made for Sophie Elise. Flooded with memories, she sat down on the bed and rocked back and forth, hugging the doll to her chest as she had so often held her two daughters.

My darling princesses! I do not know what the future holds for me—what I will do or where I will be—but life goes on, and somehow I must try to do the same.

This much is certain: Mama will never forget you.

Suddenly aware of how completely exhausted she was—physically, mentally, and emotionally—she put down the doll, laid her clothing on top of her trunk, and retired for the night.

The round-the-clock demands of caring for Friedrich and Sophie Elise in recent days had depleted her physical strength and stretched her emotional reserves to the breaking point. Having the opportunity to sleep the entire night uninterrupted seemed decadent—the height of luxury. She woke at seven o'clock the next morning, feeling better than she had in weeks. She stretched, and for a few brief moments reveled in delicious relaxation. But, glancing across the room, the sight of Sophie Elise's empty bed pierced her heart. She rose and looked out the window on leaden gray skies and drizzling rain. *The weather matches my mood. It seems the Almighty is weeping with me.*

She washed her face, dressed, and went downstairs in search of hot tea and something to eat. When she finished breakfast, she returned to her room. She spent the rest of the day repacking the trunks. She filled one of them with her own clothing and all of the small household items she'd brought with them from their home in Rheda. Friedrich and Sophie Elise's belongings went into the other one, each item of clothing carefully folded, and laid on top of Marie Louise's things. On top went the doll, carefully swaddled in the quilt from Sophie Elise's bed. She left two things out for the time being: Friedrich's journal and his pocket watch. While those tangible reminders of his loss were heartbreaking, holding the book that contained his last words and the watch that was always in the pocket over his heart were the closest things she had to being able to touch him again, and she needed those connections.

As she finished her work, she glanced up. The scene outside the rooming house window captivated her attention. The setting sun painted the western sky with blazes of orange and red, which slowly deepened into dusty pinks and mauves as twilight fell. It was a small thing, but stopping for a few moments to gaze at the striking panorama of color lightened her mood and loosed within her heart the tiniest mustard seed of hope. When the last hint of purple faded from view, she closed the trunk and prepared to retire for the evening.

After breakfast the next morning, she went back to her room and once again went over the lists in Friedrich's journal. At 8:30, there was a knock at the door. When she answered it, Sophie was greeted by one of the assistants from the German Society, who had a note for her from the clerk.

"Good morning, Madame Rieple. Herr Franke asked me to bring you this message regarding the employment you inquired about. There are instructions inside. If you have questions, please do not hesitate to return to the society office, and we will be happy to assist you."

Sophie thanked him and closed the door, hurrying to read the message.

Madame Rieple:

Please go at your earliest convenience to the tobacconist located at 141 Chartres Street. Monsieur Philippe Delaroche, the proprietor, wishes to speak with you in person regarding the sales position we discussed.

Auguste Franke, Clerk

The German Society of New Orleans

An everyday house dress will not do in this situation. Sophie once again got the white blouse, black skirt and shawl out of her trunk. Hoping to soften the somber look, she also retrieved a pair of earrings and the ironwork cross necklace that had belonged to her grandmother from her jewelry box in the bottom of the trunk. *I know it is not customary or appropriate for me to be wearing jewelry so soon after Friedrich's death, but I cannot show up in mourning attire and expect to be hired as a salesclerk in a tobacconist's shop.* Breathing an apology to her mother, she gathered the letters to Mina and Christian and Louise, and with as much courage as she could summon, headed for Chartres Street. *I will find the post office and mail the letters when I leave the tobacconist's shop.*

The morning was sunny and pleasant, and the streets of New Orleans, particularly those of the French Quarter, were beautiful, but Sophie worried as she walked. She wondered what kind of questions Monsieur Delaroche would ask her and was concerned her answers may not be satisfactory. She tried to remember as many details as she could from Friedrich and her brother-in-law Heinrich's conversations about tobacco and cigars. Just past Jackson Square, she turned down Chartres Street and located the tobacconist's shop just a few blocks ahead on the corner of Chartres and Iberville. The sign out front read *Monsieur Philippe's Fine Tobacco and Hand-Rolled Cigars* in flowing red script edged with gold.

Entering the shop, the rich earth-and-leather aroma of tobacco instantly transported her back across the sea to Rheda. She leaned against the door for a moment, eyes closed, soaking up the familiar smell and the fond memories it prompted. That very same scent lingered in the front hallway of her sister and brother-in-law's home, where the coats and jackets Heinrich wore to work in his cigar shop hung on the carved walnut hall tree. While she waited for the proprietor to finish waiting on customers, she studied the layout of the shop and the items for sale. There were glass jars of loose tobacco of various cuts on the shelves behind the cash register. A wide variety of cigars of various shapes and sizes—in elegantly embellished boxes that were works of art themselves—filled one of the display cases, some exactly like the ones Sophie remembered seeing in Heinrich's tobacco shop in Rheda. The other display case contained a selection of clay, briarwood, meerschaum, and porcelain pipes, as well as tobacco pouches, and cigarette papers.

When the last patron left the shop, she approached the counter.

"Good morning, sir. The staff at the German Society indicated that a sales position was available and that Monsieur Delaroche had requested to speak to me in person in regard to my possible employment."

The man behind the counter was tall and lithe. His coal black hair was touched with silver at the temples, and he sported a pencil-thin black mustache. The dark blue of his finely tailored suit accentuated his blue eyes, which danced as he looked up and met Sophie's gaze. His white silk shirt was distinctively French in style, as was his accent when he greeted her.

"Good morning. I am Philippe Delaroche, the proprietor, and you must be Madame Rieple. It is a pleasure to make your acquaintance. Please follow me, and I will share with you what the position requires. My office is this way."

Monsieur Philippe put an intricately engraved brass bell and a sign out on the counter instructing customers to ring for service, then led Sophie through a narrow hallway and into the back of the shop. He pulled back a damask curtain and ushered her into a small office.

"Please, Madame Rieple, be seated." Determined to make a good impression, yet apprehensive about what questions Monsieur Delaroche might ask and whether her answers would prove sufficient, Sophie sat down on the edge of the single straight wooden chair, while Monsieur Philippe settled himself in the leather wing chair behind the desk.

"I am in need of someone to work in the front of the shop assisting customers with their purchases, writing up bills of sale, receiving payments, and keeping an account of the inventory of the shop, as well as maintaining the stock in the cases and making sure the store is clean and orderly at all times. I will be frank, Madame Rieple; the fact that you lack formal sales experience is of concern. I normally would not have considered you for this position, but when it was mentioned to me that you have some knowledge of tobaccos and cigars, I decided it may be to my benefit to speak with you. If you would be so kind, please share with me what you know."

Sophie took a deep breath to steady her nerves and began. She mentioned the varieties of tobacco she had heard Friedrich and Heinrich talk about. She described the style of cigar made by her brother-in-law and members of Friedrich's family, noted its similarity to one of the brands she'd seen in the display case, and was able to articulate some of the differences between that style and some of the other cigars in Monsieur Delaroche's inventory.

"I can read and write," she assured him, "and even though I have no prior experience with sales, my husband oversaw the accounts at my father's livery stable. I remember some of the things he talked about, and if you would be willing to give me a chance, I assure you I will work as hard as I can to master whatever skills are necessary for the position."

"Most impressive, madame. You are the first woman I have met who had any knowledge whatsoever of the tobacco business. I would be willing to offer you the position on a trial basis if you are agreeable. How soon would you be able to start?"

"I have no other obligations at present, monsieur. I can start immediately."

"Very well. Shall we go back to the counter? I will show you the inventory we have in stock and will instruct you on how to write out bills of sale."

The rest of the day was spent learning the local currency, the finer points of Monsieur Philippe's system for recording sales and managing the inventory, and—under his watchful eye—actually taking customers' orders. Already somewhat familiar with different cuts of tobacco and styles of cigar, she had no trouble finding the appropriate item once she understood what the buyer was asking for. Her biggest challenge was the language. She could understand and speak German and French, and with their French roots, could also grasp Creole and Cajun, but struggled with English, Spanish, and the other local dialects and accents present in New Orleans.

She also found it difficult to keep unfamiliar monetary denominations straight in her mind and count out the correct change. Still, she worked diligently all day to master what was unfamiliar, making copious written notes as Monsieur Philippe instructed her, and refusing to let mistakes stop her from putting forth her best effort. As they prepared to close the shop late that afternoon, he complimented her on the day's work.

"I know this is all new, Madame Rieple. But it is obvious you have worked hard and made every effort to learn. It is my belief that this relationship has every opportunity to be mutually beneficial. The shop opens at nine o'clock in the morning. I look forward to seeing you then. Until tomorrow, madame."

"Until tomorrow, monsieur." Sophie nodded in farewell.

To Monsieur Philippe—and everyone else she met on the street—she projected a calm, confident, and professional exterior, but on the inside, she was dancing and shouting with joy. Her relief was palpable, welling up and overflowing to fill in the gnawing emptiness that had consumed her since Friedrich and Sophie Elise's untimely deaths. *Finally, instead of more disaster and heartbreak, I actually have something to celebrate!*

She immediately thought of her mother, Mama's mantra echoing in her mind as clearly as if Margarethe were right there beside her. *Somehow, some way—working in a tobacco shop, of all things!—at least one thing has turned out all right. I have employment. It is just my first day, and I have much to learn, but I have hope that I will be able to support myself. That is an immense relief. Just two days ago, I was utterly hopeless.* The walk back to the rooming house went by quickly. Sophie stopped briefly to say hello to Mrs. Muller, and then got something to eat. After supper she opened her trunk once again, going through her clothing piece by piece to see which of her dresses she might be able to quickly alter in order to be appropriately dressed for work the next morning. The tobacco shop, where she was the one behind the counter dealing directly with customers, was a much different environment than Madame DuVall's dress shop, where she had spent all of her time behind a mountain of fabric at a worktable in the back of the shop, never personally interacting with the clientele.

Looking at the garments laid out on her bed, she found several that would be suitable once she completed the alterations necessary to make them fit again. She started with a pale gray windowpane-checked dress with gathered pleats at the waist and hand-tatted lace trim at the neckline and on the edges of the sleeves. By taking in the side seams and each of the pleats, she hoped to make it wearable. When she finished stitching, she slipped out of her skirt and blouse and tried on her handiwork. To her relief, the dress once again fit perfectly. *I will keep working at this each evening when I get home from the tobacconist's shop,* she told herself.

And within a few weeks' time, all of my garments will be serviceable again.

She hung up the dress, put the pins, needle, and thread back in her sewing basket, and prepared to retire for the night. As she folded her skirt and blouse so they could be put back into the trunk, she found the letters she'd written to Mina and Christian and Louise tucked in the skirt's side pocket. *I must remember to mail these letters tomorrow,* she reminded herself. *Perhaps, if the shop is not too busy, Monsieur Philippe will allow me to leave a few moments early so I can go to the post office before it closes for the evening.*

Chapter Fourteen

She rose the next morning, dressed, had breakfast, and was at the tobacco shop ten minutes before nine o'clock. Monsieur Philippe arrived seconds later, unlocked the door, and escorted her in.

"Madame Rieple! You are a vision of loveliness this morning. I trust you rested well and are ready for the day."

Sophie blushed, unused to receiving such direct and personal attention from anyone but Friedrich. She and Monsieur Philippe did not know each other at all; they had just met the day before, and all of the conversations that day had centered around the necessary tasks for conducting the business of the shop. She was not at all sure it was appropriate for him to inquire about how well she had slept, under the circumstances. It would not have been appropriate in the least in Rheda, she was sure. *But*, she reminded herself, *this is not Rheda. This is America—New Orleans—and things are different here.* She did not want to risk doing anything to anger her new employer as she had Madame DuVall, so she fixed a gracious smile on her face and returned Monsieur Philippe's greeting, but without any specific references to how she slept. "Thank you for your kind words, Monsieur. I am indeed ready for the day."

"Shall we begin by taking stock of what we have on hand, madame? One of my suppliers will be calling later today, and I will need to determine what, if anything, I need to order from his company."

While Monsieur Philippe observed, Sophie went through each box and case, making lists of every item they had on inventory, noting which items they were out of and which were in short supply. She paused occasionally to wait on customers, each time carefully marking where she had stopped counting so that when she returned to the task, her final tally would be accurate. When she finished, she handed the list to Monsieur Philippe.

"You have done well, madame. And I thank you. If you would be so kind as to wipe down the cases and straighten the sales area, I will go prepare the order. When my supplier arrives, please show him to my office."

"Yes, monsieur."

Sophie busied herself polishing the glass cases with a soft cloth, dusting the carved oak cabinets behind the counter, and making sure the sales book and cash drawer

were in order. As she was finishing, a well-dressed gentleman arrived, carrying a brown leather case similar to the
bag Dr. Foster had.

"Good morning, madame. I am in the employ of the
Trellis Tobacco Company." He removed his hat and bowed
slightly, then handed her a card with his name on it. "I have
an appointment to see Monsieur Philippe."

"Of course, sir. He is expecting you. If you would please
follow me." Sophie led him behind the counter and through
the curtain and showed him into Monsieur Philippe's office.
Just before the noon hour, Monsieur Philippe and the salesman emerged, both wearing their hats and gloves.

"We will be going to the St. Louis Hotel for our midday
meal, madame," Monsieur Philippe said. "I will return later
in the afternoon."

"Of course, monsieur."

Sophie didn't realize until after Monsieur Philippe and
the salesman left the shop that in her haste to make sure
she arrived for work on time, she had neglected to make
any provision for her own midday meal. *Ah, well,* she told
herself, *it is possible I will be so busy with customers that
I would not have had much time to eat anyway.* She was
correct. Customers came and went in a steady stream all
afternoon. Monsieur Philippe was pleased when he returned
to the shop to see Sophie double-checking a large stack of
sales receipts.

"Ah, Madame Rieple," he greeted her enthusiastically and leaned over the counter to look at the figures she was working on. "How have sales gone in my absence?"

Unused to such familiarity, Sophie instinctively took a step back. "Very well, monsieur," she replied matter-of-factly, being careful to maintain a neutral expression. "I have been quite busy since you left to go to the hotel."

"Very good. If you would be so kind, please bring the sales book and join me in my office."

She gathered the ledger and the day's receipts and joined Monsieur Philippe in his office. He double-checked the total and her entries of the purchases made during the time he'd been away.

"You are correct, madame. A very good day so far, indeed! I am most pleased, both with the sales, and with your work."

"Thank you, monsieur." She paused before continuing, fidgeting in her chair. "There is one small thing I need to discuss with you. I do not want to be a bother; I realize I just began my employment, and I do not wish to make things inconvenient, but there is something I am in need of."

"Of course, madame," he said graciously, smiling to put her at ease. "Anything at all. Just ask."

"Thank you. You are most kind. I was wondering if it would be permissible for me to leave just a few moments early this evening. I need to go to the post office and mail a letter to my sister, and one to my late husband's family.

They were already on their way to Illinois when he died, and I need to let them know of his passing."

"My deepest condolences on your loss, madame. As it turns out, I have correspondence of my own to post. We will close the shop at four thirty, and I will escort you to the post office. When we have concluded our business there, I will make sure you arrive safely back at your residence."

Something in the way Monsieur Philippe phrased his response coupled with the look in his eyes gave Sophie pause. *His expression was somber when I explained why I needed to leave early, but when he mentioned escorting me back to my residence, his eyes were almost dancing. Why? Was he offering to accompany me simply out of kindness, to ensure my safety, as he said? Or might he have something more in mind?* "That will not be necessary, monsieur," she protested. "I have the address of the post office, and I am sure I can find my way. There is no need for you to take up your valuable time with my personal concerns."

"I insist, madame. As I said, I have letters to post as well. Make sure everything is ready for closing at four thirty. I will be in my office until then."

Although she was nervous being in Monsieur Philippe's presence—she was cautious by nature around people she did not know well and was keenly aware of her vulnerability as a widow alone in an unfamiliar place where she knew almost no one—she had to admit the walk to the post office was quite pleasant, through a part of town Sophie hadn't had a chance to fully explore yet. The architecture of the French Quarter with its bold colors and whimsical embellishments was vastly different from the buildings in Rheda. She found the combination of the intricate wrought-iron accents on the stylish buildings and the lush tropical landscaping enchanting. As they walked, Monsieur Philippe pointed out various locations of interest: the Supreme Court building, the majestic and elegant St. Louis Hotel where he and the tobacco supplier had eaten their midday meal that afternoon, and historic Jackson Square. As they continued down Chartres Street, Sophie noticed what looked like a graveyard a few blocks away to her left.

"I beg your pardon, monsieur; I am not familiar with the city. Is that a cemetery off in the distance?"

"Yes, madame. That is the St. Louis Cemetery, named after the street on which it is located. Why do you ask?"

"My late husband is buried in the Charity Hospital Cemetery. I did not know the exact location and wondered if this was that cemetery."

"Again, my deepest sympathies, madame. The Charity Hospital Cemetery is a good distance away from here to the north on Canal Street. Much too far to walk in the late-afternoon heat, I am afraid. After we conclude our business at the post office, I would be happy to arrange for a carriage, should you desire to pay your respects."

"Thank you, monsieur, but I have no wish to visit at present." While she very much wanted—at some point—to see Friedrich and Sophie Elise's final resting places, she was not prepared to do so yet, and certainly had no wish to visit Friedrich's grave with Monsieur Philippe in attendance. Barely able to face her grief herself, she was in no way ready or willing to share it with someone she hardly knew.

They turned right at the next corner, onto Toulouse Street, then walked another block and a half. The post office was on their right in the middle of the block. When they walked in, the postmaster greeted Monsieur Delaroche by name.

"Ah, Philippe! How are you, today? I trust business is good!"

"It is, mon ami. Quite good. May I present Madame Rieple? She has recently joined my staff as a sales associate. She may from time to time be here to conduct business on my behalf."

"It is my pleasure to make your acquaintance, Madame Rieple," the postmaster replied, bowing deeply in Sophie's direction.

"And mine as well, sir." She nodded in acknowledgment.

Monsieur Philippe pulled a stack of letters from his waistcoat pocket and handed them to the postmaster, who began sorting them and affixing postage. "I believe you also have correspondence that needs to be posted, madame," he said, turning to Sophie and gesturing for her to hand him the letters to Mina and Christian and Louise.

"I was prepared to attend to this matter myself, monsieur," she insisted. "You do not need to trouble yourself on my account."

"It is no trouble at all, madame, I assure you."

She handed him the letters and the card with the name of the town where Christian and Louise's letter was to be sent. With a few quick pen strokes, Philippe had the letter addressed and handed it to the postmaster to be stamped and placed in the bag with the rest of the outgoing mail. Monsieur Philippe paid for the postage and bade the postmaster goodbye.

When they were outside once again, Sophie spoke. "Thank you again, monsieur. It was not necessary for you to do that, but I do appreciate your kindness. You have been most gracious to me."

"It is truly my pleasure, Madame Rieple. Would you like to join me for dinner? I can arrange for a carriage to take us to the Hotel St. Louis."

Sophie stiffened, uncertain how to respond. After what happened at Madame DuVall's, she was keenly aware that keeping her employer happy was an important consideration if she wanted to remain employed. But having dinner with another man—one she barely knew—just two days after Friedrich's death was improper in the extreme. She did not want to disappoint or anger him, but she could not in good conscience accept.

"I am sorry, monsieur, but that will not be possible. There are several things I must attend to this evening. But I do thank you for your thoughtful invitation."

"I am thoroughly disappointed, madame," Monsieur Philippe said, "but I understand. As I promised earlier, I shall escort you to your residence, with your permission."

Once back at the rooming house, Sophie had a light supper, then spent the evening continuing to make alterations to the dresses in her trunk that were suitable to wear to work at the tobacconist's shop.

Monsieur Philippe returned to the hotel for dinner and then retired to the bar for a cigar and an after-dinner drink. He sat sipping cognac and thinking of Sophie well into the evening.

Chapter Fifteen

The days sped by for Sophie, each one a flurry of activity full of new things to learn and do. The heat and humidity of summer gave way to cooler, shorter fall days, followed by what passed for winter in New Orleans—vastly different from the snowy season she was accustomed to in Rheda. She threw herself into her work, concentrating on learning the languages and local dialects of Monsieur Philippe's regular customers, and by the new year—just months after she'd begun her employment—was proficient in all of them. She had a knack for remembering faces and preferences, and would often have a customer's usual choices out on the counter as soon as she saw them walk into the shop. When new stock arrived in the store, she did not hesitate to make recommendations if she thought it was something the customer would enjoy. Monsieur

Philippe's clientele found Sophie's gracious manner and the personal attention she provided most appealing, and sales increased steadily.

As she was completing a sale on the morning of February 20, the representative from the Trellis Tobacco Company walked in. When she finished with the customer she was waiting on, he greeted her. "Good morning, Madame Rieple."

"Ah, good morning, Mr. Francis. Monsieur Philippe is in his office and is awaiting your arrival. Please, go on in."

"Thank you, madame."

Monsieur Philippe had the inventory in front of him when Mr. Francis walked in, and with Sophie's expertly categorized and labeled lists, it took less than half an hour for the order to be completed. "Shall we head to the hotel?" he asked the salesman. "It is a little early, but this will give us a chance to enjoy a glass of wine and converse before our meal."

"Absolutely," the salesman replied. "I could use a drink."

They left the office and made their way down the narrow hallway to the front of the shop. "We will be going to the hotel for the midday meal as usual, Madame Rieple. I will return later this afternoon."

"Of course, monsieur."

Mr. Francis bowed and tipped his hat in Sophie's direction but did not speak.

When they arrived at the hotel dining room, the maître d' immediately showed them to Monsieur Philippe's regular table. Tucked into the far corner of the room away from the noise of the street and the auctions of real estate, goods, and slaves that regularly took place in the grand rotunda, it was secluded and quiet enough for intimate conversations, yet still allowed those seated a view of the entire dining room. And what a glorious sight it was. Lavishly appointed, the tables were set with pristine white table covers, gleaming silverware, and spotless crystal wine and water goblets. Elegantly folded napkins with razor-sharp creases stood at attention beside gold-edged Haviland China plates.

"I must say, Philippe," the salesman observed between sips of wine, "you have always had a well-appointed and well-run shop, but that new saleswoman of yours has improved things a thousand-fold."

"She is quite something, isn't she?"

"She is. I have had a chance, these past few months, to observe how she interacts with customers, and I am amazed every time I see her. She knows the stock and your clientele frontward and back. And sales have increased steadily since you took her on; you order more from me each month. Wherever did you find her?"

"Herr Franke at the German Society sent her over. She arrived a few months ago from Prussia. I had significant reservations in the beginning about whether things would work out or not. She had no sales experience, and I did not know how fast she would be able to learn, but I am eternally grateful now that I took a chance on her."

"I did not want to say anything while we were at the shop for fear she would overhear, but her physical appearance is quite striking as well. Those eyes! That hair! She is one of the most beautiful women I have ever seen."

"A vision of loveliness," Philippe agreed. "However, I must warn you: she is absolutely and completely unavailable."

"How so? Married? That is not much of an obstacle, Philippe, as you well know."

"She is widowed, newly so, and in deep mourning. My advice, Stephen? Stay away from her."

"Are you seeing her yourself?" Mr. Francis asked, with a sly smile.

"I am simply protecting my investment," Philippe replied. He found Mr. Francis's interest in Sophie and the way he doggedly continued to press the issue irritating, yet did not want to divulge his own feelings. "As you so astutely pointed out, business at the shop is booming. I have made larger profits in the last six months than I ever have, due exclusively, I am convinced, to the efforts of the lovely and capable Madame Rieple. Should a suitor appear and propose marriage, she would no longer need employment. That is a risk I am disinclined to take. I appreciate your kind words about her, and I do not disagree with you, but she is not available."

Monsieur Philippe had, in fact, been trying to woo Sophie since the day she started working at the shop. He had been careful in his approach, given the recent loss of her husband and the depth of her grief, but he had made his interest clear. The more diligently he pursued her, the harder she worked to keep him at arm's length, but he hadn't given up, and had no plans to, nor was he interested in competing with anyone else for her affections.

"It is most regrettable," the salesman sighed, "but I understand completely. Shall we get on with ordering our meal, then?"

When they finished eating, they left the hotel. "Until next month, Stephen," Monsieur Philippe said.

"Yes, Philippe. I'll see you then."

After shaking hands, Mr. Francis turned and continued down St. Louis street. Monsieur Philippe walked back down Chartres Street, stopped by the tailor's, then went to the stationer's and ordered more letterhead before going back to the shop. When he returned, he called Sophie into his office to apprise him of how things had gone while he had been out. It had been another very busy afternoon, and it took an extended period of time for them to go over the day's sales. It was well past five o'clock and already nearly dark when they finally closed the shop.

Sophie left the shop, crossed Iberville Street, then continued east on Chartres Street, as she usually did, but before she got to the end of the next block, she became engulfed in a huge crowd. Music was blaring, and there were more people out in the street than she had ever seen in her life: some walking, some riding on wildly decorated wagons, all dressed in strange costumes and throwing beads and coins into the crowds lining the streets. She tried to pick her way carefully through the raucous mob, but no matter where she stepped or which way she turned, she was bumped and jostled as the multitudes around her rushed to follow the wagons and carriages. She was nearly knocked to the ground several times when revelers behind her leaped up to catch the trinkets being thrown and, on more than one occasion, had to duck to keep from being pelted in the face with coins. The nonstop music and cheering and screaming that erupted at various intervals along the parade route made her head pound. It was useless trying to politely ask those in front of her to make room for her to pass; she could not make herself heard over the din. She realized it would be quite impossible to fight her way through the crowd and get back to the rooming house in a reasonable length of time. In a panic—fearing for her physical safety in the seemingly out-of-control crowd—and not knowing what else to do, she turned around and headed back toward the tobacco shop. Monsieur Philippe was still out in front, conversing with one of the other shopkeepers.

"Madame Rieple. Did you forget something?"

"No, monsieur. But there is a gathering of some sort down the street, and I cannot get through the crowd to return to my residence by my usual route. I thought perhaps I would wait here for a few moments and see if they disperse, and then try once again to make my way home."

An amused smile flashed across Philippe's face. "Ah, madame, I apologize for the inconvenience. Regrettably, it will be many hours before the crowds disperse. Likely tomorrow morning."

"Tomorrow morning?" Sophie asked in bewilderment. "I am sorry, monsieur. I do not understand."

"It is one of our quaint local customs. What you are seeing is the Mardi Gras Parade. Each year, the city engages in one last night of revelry before the somber disciplines of the Lenten season are thrust upon us. The merriment will last until the wee hours of the morning, and will be quite boisterous, as you have already seen."

"But then how will I get home?" Sophie asked frantically, her concern causing her voice to rise.

"If you will permit me, madame, I will call for a carriage and escort you back to your residence myself. It will be safer that way. If you will come with me, please?" Without waiting for her to respond, Monsieur Philippe bowed slightly, took Sophie by the arm, and whisked her off in the opposite direction.

She was more than a little uneasy about the prospect of being alone in a carriage with Monsieur Philippe; he had expressed obvious interest in her early on in her employment and had consistently made bolder and bolder overtures for her affections over the past few months. Up until now, she had regularly but politely rebuffed him and, under other circumstances, would never have considered getting into a carriage alone with him, but the huge, high-spirited crowd had completely unnerved her. Even as fraught with peril as it could potentially be, a carriage ride with Monsieur Philippe seemed safer at the moment than trying to brave the mob and walk home alone. When they reached the end of the block, Monsieur Philippe hailed a carriage and gave the driver an address on St. Louis Street.

"That is not the street the rooming house is on, monsieur," she reminded him.

"No, madame, I am aware of that. But we closed the shop much later than usual, and by now it is well into the supper hour. We are both in need of sustenance. I know a café that is not directly on the parade route and will be able to accommodate us. Once we have had our evening meal, I will return you to your home. In the meantime, please, do your best to relax and enjoy the ride."

Still shaking from her experience with the Mardi Gras crowd and apprehensive about her employer's true intentions, Sophie huddled on one side of the carriage. Grateful Monsieur Philippe made no attempt to engage in conversation, she turned her attention to the view outside the carriage window. This section of the city was grand and glorious in the daytime, but in the evening, the twinkling street lights and the warm glow of oil lamps, candles, and fireplaces visible through the windows of homes, shops, and cafés gave the neighborhood an almost magical appearance. Lulled by the soft, golden light and the rhythmic clopping of the horses' hooves, by the time they arrived at their destination, her trembling had eased considerably. She was not familiar with the café, but Monsieur Philippe was well-known there.

"Ah, Monsieur Delaroche!" The maître d' greeted them enthusiastically. "So good to see you! I will let Antoine know you are here. Your usual table is waiting. Please, follow me." They wound their way through the café to a table in the back overlooking a small courtyard garden, now mostly obscured by shadows.

"I apologize, Madame Rieple," Philippe said as the maître d' seated them. "The view is much lovelier in the daytime when the garden is visible. But this does offer us a respite from the noise of the street. I know the large crowd was most upsetting to you; you were quite shaken. I am hopeful a quiet meal will put you at ease."

Sophie was not at all certain that spending time alone with Monsieur Philippe would put her at ease, but she kept her concerns to herself. "I appreciate your thoughtfulness, monsieur," she murmured noncommittally. "Thank you."

A tall man in a well-tailored dark suit appeared, acknowledging Sophie with a smile and slight bow, then greeting Monsieur Philippe effusively. "Welcome, Monsieur Delaroche. It is wonderful to see you on such a lovely evening!" The man raised one hand in the air and a waiter immediately appeared at their table carrying a loaf of bread and a carafe of red wine. This, Sophie realized, must be Antoine, the café's proprietor.

"May I offer you and madame a beverage?"

"Yes, please, Antoine. Wine for each of us. And thank you. It is indeed a lovely evening."

Monsieur Philippe glanced briefly at the menu while the waiter filled their glasses, then turned his attention back to Sophie. While she slowly sipped her wine, he regaled her with stories about the history and traditions of Mardi Gras. There was nothing like Carnival celebrations in her experience, and she was fascinated by his tales of the various secret societies and graphic descriptions of the unbridled revelry that took place. His soothing voice, the comforting aroma of tomato sauce, onions and peppers, and baking bread wafting from the kitchen (and the effects of the wine) calmed her nerves. The tension in her neck and shoulders ebbed away.

He paused, then asked, "Madame Rieple, do you mind if I change the subject to something of a more personal nature?"

His question immediately put Sophie on edge again. *Something more personal? What in the world does he want to know?* Worried her voice would betray her fear and concern, she simply shook her head and continued to sip her wine.

"Please, do not think me too forward, but we have known each other for several months by now. Since it is outside of working hours and we are not at the shop, I would ask your permission to address you by your first name. If you prefer otherwise, I will, of course, honor your wishes, but under the circumstances, I see no need to continue to use formal titles. May I?"

Sophie flinched, warnings flashing across her mind. She was put off by his words, unsure that becoming more familiar with Monsieur Philippe was prudent, particularly given the fact that she had so far only spent eight months of the requisite year in mourning. But as she considered his request, her thoughts once again went back to her previous employer and the debacle that ensued when she did not comply with Madame DuVall's wishes.

As much as I want to keep him at arm's length, it may be best to allow him to use my first name. I know from bitter experience the happier I am able to keep him, the better my chances of keeping my employment, and alone and on my own, I have to be able to earn a living.

"If monsieur prefers. My given name is Charlotte Sophia, but I was most often addressed by those who knew me as Sophie."

"Ah, Sophie! It fits you perfectly. An elegant and charming name for an elegant and charming lady. You, of course, already know my given name is Philippe."

The waiter returned just then to discuss the menu with Monsieur Philippe, so Sophie didn't have to meet his eyes or respond directly. He ordered shrimp étouffée and another glass of wine for each of them. Accustomed to the simple fare at her boardinghouse in one of the predominantly German neighborhoods on the other side of the French Quarter, Sophie had never tasted anything like it in her life. She savored every bite of the succulent shrimp, spicy sauce, and fluffy rice. When they were finished with the main course, the waiter cleared the plates and spoke briefly to Monsieur Philippe. Moments later, he returned with brandy and coffee, and a rich custard dessert with a burnt sugar topping.

"They call it crème brulée. What do you think, Sophie?" Monsieur Philippe asked.

"It is delicious," she had to admit. "The entire meal has been unlike anything I have ever eaten before, but all of it was wonderful."

"I am happy to hear you enjoyed it. If you are ready, it will be my pleasure to see you to your residence."

"Thank you, monsieur."

"Philippe, Sophie."

"Thank you, Philippe," she said reluctantly, hoping the use of Philippe's first name would not encourage him further.

A carriage was waiting for them when they left the café, and they settled themselves inside for the ride back to the rooming house. "I did not want to ask publicly at the café, Sophie," Philippe said, turning to face her, "but I am curious; I wondered if you would be willing to tell me a bit about your late husband."

Waves of sorrow instantly swept over her, filling her eyes with tears and leaving her bewildered, frustrated, and embarrassed. *What is wrong with me? I have not wept over Friedrich in weeks.* Her grief over losing her family still burned raw in her soul, but with work at the tobacco shop demanding so much of her attention, she was able to get through most days without breaking down. *Why tonight, of all nights, is it so difficult for me to keep my emotions under control? I cannot allow Monsieur Delaroche to see me distraught and sobbing,* she told herself. *He will think me weak and insufferable, and he will regret ever offering me employment.* She stared out the window of the carriage for several minutes, struggling to regain her composure. After several deep breaths, she cleared her throat and spoke, her voice barely above a whisper. "I am sorry, monsieur. I cannot." She again looked away in hopes of concealing her tears.

"Of course, Sophie," he said gently, settling back in his seat. "Forgive me. I did not mean to cause you undue pain or distress." They rode the rest of the way in silence.

Sophie could feel Philippe's eyes on her as she stared out the carriage window, but she did not turn and meet his gaze until the carriage stopped in front of the rooming house.

She was almost too afraid to try speaking again, but courtesy required that she convey her gratitude for the evening. "Thank you again, monsieur," she said as she gathered her skirt and prepared to climb down out of the carriage. "The evening meal was lovely, and I very much appreciate you taking the time to escort me home. You are most kind."

"It was my pleasure, Sophie." He stepped in front of her and gracefully alighted from the carriage, extending his hand to help her down the steps. Still holding her hand, he bent down and allowed his lips to brush it ever so slightly. Raising his head, he looked directly into her eyes for several long seconds—seconds that to her seemed like years—before continuing to speak. "Again, please forgive me for any distress my question may have caused you. It was not at all my intention to upset you. I will see you to the door."

Sophie was grateful that it was fully dark by now, with clouds obscuring the moon; she could feel her cheeks flaming after his familiar gesture, and she did not want Monsieur Philippe to see her embarrassment. When they reached the entrance to the rooming house, he kissed her hand once again, this time purposefully allowing his lips to linger.

"May you enjoy sweet dreams, Sophie. I will see you in the morning."

"Goodnight, monsieur," she stammered, letting herself in and shutting the door behind her as quickly as possible. She leaned her back against the closed door and heard his voice come through.

"Philippe, Sophie."

Chapter Sixteen

Unable to get the evening's encounter out of her mind, Sophie spent the rest of the night tossing and turning. She did have dreams, several in fact, but she would not have described any of them as "sweet." They started out pleasantly enough, with her and Philippe enjoying a carriage ride, a leisurely stroll through the park, or an intimate meal together, but they always ended with an accusing face from her past questioning her loyalties and hinting at betrayal. Sometimes it was Mama, sometimes it was Papa, once it was even Sophie Elise. She would jolt awake each time, racked with shame and guilt. *What am I going to do?* Philippe's thin veneer of concern no longer covered the blatant desire underneath it; she wasn't sure how long she could continue to put off his overtures. And if she told herself the truth about it, after the evening they'd just spent together, she was not entirely sure she wanted to.

There had been no other suitors, or even any "passing fancies" in her life. She'd never been in love with anyone but Friedrich. Had anyone asked her, before tonight, she would have insisted she could never love anyone else—was not interested in even considering marrying again after Friedrich's death. But the carriage rides and dinner she had shared with Philippe that evening unleashed a tempest of thoughts and feelings. She could no longer ignore or push aside how achingly lonely she was. Her only friends, the Mullers, had moved months ago, after their niece and nephew had arrived and settled upriver in Carrollton.

Her terrifying experience with the crowd as she left the tobacco shop that evening reminded her just how much she missed Friedrich's solicitous attention and how vulnerable she was without him—or anyone else—there to protect her. Her cheeks flamed again as she recalled Philippe bidding her goodnight at the front door of the rooming house. The touch of his lips on the back of her hand set her skin on fire. Desire rippled through her each time she thought of it, forcing her to admit she missed all of *those* feelings, too. She was shocked, in fact, to be confronted face-to-face, as it were, with just how much she yearned to be held, kissed, touched, caressed, fondled, stroked . . .

Stop it, Sophie! she admonished herself. *It is improper in the extreme for you to entertain such thoughts while you are still in mourning. Just stop!* But she could not stop. Pandora's box was open, and try as she might, there was no way to stuff those feelings back inside.

She dozed fitfully the rest of the night but never truly rested. She rose at her accustomed time and dressed for work. She had hoped that by morning her mind would have quieted, but that was not the case. The more she tried to stop thinking about Monsieur Philippe and the events of the previous evening, the farther out of control her thoughts spiraled. Every step of the walk to the tobacco shop was filled with anxiety, apprehension, and trepidation.

I am a bundle of nerves just thinking about Monsieur Delaroche. How am I to be in the same room with him? In hopes of maintaining some shred of clarity and objectivity, she forced herself to refer to him formally. *What will happen when he is out on the sales floor? Will he expect the same level of familiarity here in the shop as he did last night in the café? How shall I answer if he asks me to dinner again or insists on offering me a carriage ride home? And if he tries to kiss my hand, or heaven forbid, insists on being even more intimate, what then?*

Thankfully, the door of the tobacco shop was unlocked, and he was already in his office when she arrived at her usual time ten minutes before nine. She set about uncovering the display cases and readying the cash register and sales ledger. At precisely nine o'clock, he walked out of his office and greeted her.

"Good morning, Madame Rieple. I trust you rested well?"

"I did, monsieur," she lied. She did not return the inquiry, instead asking, "Are there any special instructions for the day?"

"No, madame. I will be going to the hotel for my midday meal as usual, but I have no appointments on my schedule. I will be in my office, should anyone desire to speak to me."

"Very good, monsieur."

After the boisterous revelry of the Fat Tuesday celebration the night before, it was a quiet day in the tobacco shop. Monsieur Philippe, to her great relief, spent the entire day—with the exception of a brief trip to the St. Louis Hotel at noon to dine—behind the curtain in his office, leaving her in blessed solitude and with plenty of time to think. She did little else.

Who is he, really? She knew nothing about him outside of what she had observed of his interactions in the tobacco shop, the post office, and last night in the carriage and at the café. *He deals fairly and respectfully with the salespeople and customers, but is that because he values respect and fairness, or is it simply one of the strategies he employs to ensure the success of his business? The postmaster and the staff at the café greeted him enthusiastically and treated him with deference, but is that because they genuinely like him, or because they are aware of his wealth and position and want to keep his patronage? He treats me with kindness and courtesy, but is that* the kind of person he is in his heart of hearts, or is his doing so motivated only by his desire to pursue me romantically?

All these uncertainties were concerning enough in and of themselves. What was even more unsettling was the fact that as little as she knew about Monsieur Delaroche, she knew even less about herself these days. There was a time—not all that long ago—when she knew exactly who she was and where she fit in the world: she was a wife, mother, confidant, helper, and friend. *Now I am none of those things. Caught between nothing and forever—between a life that no longer exists and a future I cannot even imagine—stripped of everything that meant anything to me, I no longer have any sense of identity or belonging, no idea where to go or what to do.*

Could New Orleans ever feel like home? Everything outside of her own neighborhood was so "other" to her. She felt confused, intimidated, and uncomfortable most of the time. The Mardi Gras crowd outside the shop last night was so large and so raucous, she had been too frightened to walk back to the rooming house alone. Even the weather was strange and exhausting; she wilted in the summer heat and humidity, and the storms that rolled in off the river were terrifying. If she accepted Monsieur Delaroche's advances, this was where she would stay.

Do I want to spend the rest of my life in a place where I am afraid as often as I am anything? Will I be betraying

Friedrich and our love if I choose to stay here instead of going to Illinois with the rest of his family as he planned?

I do not know.

But saying no to Monsieur Delaroche could cost me my job. By refusing his advances I may anger him enough to not only terminate my employment, but—because he is wealthy and well-known—also cause him to openly discourage others from hiring me as well. If the choice is between the word of an established and popular local businessman and a no-name foreigner, who also happens to be a woman, and a widow, there is no question which one they will choose.

I know what you always said, Mama. You told us to "Stop and think!" I am trying to, but all I have is questions—questions that have no answers. And even though you insisted that somehow things would turn out all right, right now I cannot see how.

Just a few yards away, secluded behind the damask curtain in the office at the back of the store, Philippe Delaroche sat at his desk considering some of the very same questions plaguing Sophie. As he replayed last night's encounter with her over and over in his mind, he found himself both mystified and frustrated by his utter lack of certainty regarding his desires and how to proceed—all of which was brand-new territory for him. Never before had Philippe Delaroche experienced any problem whatsoever articulating exactly what it was he wanted, or any hesitation or reservation about pursuing those things.

All right, Philippe, he told himself, *enough of this mental meandering; you need to get this sorted out. She is beautiful. Breathtaking, still, even after everything the poor woman has been through. The combination of her platinum hair, those cerulean eyes, and that thin, willowy frame that is still amply curved in all the right places is striking to say the least. So striking I am no longer certain how many of my customers actually come to the shop just for tobacco or cigars; I think most of them show up first and foremost to feast their eyes on Madame Rieple.*

She is capable, efficient, and obviously highly intelligent. It took no time at all for her to master all the skills necessary to run the shop. In just a handful of months, she has become fluent in all the local dialects, learned a new currency, mastered the inventory, and figured out the accounting system. It makes me doubly curious as to what else she might be persuaded to learn and how accomplished she might become at those tasks . . .

By intention, because of her recent bereavement, I have not pursued her as aggressively as I would normally pursue a woman I was interested in, but even so, she was abundantly aware of my attraction to her long before last night, I am sure. And I must admit my patience has been wearing thin of late, particularly when others—that Francis fellow who works for Trellis Tobacco for one—have expressed interest in her as well. Her being so frightened by the parade crowd last night was a serendipitous coincidence, creating the perfect opportunity to spend time alone with her without any fabrication on my part, and no awkward questions on her part. And things went very well up until the carriage ride back from the café.

I was hoping that by asking about her late husband I could get a clear sense of where things were between us, how receptive she might be to a relationship with me, and how to proceed. Alas, she could not even bring herself to speak of him, and though she tried valiantly to hide them, I could see the tears welling in her eyes and sense the depth of emotion she was struggling with. I had thought, then, that it was best to leave things as they were and forgo the idea of pursuing her, and that is what I intended to do. Kissing her hand after helping her down from the carriage was meant to be nothing more than a polite goodnight, but it turned out to be anything but.

When my lips touched the back of her hand, I felt an instant connection with her. It was so powerful—so visceral and deep, and yet so tender and so sweet—I could not help myself; I had to kiss her hand again when we reached the front door of the rooming house. I heard her gasp and felt her start to tremble when my lips lingered for those few seconds; I know she experienced it too. But she offered no comment, nor did she reciprocate in any way.

So where do things go from here? Do I forge ahead and continue to pursue her? Do I wait for her to offer some sort of response? Or should I follow my first inclination from last night and simply leave her be?

Checking his pocket watch, Philippe saw that it was nearly time to close the shop. No closer to a definitive conclusion regarding his relationship with Sophie than he was when he entered his office that morning, he prepared to leave for the day. *I will remain formal and businesslike for the time being,* he told himself, *and wait to see if and how she responds.*

Hat and gloves in hand, he left his office and walked out to the counter where Sophie was tidying the display cases. "It is nearly five p.m., Madame Rieple. Is everything in order for the evening?"

"It is, monsieur. Do you wish to go over the accounts for the day before closing?"

"I think not. I will check the ledger first thing in the morning when I arrive."

Sophie covered the display cases while Monsieur Philippe put the ledger and the day's receipts in the safe.

"Is there anything I can assist you with before we leave for the day?" he asked.

"Nothing I can think of, monsieur; I will get my handbag and gloves and be on my way. Good evening to you, sir."

"Good evening, madame. I will see you at nine tomorrow morning."

They left the shop and went their separate ways, Sophie to her residence, and Philippe to the Hotel St. Louis.

Chapter Seventeen

*A*t his usual table in the corner of the main dining room, wreathed in a cloud of earth-and-leather-scented smoke, Philippe savored one of his favorite cigars—a La Belle Creole—and a glass of burgundy before he ordered dinner, continuing to consider the conundrum that was Sophie Rieple. *If I choose to pursue this*, he mused to himself, *what exactly am I pursuing?* He realized that in all his ruminations earlier in the day, he had never asked himself that particular question. *Am I pursuing her just for the pleasure I would most assuredly have in her company? Or is there something deeper here? Could I be falling in love with her, and might marriage be in our future? Would she consider marrying me if I asked?*

Philippe Delaroche was no stranger to pleasure; it was what he lived for, and there was no place on the planet at this point in history more suited to pursuing that predilection in all its forms than populous and permissive New Orleans. There were beautiful women—and men!—everywhere one turned, and new faces arrived by the boatload daily from around the globe. He had had a constant string of casual relationships and was often seen about town with beautiful companions, but until the present moment, he had been a confirmed bachelor. The thought of marriage or, truth be told, any sort of commitment, had never interested him in the least. *Much too constraining*, he told himself. *Not enough spontaneity.* He loved the freedom of having to please no one but himself—and being able to pursue that pleasure at any moment—that being single and unattached offered. And yet here he was asking the question. He drained his glass and motioned to the waiter for another.

On Decatur Street in Faubourg Marigny, Sophie lingered over the last morsels of the simple evening meal offered by the proprietress of the rooming house—cold cuts and cheese served with baguettes, fruit, and tea. When she finished, she took her empty plate and silverware to the kitchen, then went up to her room to finish the alterations on the last dress in her trunk—a dark-blue watered silk evening gown with a V neckline overlaid with beaded lace in a soft ivory shade. Laying the garment out on the bed, she smoothed it out so it was perfectly flat, and one by one, marked the seams of the bodice with tailor's chalk.

I have always loved this dress. I loved the challenge of crafting something this intricate and elegant, and the sense of accomplishment I had when it turned out so well. And I especially loved how beautiful I looked and felt in it.

As she snipped and pinned and stitched, she recalled the last time she wore the gown—in March of the previous year—for her beloved sister Mina's wedding.

It was such a glorious day. The weather was perfect, the service was perfect, dinner was a delight, and dancing into the night with Friedrich was simply divine. It was the last truly happy day she could recall, where there were no cares or concerns, no arguments or contention, just celebration and joy. Life seemed full of possibility and promise that day. And then just weeks later, they were on their way across the sea. All that promise turned to ashes; life had been nothing but death and death and more death ever since.

Recalling each of those specific losses—Marie Louise, then Friedrich, then Sophie Elise—led her back to her present circumstances, Monsieur Delaroche, and all the questions she had asked herself earlier in the day. *While he has been discreet and reserved in his approach, he has pursued me relentlessly since the very day I began working at the shop. But what does he really want? Is he showering me with attention because he is considering entering into a courtship that might one day lead to marriage, or is this just a dalliance? Could I—once I became acquainted with him on a deeper level—ever be interested enough in him to consider it? He is incredibly handsome, always impeccably dressed, and has connections all over town. But that is not enough of a foundation to build a marriage on. I am not a socialite and have no desire to become one. Hearth and home are what hold my heart. But are they enough to hold his?*

She sat with those questions, turning them over and over in her mind while she continued to sew. After an hour of painstakingly taking in each of the bodice's intricately curved seams and full skirt, the alterations were complete. She slipped out of the dress she had on and stepped into the blue gown to check the fit. She was stunned when she finished buttoning it and looked up at her reflection in the mirror. *I still love this dress. And I still feel beautiful in it.* Reaching up, she pulled the pins out of her bun and let her hair fall around her shoulders. Caught up in the moment— captivated by a stab of pure joy, something she hadn't felt in months—she smiled and twirled in front of the mirror. But as she came full circle, the bodice of the dress caught her eye, and that joy instantly faded. It had been so long since she'd worn it, she had forgotten how revealing this garment was compared to her other clothing, even with the over-lay of lace. She sighed. *It's the most beautiful dress I've ever owned, but there is no place I can wear it. Even if my year of mourning was complete, it is in no way appropriate for the tobacco shop. Back in the trunk it goes.*

Philippe mopped up the remaining Bearnaise sauce on his plate with the last crust of baguette from the breadbasket. Deciding to forgo his usual custom of finishing his evening meal with dessert and brandy or cognac, he paid his bill, left a tip for the waiter, and walked out onto St. Louis Street. *It is time*, he told himself. *Time to settle this once and for all.* Hailing a carriage, he gave the driver the address of Sophie's rooming house and climbed inside.

Sophie was still in front of the mirror, taking one last look at her handiwork before she packed away the evening gown for good, when there was a knock at her door. The proprietress was there, with a message that Sophie's employer was downstairs asking to speak to her. "I will be down at once, madame. Thank you for letting me know." She glanced in the mirror, smoothed her hair, and hurried downstairs.

"Monsieur Delaroche! I was not expecting you." Confused as to his reason for coming to the rooming house, rather than inviting him into the parlor, she motioned him out onto the porch and closed the front door behind them. "Is there something I can do for you?"

"I most assuredly hope so. I believe it would be best if we spoke privately. I have a carriage waiting." Without asking if she was willing to accompany him, he grasped her arm and whisked her down the steps and out into the cloudless, moonlit night. Philippe helped her into the carriage, then after giving the driver instructions, climbed in beside her, slipping his arm around her shoulder and resting his right hand on hers.

"Forgive me if this seems too forward, Sophie," he began, "but since last night, I have thought of nothing else but you."

In the silver light of the full moon shining through the carriage window, every detail of Monsieur Philippe's face was visible. Apprehensive about where the conversation may be going, Sophie was grateful for the moonlight. She carefully studied his expression in order to glean as much as she could about his emotional state and his intent.

"I know it was extremely distressing to you when I asked about your late husband," Philippe continued. "I thought hearing you speak about him would give me some sense of where and how you are and whether or not there was any point in pursuing you any further. You were well aware of my interest even before last evening, I am certain. Alas, my inquiry upset you greatly; you were not able to speak of him at all."

Please, Sophie pleaded inwardly, recalling the intense emotions of the previous evening. *No more weeping. Tonight of all nights, I need to stay calm so I can think clearly.*

"I took your tears to mean you were still mourning so deeply you had no wish to even consider any sort of relationship," Philippe went on. "I was prepared at that very moment to refrain from pursuing any romantic involvement with you, and indeed, as God is my witness, that was the only intent behind my kissing your hand. I meant it only as a respectful—but extremely fond—ending to that part of our relationship. But that kiss was so exquisite, I could not help myself. I had to do it again. You sensed it, too, Sophie. I heard you gasp, noticed your trembling, felt the warmth spread across your hand when my lips touched your skin. So, where do we go from here?"

"Forgive me, monsieur," she stammered, her heart hammering. "I am not accustomed to having gentlemen speak with such candor, but I will do my best to answer your question as honestly as I can. I have been thinking a great deal about last evening as well, and there are many things to consider. It will be June before my year of mourning is completed. Because of that, and for several other reasons, I had not given any thought whatsoever to the possibility of being courted by anyone. The events of last evening have brought that possibility, and with it, many questions, to the fore. But I must advise you that before I could fully and completely entertain such a thing, I would need to know your intentions—and truly discern my own."

"That is what I am trying so desperately to sort out!" Philippe said, throwing his hands up in exasperation. "It is the very reason I am here."

"Your intentions, monsieur?" she asked again, her eyes locked on his. "Were you thinking of a formal courtship and marriage?"

"That is the problem, Sophie. I do not know." He looked away in silence. At last, he turned back to her and spoke. "You are organized and capable; you run the shop like clockwork, and sales are booming. I cannot even imagine what other gifts and talents you may possess." He shook his head briefly, then continued. "Not only are you efficient and intelligent, your beauty bewitches me, which I find most exhilarating; when I am in your presence, I can barely concentrate. With your hair down—and in that dress—you look positively ravishing. All I can think about is what it would be like to feel your lips against mine, to hold and caress you from head to foot." He brought her hand to his lips. As he did so, Sophie both saw—and felt—his eyes drop ever so briefly. She pulled her hand away before his kiss could linger, realizing with horror that she was still wearing the low-cut evening gown. Her cheeks burned with embarrassment, because of the revealing way she was dressed, the hunger that flamed in his eyes when they drifted across her bodice, and the directness with which he spoke.

"Please, hear me out," he implored, grasping her hand again. "You would make a wonderful wife for me—or any man—but the truth is, I have been completely happy as a bachelor and never planned on marrying anyone; indeed, I have never once considered it. And as of this moment, I am still not sure. In time, and perhaps only a very short time, I could decide that I am quite in love with you—that you are the only woman for me—and be ready to propose marriage. But right now, I am not completely certain of that fact."

"I see." It was her turn to look away.

His position is clear. What about mine? Where am I in all of this, and what do I really want?

After spending many minutes silently contemplating his words and her own thoughts and emotions, the barest hint of certainty settled in her soul.

She was painfully aware, by virtue of her own circumstances and experience, that she did not know—and could not predict—what the future might hold. She would never have all the answers to every question. All she could do was make the wisest choices possible with the information she had. And, at present, what she knew was this: she was more than a pretty face, more than a "capable and efficient worker." And she had no interest in risking her future on a possibility that might never become reality. He was handsome, courteous, well-respected in the city, and extremely successful. Life with Monsieur Delaroche would no doubt be comfortable—luxurious even—and for the first time in a long time, she would not have to worry about either financial matters or her physical safety. But unless their lives were legally bound together in matrimony, she would be no more secure than she was at present, and likely even less so.

There is no denying the physical attraction between us. He is infatuated with me now, but when my beauty begins to fade—and one day it surely will—would he remain by my side? I want more than casual companionship—regardless of how delicious the companionship of Monsieur Delaroche might prove to be. I want to matter, to belong—to find a place and people I can spend the rest of my life with, connections that will anchor my soul—a commitment Philippe is, by his own admission, not ready to make at the moment, and might never be.

She turned and studied his face for several more minutes, then spoke again.

"I respect your willingness to be honest with me, monsieur," she said calmly, once again looking him directly in the eye. "You have been most kind and gracious to me, which I very much appreciate. Even though you made no secret of your considerable interest in me, up until last evening, you have been entirely discreet and chaste, for which I am also grateful. In addition to the fact that I am still in mourning, and will be for several more months, I know nothing about you outside of the way you conduct yourself in the tobacco shop. I have no knowledge of your family or any details about the rest of your life. By your own admission, you cannot tell me whether marriage is something you could seriously consider; right now, in your very own words, you 'are not sure.' That is not enough." She pulled her hand away and turned to face him more directly. "Everything I loved has been taken from me. My life is full of uncertainty and unknowns. As I move forward into whatever my future holds, what I need most are things and people I can count on, not more uncertainty and ambiguity. Given those realities, I do not believe we have a future together. I am sorry if my answer is disappointing to you, monsieur. But since you were kind enough to be honest with me, I can do no less for you."

"But, Sophie!" he protested. "Can I not convince you to even try? To give me a chance and see if there is truly something between us worth pursuing?"

"I am sorry. I cannot. If you will excuse me, I must return to my room." She started to rise and exit the carriage, then stopped. There was one more issue she knew she had to address, even though she was dreading what Philippe's answer might be. "One last question, monsieur. Will you be expecting me at the shop tomorrow as usual, or has our conversation changed that circumstance and rendered my services unnecessary?"

"Of course you are expected at the shop in the morning! While I obviously would have preferred a different answer, your employment is not incumbent on maintaining an intimate relationship with me," he assured her.

"Thank you, monsieur," Sophie said with a deep sigh of relief. "I deeply appreciate your kindness and understanding."

"You are an extremely valuable asset to my business, Sophie—one I cannot afford to be without. And please, do not worry. I will maintain a proper and appropriate professional distance from this moment forward. You can count on it. I thank you for your frank and direct responses, and again, I offer my deepest and most sincere apologies for any distress or discomfort I may have caused you." He rose, helped her down from the carriage, and walked her to the door, but made no attempt to kiss her hand.

Sophie went upstairs to her room and prepared to retire for the evening. She removed the lace-trimmed dress and packed it away in the bottom of her trunk, brushed her hair, then slipped on a nightgown. Piling the pillows at the head of the bed, she propped herself up, picked up Friedrich's journal, and reread the lists he had made for traveling to Illinois, making notes of her own as she went.

Despite Monsieur Philippe's assurances that he would maintain a discreet professional boundary at all times, the next day was awkward for Sophie. Edgy and tense, she struggled throughout the day to maintain her concentration and worried about each interaction with Monsieur Philippe. *I want to believe what he said last night in the carriage, but I still do not know him well enough to know whether I can trust him completely. He sounded sincere, but perhaps he only said those things because he knew that was what I wanted to hear. Even if he meant it then, he could always renege.*

I wondered last night if perhaps I should seek out Friedrich's family, as he had originally planned, and I believe now that it would be best to do so. I will go to the German Society at my earliest convenience and inquire about securing passage to St. Louis, then traveling on to Havana.

When she walked into the rooming house after work that day, the proprietress handed her a letter. Glancing at the postmark, she was surprised to see the letter was from Christian. Weary from her awkward and tiring day at the tobacco shop, she decided to eat dinner first, then read it.

When she returned to her room, she retrieved the letter, then, hands shaking, sat down on the bed, tore the envelope open, and began to read.

5 March 1855

Dear Sophie,

I am hopeful that this letter finds you well, and that you were able to find adequate employment. Louise and I were greatly saddened to hear of the deaths of Friedrich and Sophie Elise. I am sure you are utterly and completely heartbroken, and I cannot imagine how lonely you have been all these months alone in a strange city where you know no one. Forgive me for taking so long to write. It was grievous news for me as well, and I have been very busy. It takes a great deal of effort to settle new territory.

I can tell you that the Illinois prairie is much to our liking so far. I am sure Friedrich would have loved living here, and I am sorry that his dream of building a new life in America was so tragically cut short.

You did not mention in your letter whether you were going to stay in New Orleans permanently or not. I was wondering if you had come to a decision by now. I realize that if you have found employment and begun making a life for yourself there, it may be easier and more prudent for you to stay. If, however, that is not the case—if you have not found New Orleans satisfactory and were inclined to make the effort to honor Friedrich's wishes—we and the rest of the Rieple family who are here would be happy to welcome you to Illinois. Havana is a prosperous and growing river town, so ample opportunity awaits you here. As far as the trip itself, traveling by boat up the Mississippi is quite pleasant; the voyage is a short one, just a matter of days.

Please, let us know what your plans are. If in fact you do choose to come to Illinois and join us, rest assured that we will do whatever we can to assist you. Once again, we are so sorry that Friedrich and Sophie Elise are gone.

Most sincerely,

Your cousin Christian

Christian and Louise. It had been nearly a year since Sophie wrote to them of Friedrich's death—long enough that by now, she had given up any expectation of ever hearing from them. *But,* she reasoned, *our parting on the* John Schmidt *was so acrimonious, Christian may have been as hesitant to respond to me as I was to write to him.*

It was a curious coincidence to hear from them after she just last night concluded that she should make her way to Illinois after all. *What he says is compelling. He speaks well of the location they have settled in; he and Louise are obviously happy there. And he seems certain Friedrich would have been too. It does indeed sound like I will have a far better chance of finding a place I can belong there than I will ever have here.*

But there was much he did not say. He did not apologize for leaving us in New Orleans when we needed his help most, and that still hurts. Yet he is offering his assistance now. That is something.

I can hear you now, Mama, reminding me again that things will be all right. I did not see how that could be when we left for America, certainly not when those I loved most in the world were taken from me in such quick succession. I could not even see it night before last when I was struggling with what to do about Monsieur Philippe's overtures. I want things to happen—I want answers and resolution—immediately; that is not always how life unfolds. But in time, with patience—"somehow, some way," as you always said—things do work out. Christian's words seemed to be a direct confirmation that her decision to go to Illinois was the right one. For the first time in a long time, she had hope that things would be all right—or at the very least, far better than she had envisioned them.

As she had planned, she went later that week and secured the assistance of the staff at the German Society in planning to travel to Illinois. When the details were complete, she posted another letter to Christian, letting him know approximately when she would be leaving New Orleans and arriving in Havana.

She continued working at Monsieur Philippe's tobacco shop through the late spring. True to his word, their relationship remained cordial but professional. When the last of the winter snows had melted in the north, the resulting high water along the Mississippi had begun to recede, and riverboat travel was safe once again, she set sail on a steamer the first week of June, one year after arriving in New Orleans.

Chapter Eighteen

Before sunrise on the morning of June 3, 1855, Sophie stood facing the Mississippi River, waiting to board the *Mayflower*. While the streets between her Decatur Street rooming house and the riverfront were nearly vacant at that hour, the docks themselves were crowded and bustling. Steamboats departed early in order to ensure there would be as many hours of daylight to travel in as possible.

It was strange to think about how much had changed in a year's time. It was just a year ago that Friedrich and Sophie Elise and Sophie arrived in New Orleans. And now she was preparing to sail again. She was anxious to move on with her life, but she could not help but think of what that voyage a year ago was like. Those days on the *John Schmidt* were filled with unspeakable horror; she could not wait to leave them behind. This time, thankfully, she would not be traveling in steerage. She would at least have some measure of privacy and adequate food and drink.

While this decision felt right, still she had concerns. She would once again be going to an unfamiliar place where she would have to learn new customs and skills. And she would know no one but Christian and Louise. Their letter was courteous enough, and it was kind of them to offer to assist her in getting settled, but she had reservations. Christian promised to help when they arrived in New Orleans and then changed his mind. He could do so again. She also had questions about his motivation for offering help after such a long time. *Does he feel sorry for me? Guilty for leaving us, when Friedrich died so soon?*

Sophie's thoughts were interrupted by the call to board. This time, instead of huddling on her berth, she stood on the deck and watched the city slowly slip into the background as the craft made its way into the middle of the river and churned north. It was an experience she would never forget. Watching the sun rise over New Orleans was breathtaking, and the sound of the steam whistle blowing as they got under way gave her chills.

Just as Christian had indicated in his letter, Sophie's trip north from New Orleans on the *Mayflower* was the polar opposite of her voyage from Bremen to America on the *John Schmidt*. Having worked in Monsieur Philippe's tobacco shop for nearly a year, she had the wherewithal to book a cabin on the upper deck, which allowed her to travel in relative comfort. For those who could not afford a cabin, conditions were much like what she experienced on the *John Schmidt*, and in some cases, worse. The Mississippi was an important trade and supply route; the majority of the steamboats that plied her waters were not exclusively for passenger travel. They were also shipping vessels carrying a wide range of cargo. Passengers on the lower decks often shared space with the freight—goods and supplies such as rice, cotton bales, timber, tobacco, molasses, grain—and even livestock.

It was a mere handful of days from New Orleans to St. Louis, nothing compared to the weeks-long nightmare of crossing the Atlantic. Sophie particularly enjoyed the fact that there was breathtaking scenery to enjoy throughout the trip, a much different experience from the monotony of ocean travel where all one saw was water in every direction, every single day. The riverboat was steam-powered and the river was wide and deep, offering them a smooth ride devoid of the exaggerated rocking motion of an ocean-going vessel. The rhythmic lapping of the paddle wheel and hum of the engines lulled her to sleep each night, and the bluffs, towns, forests, and farmland that framed the mighty Mississippi on either side intrigued and enchanted her each day.

When they arrived in St. Louis, a porter came for her trunks and assisted her in getting settled on the packet boat that would take her up the Illinois River to Havana.

Although the Illinois was not as expansive as the Mississippi, the view as they traveled the river was every bit as beautiful. Just two days later, they arrived in Havana. High limestone cliffs dotted the shore to the north and west while the town itself spread out over bluffs that rose and fell on the opposite shore. The streets were laid out in orderly squares that made it quite simple to travel about and easy for newcomers to locate particular homes and businesses. By midafternoon on June 14, the boat was docked, passengers and baggage unloaded, and she was on her way to the Ross Hotel, near the center of town.

When she identified herself and signed the hotel register, the clerk immediately produced a message for her. He pointed out the location of the dining room, described the amenities and restaurants available nearby, then showed her to her second-floor room. A few moments later, two gentlemen arrived with her trunks. Once alone, she opened the envelope and found a letter from Christian.

8 June 1855

Dear cousin Sophie,

We are so glad you have made the decision to join us here in Illinois. Were he here, I am certain Friedrich would be pleased as well. We hope the voyage upriver was uneventful, and that this note finds

you well and comfortably settled in the hotel. We
plan to travel to town next Friday, June 15, and
are anxious to see you. If all goes well, we expect to
arrive at the hotel shortly after midday.

We are looking forward to your visit, to showing
you the sights of the city and surrounding country-
side, and are especially pleased to be able to give
you a tour of our farm and introduce you to the
rest of the family here.

Most sincerely,

Christian and Louise

Sophie put the note on the dresser, relieved at the gracious
tone of Christian's words and grateful to read that they
were looking forward to seeing her. After unpacking Friedrich's journal, her comb, hairbrush, hairpins, and the rest
of the things she would need for the evening, she donned
her hat and gloves and went downstairs to explore the city.
Minuscule compared to New Orleans, and much less of
a melting pot, Havana nonetheless appeared prosperous
and industrious. Stately trees—elm, oak, maple, birch,
walnut, and pine—but without New Orleans' ever-present
moss—lined the downtown streets and dotted the yards
of residences. Markedly different from the landscape and
climate of the Crescent City, to Sophie, it felt familiar and

deeply comforting. Similar varieties of oak and pine had populated the forests in her native land, and the absence of New Orleans' excessive heat and humidity was most welcome. The wood-frame buildings were far less ornate than the architecture she was accustomed to seeing either in New Orleans or back home in Prussia, but they were well-constructed and pleasing to the eye. While sedate compared to the boisterous crowds of New Orleans' French Quarter and business districts, the people she encountered were friendly, the shops and businesses orderly and well-kept, and there was a sense of optimism and determination that appealed to her greatly.

Within the blocks surrounding the square were grocery stores, livery stables, wagon sellers, restaurants, and hotels. She was also pleased to see dry goods stores, a tailor shop, a cigar store, and a millinery—all possibilities for employment. As she passed various storefronts, businesses, and people on the street, she heard bits of German, Swedish, and English, as well as Scottish accents and the occasional Irish brogue. On the bluff northeast of the town square stood the Methodist Episcopal Church and the German Evangelical Lutheran Church. Taking in the scenery and getting a sense of what Havana and its citizens were like was most pleasant; after several days of travel by boat, the long walk felt good. Sophie returned to the hotel just before the dinner hour hopeful and relaxed. After a brief rest, she brushed and repinned her hair, washed her face and hands, and at six o'clock, went downstairs to the dining room for the evening meal.

Just like everything else she had seen that day, the hotel dining room was much plainer than the hotels and restaurants she had dined in in New Orleans. Instead of white, starched tablecloths, the tables were bare varnished wood set with stoneware rather than fine china. There were no fresh flowers on the tables, no exotic aromas wafting from the kitchen. But everything was neat and clean, and the staff attentive and gracious.

"Good evening, madame," the waiter greeted her courteously when she walked in, and he seated her immediately. "May I bring you a beverage to enjoy while your meal is readied?"

"Thank you," she replied. "May I have hot tea, please?"

"Certainly, madame."

The waiter returned momentarily with a steaming cup of tea and a jar of honey with which to sweeten it.

"We have sauerbraten tonight, madame, served with red cabbage and spaetzli. We also have freshly caught fried catfish with pan-fried potatoes, slices of onion, and rye bread. What may I bring you?"

"The sauerbraten, please. It sounds delicious." She sipped her tea appreciatively while she waited for her meal to be served. When the waiter returned, he brought a steaming plate piled high with succulent slices of tender beef smothered in a delicious sauce, tiny golden dumplings, and tangy shreds of red cabbage. It reminded her of Rheda—of home, of childhood dinners with her siblings crowded around the table, of her mother's cooking, and of holiday meals when the entire family gathered at her grandparents' home. For dessert, she had a piece of spice cake topped with sweetened whipped cream and another cup of tea. When she finished, she went out for a twilight stroll around the block and then retired to her room.

As she turned her thoughts toward the next day, her heart sank; grief, doubt, uncertainty, and anger swirled around her like the storm clouds that rolled in off the Mississippi during New Orleans summers. Preoccupied by the sights and sounds of a new place, she had not given any thought to what seeing Christian and Louise again would be like. The moment she did, all the anger and resentment associated with their parting when the ship arrived in New Orleans came flooding back. To her, it had not been a parting at all; it had been an abandonment, and it still hurt.

We are so glad you have made the decision to join us here in Illinois, they'd said. But could she trust them to mean that? *I have no way of knowing, at this moment, whether they are truly glad I am here or not. And I do not know whether this is someplace I want to stay, or if making a life here is even possible. What I do know is this: The last time Christian gave me his word—promising to help us when the* John Schmidt *docked—he left without doing a thing.*

Will I be able to put my hurt aside and be courteous when I see them tomorrow, or will the very sight of them send me once again into a rage? She did not know the answer to that question either. She was able to take her time in composing the letters she exchanged with them and use a cordial matter-of-fact tone, but being face-to-face with someone is a far different thing than putting words on a page. *If I cannot put my hurt aside, forging a positive relationship with them will not be possible. And they will know exactly how I feel; I have never been good at concealing my emotions. If I am upset with them, it will be written all over my face.*

Even though Christian's letters back to me were courteous, there may be some ill feelings toward me on his part as well. He may be angry and resentful that I expected him to help take care of Friedrich—his cousin—before and instead of seeing to the needs of his own wife and children. Dear Lord in heaven, forgive me. I had not considered how strident and selfish my demands likely seemed to him. And I was demanding, I know it. With my entire life disintegrating before my very eyes, I was desperate for any kind of help I could get, any way I could get it.

I hope, for all of our sakes, things go smoothly and there is no discord. In spite of my displeasure, I am truly curious to see how different it is to be involved in farming in this part of the world compared to the life we led in Rheda, and I'm anxious to learn more about whether it will be possible for me to make a life here. So much had happened in a year's time. She wondered how much Christian and Louise had changed since she saw them last, and how much the children had grown. Would she even recognize them?

The children! Thoughts of Christian and Louise's children set off a string of memories of her own daughters and their untimely deaths. *My beautiful baby girls! I miss you so. I pray, for Christian and Louise's sakes, that their children are all well; that they have not had to face the grief and tragedy I have endured. There is absolutely nothing in the world that is worse for a parent than to bury one of your children. I would not wish that agony on my worst enemy, and even though I have been angry with them, I truly hope Christian and Louise have been spared this pain.*

Thinking back once again to the message waiting for her at the hotel, she remembered Christian talking about how much he was looking forward to introducing her to the other Rieple family members living in the area. She wondered who they were and exactly how they were related to Friedrich. They had visited his parents regularly until their deaths, and she knew his siblings but was not well acquainted with his extended family, and by now she could not remember any of their names except for Christian and Louise. Were those here cousins as well? Or had some of Friedrich's aunts and uncles come to America even earlier?

She also wanted to ask Christian about the other German families in the area. She could tell from the names on some of the businesses—Krebaum, Holzgraefe, Dierker—

and the fact that of the two church buildings in town, one was a German Lutheran Church, that there was a significant number of the population here who had emigrated from Germany just as she had. She was curious about where they were from and what caused them to make the choice to come to America. *Those are questions for tomorrow, Sophie,* she told herself. *Get some rest so you are ready for the day.*

Her room was well appointed and comfortable, with an iron bed, a hand-carved oak dresser with a gray-and-white-streaked marble top and matching washstand. She washed her face, took down her hair and brushed it, then dressed for bed. The very last thing she did before blowing out the lamp was pick up Friedrich's journal. In the days immediately following his death, and particularly after she made the decision to come north to Havana, it became a nightly ritual for her to reread the first few pages where Friedrich had made his lists and notes, and to make notes of her own. Some nights she was able to make it through those entries without dissolving into tears, but that was not always the case. At times, she could take the sadness in stride, let the tears flow. But on other occasions—like that Mardi Gras night in Monsieur Philippe's carriage—the randomness of grief and its intensity angered and frustrated her. She found herself chafing to get through it, wanting to move on as quickly as possible.

She worked hard to hide her pain, worried others would think less of her, and most times she hid it well.

To anyone who had seen her as she walked about town that afternoon, had encountered her in the hotel dining room, or had witnessed her as she took her evening stroll around the block, nothing would have seemed amiss. Indeed, anyone who had seen her in Monsieur Philippe's tobacco shop in New Orleans would have thought the same thing. Yet she still grieved deeply.

Tonight, given her uncertainty and apprehension in regard to seeing Christian and Louise and meeting the rest of the family and the poignant and painful memories of Sophie Elise, Marie Louise, and Friedrich that thoughts of Christian and Louise's children had dredged up, her emotions were closer to the surface than they had been in several days. Rather than stopping at the end of Friedrich's lists as she usually did, she continued reading all of the letters he had written to her, holding onto his every word with all her heart. When she finished the last letter, she blew out the lamp and lay down. Yet on this night when she most needed to rest, sleep would not come; she was haunted by thoughts of Friedrich and her darling girls and was full of regrets and remorse and questions about tomorrow.

Oh, my sweet prince! How I miss you! When Catharine died, I chafed at an entire year of mourning, thinking it much too long a time. What a silly girl I was! A year is nothing. I could mourn you for a thousand lifetimes and it would not be enough! I will never stop missing you. I know you did not want to leave me and would have given anything to have had things turn out differently. You tried with all of your strength to hang on as long as you possibly could. And I also know you kept the extent and severity of your illness from me until the last possible moment, doing everything within your power to shield me from worry. You always went out of your way to protect me, my prince, and that is one of the things I miss most about you.

Looking back, after reading his journal, she realized he carried many other concerns he did not share with her. And she understood why; he did it in order to keep peace between them. *I railed like a selfish shrew when you told me you thought our best chance for a future was to leave Prussia and start over in America. I treated you hatefully! I am so sorry, Friedrich. Forgive me for all of the turmoil and distress I added to your life by being so angry! I am sure having me question your decision, when you were doing your very best to take care of us, was heartbreaking to you. You blamed yourself for all of our misery, and the amount of grief and guilt you felt when our beautiful Marie Louise died on the ship was overwhelming. Again, I am so sorry, my prince! It was not your fault. You did not know—you could not know—what was going to happen, and if there had been any way of preventing it, I know you would have.*

Ah, Friedrich. Had I been more gracious about the decision to move, I would likely be in less distress right now as well. Had I not been so angry and stubborn, arrangements might have been made to travel from Rheda to Bremen with Christian and Louise and their family and a connection between us—something I now sorely need!—might have been forged. Traveling together, we may have arrived in time to secure a cabin to share, which would have made the voyage much more tolerable, and may even have preserved Marie Louise's life.

I kept things from you as well, when I should not have. I refused to tell you the details of my conversations with Christian on the John Schmidt *when you asked. You guessed things had not ended well anyway; I saw the disappointment on your face when I said they had made other plans. But I should have told you the truth. Not being honest with you demeaned and diminished you even further, when you were already sick, tired, grieving, and feeling incapable and incompetent.*

I am sorry for the pain that caused you. And I am sorry for myself that I am now preparing to meet them again, dependent on their help to rebuild my life, and unsure how I will be received. I can only hope and pray that they will be more gracious to me than I have been to them. I remember with deep regret my comments about not wanting to travel with them, and my accusation that your family did not like me. You insisted that they adored me. I sincerely hope you judged them correctly, my prince. Christian says there are several other relatives here. Had we spent even half as much time with your side of the family as we spent with mine, I would have at least known of them, if I did not know them personally, and they would not be strangers to me now. I regret that as well.

I have tried very hard to think things through carefully, my love. I have studied the lists you left in your journal, and I am grateful for your words. I have some idea of what will be necessary for me to move forward and make a life for myself in America. My only question now is whether it will be possible for me—a woman alone; a widow—to accomplish those things. It will be much easier if Christian and Louise are in fact willing to help. I am hopeful, since they encouraged me to make the trip north, that they will honor their promise to assist me, but I will not know for certain until I meet them tomorrow.

Friedrich, I am so worried! Whatever will I do if Christian and Louise are not able or willing to help me, if the words in the letter were just that—words? She was once again in a strange place where she knew almost no one. She was not familiar with the countryside or the customs here. While Havana seemed to be a nice town—it did remind her of home—and showed every indication of being prosperous, it was much smaller than New Orleans; Sophie did not know if she would in fact be able to find employment. Christian seemed to think so—in his letter he spoke of there being "ample opportunity" in Havana—but what if he was mistaken, or things had changed in the time between his reply and her arrival? If she could not find work, she would need to go somewhere else and try again to make her way. But where? She did not know.

I am trying, my prince, to live with the resolve I was able to marshal after Marie Louise's death. To make a conscious effort to choose life, even in the face of death. But it is so very difficult, especially now when you and Sophie Elise are gone too. I am not sure how many times I can keep choosing. If Christian and Louise are unkind, or for some reason not able to help me, I fear I may not be able to go on.

It has been a year since I kissed you goodbye the last time, my prince, and yet I still weep for you and for our beautiful girls. You occupy so many of my thoughts and I still miss you so much! She still felt the sting of grief when she saw couples and children walk down the street. And she felt so, so alone; she did not feel at home in the least in New Orleans, and she was not sure it would ever be possible for her to feel as though she belonged anywhere again. Whatever was she going to do? *I still have so many questions! Leaving New Orleans was the right thing to do. That, I know. Yet even in knowing there is uncertainty.*

An insistent rustling sound interrupted Sophie's thoughts. Raising her head from the pillow, she saw the curtains billow and flap. Wiping her tears with the back of her hand, she slipped out of bed and went to the window to see if a storm was approaching. Strangely, the night air was calm; there was no breeze stirring the tree branches outlined outside her window in the cloudless moonlit night.

No one was out on the streets; the shops and storefronts she could see were all dark. As she looked up at the stars, she sensed something behind her. Turning to look, she saw nothing, she heard nothing, but she felt *something*. Rather than cold and frightening, whatever it was—spirit, angel, the Almighty?—Friedrich? Mama?—was a decidedly kind and gracious presence, with no hint of malevolence or evil. Her tears ceased, her restless mind stopped racing, her tensions eased.

"Is that you, my prince?" she whispered. No voice answered, but her mother's words echoed in her heart. *It will be all right. Somehow, some way, everything will be all right.*

Turning back to the window and seeing nothing but the town square, the trees, the full moon, and a million winking stars, Sophie went back to bed and fell into a deep, dreamless sleep. She rose at her usual hour, brushed and put up her hair, dressed, and went downstairs to the dining room, drawn by the aroma of freshly baked biscuits and coffee. After breakfasting on scrambled eggs, sausage patties, biscuits with butter and strawberry jam and steaming mugs of coffee with cream, she took another leisurely walk through the center of town. Returning to the hotel just before noon, she had a light midday meal of cheese, fruit, and bread, then readied herself to meet Christian and Louise.

As she sat waiting for them in the lobby, she mused over last night's encounter at the window. She had no idea who or what had been in the room with her, but whatever that something was, it had given her a measure of peace and release.

I will be kind and gracious. I will listen carefully, with an open heart; I will think through my responses before I speak. And I will trust that all will be well.

Chapter Nineteen

Just past 1:30 that afternoon, a wagon pulled up at the front door of the hotel. Sophie instantly recognized Christian, Louise, and their children. To her great relief, they looked much the same as they had when she had last seen them leaving the *John Schmidt*. Christian was a bit thinner, but that was probably due to the strenuous activity involved in building a farm from the ground up, she reasoned.

"Sophie!" Louise clambered down from the wagon and wrapped her in a tight embrace. "I trust the trip north from New Orleans was uneventful, and much more pleasant than our time on board the *John Schmidt*!"

"It was, Louise. Having been employed for some months in New Orleans, I was able to secure a cabin. And the scenery on both the Mississippi and the Illinois Rivers was quite beautiful."

The children piled out of the back of the wagon and rushed up to Sophie. "Welcome to Illinois, cousin Sophie," Friedrich said, offering her his hand. Carl nodded solemnly and offered his hand as well.

"We are glad you are here," Johanna said, as she and Anna offered hugs.

"Thank you so much for the warm welcome," Sophie said. "I appreciate it very much and am glad to be here. You have grown so much since I last saw you. You are quite the young gentlemen and ladies!"

Christian walked around the wagon and tipped his hat. "It is good to see you, Sophie. I am glad to hear the trip was good and pleased you are finally here. A lot has happened in the past year, and we have much to catch up on."

"Yes." She nodded and offered what she hoped was a gracious smile. "I am anxious to hear about everything."

She found Christian's choice of words telling. *There is much indeed the two of us need to "catch up on" and say to one another.* It was obvious he preferred not to address those things at the moment, in a public place, in front of Louise and the children. She understood, but she hoped it would not be long before they had a chance to speak privately and clear the air.

"If you like, Sophie, we would love to show you around town," Christian said.

"Of course," she replied.

Christian helped Louise onto the front seat of the wagon, then offered his hand to Sophie. Once she was comfortably settled next to Louise, he lifted the girls into the back of the wagon. The boys climbed in behind them. While Christian unhitched the horses, Louise peppered Sophie with questions. She wanted to know all about everything, immediately. "Oh, Sophie! I cannot begin to imagine how difficult things were for you! How in the world did you survive? Where did you wind up living? How did you find work?"

"The staff at the German Society found us a room in one of the boardinghouses and helped me secure a position in one of the dressmaker's shops as soon as we got settled, but when Friedrich and Sophie Elise became sick, I had to care for them and was not able to continue working." Sophie paused, her throat tightening and tears stinging her eyes. Taking a deep breath helped her maintain her composure, and after a moment, she was able to continue speaking. "After their passing, I returned to the German Society for assistance. By that time, there were no positions at any of the dressmaker's or tailor's shops, but they found work for me as a salesclerk in one of the tobacconist's shops in the French Quarter. I worked there until just a few days before the *Mayflower* sailed. And there was a lovely older couple from Bavaria next door who helped me immensely when

Friedrich and Sophie Elise were so ill. Mr. and Mrs. Muller were angels. I was so sad when they moved."

"A salesclerk in a tobacco shop—in the French Quarter!" Louise's eyes widened in surprise. "My goodness, that sounds so exotic and exciting! I am so grateful you were able to find employment and people to help you, Sophie," Louise said with relief. "We were worried about you being alone in a huge city like New Orleans."

"It can be quite raucous and boisterous," Sophie agreed. "I was very careful; I spent most of my time in my neighborhood, which was predominantly German, and my employer was very kind. In the end, though, I just never felt completely at home there, and I doubted I ever would. I am very much looking forward to seeing what life is like here." She tried to say enough to quell Louise's curiosity but did not want to go into too much detail until she had a chance to speak with Christian and sort out exactly where things were between them. Anxious to divert attention from herself and her circumstances, she changed the subject.

"I am curious about the name of the town, Christian. My employer regularly received shipments from Havana, Cuba, and New Orleans had a significant population of Cuban residents. Their language, art, and customs were evident throughout the city. Many were master cigar makers or otherwise involved in the tobacco trade, and I saw them regularly in the shop. There is nothing like that here. Most of the names I saw on the businesses when I was out walking yesterday are either European or American. How did a settlement in the middle of the country—far from the sea, and with no apparent ties to anything Cuban—come to be known as Havana?"

"Well, there is a connection, but not an obvious one, unless you live here and are familiar with the locality. Just upriver to the north from where your boat docked, there is an island. It is the same shape as the island of Cuba, and that is how it has always been known; as Cuba Island or 'Little Cuba.' Since that was already part of the history of the area, when the town was organized in 1848, they chose to name it Havana, after the capitol of Cuba."

"How fascinating. I would never have dreamed of encountering a story like that here. Now, tell me, how are things on the farm?"

"It has been a challenge starting from scratch," Christian admitted, "but the land is good, and we enjoy it here. We have a few errands in town; you can join us and meet some of the townspeople, then we will take you out to the farm and show you around. We will stop at the hotel and get your things on our way out of town. We would love to have you stay at the farm with us."

Sophie was surprised by the generous offer, and at the same time wary of the possibility of being stuck in an uncomfortable situation if their conversations did not go well. "Are you sure, Christian? I know you have much to do. I do not want to be a burden or inconvenience you in any way."

"No, please, Sophie," Louise insisted, her eyes shining with tears. "It would be our honor to welcome you to our home."

"Thank you, both of you. As I said, I did spend some time walking around yesterday after I arrived but have not been formally introduced or spoken with anyone. I would very much like to meet some of the people, and I am most interested in seeing the farm and the rest of the family."

Sophie enjoyed making the rounds of the various businesses and meeting the proprietors Christian and Louise did business with. Many of them were from Germany, some from the same region of Prussia she and Friedrich's families were from, and as conversations unfolded, it became obvious they had made the trip to America for the same reason Friedrich and Christian had chosen to come: opportunity. When the errands were finished, they went back to the hotel. Sophie paid her bill and checked out while Christian and the boys loaded her trunks into the back of the wagon.

They took the main road out of town to the south. On that side of the river bluff, thousands of acres of land stretched out in front of them from horizon to horizon, with houses, cultivated fields, pastures, and outbuildings randomly dotting the landscape. After an hour's ride, Christian turned west and traveled for another few miles.

On the south side of the road, there was a long lane, at the end of which stood a newly built cabin. Vegetables stood at attention in orderly rows in the large garden east of the house. There was a chicken house in the side yard, hogs, cattle, and sheep in pens across the back of the property, and a barn for the horses on the west side of the lane. Christian halted the wagon in front of the house and instructed their sons, one of whom was Friedrich's namesake, to help him unload Sophie's trunks, then helped Sophie down from the wagon.

"The other relatives I spoke of in my letter live close by," he said. "We will meet some of them tomorrow afternoon."

"Thank you again, Christian," Sophie said. "I appreciate everything you have done. It is good to see all of you, and I will be glad to meet the rest of the family." She and Louise and the girls went into the house where Louise showed her the room she would be using while Christian and the boys took care of the wagon and horses.

"Is there something I can do to help you, Louise?" Sophie asked as they walked back into the kitchen. "It is nearly time for supper."

"Johanna and Anna will help me. You and Christian have many things to discuss; he will want to know more about what happened to Friedrich, I am sure. Evening chores do not take long; the two of you can talk while we get the food ready." Just then, Christian and the boys returned from the barn.

"If you would like, Sophie, I will show you around the farmstead," Christian offered. He led her out the back door, noting how many acres he had purchased and pointing out where the boundaries of his fields were. Several other members of the Rieple family lived along the same road, and he described the general locations of their farms as well. They walked behind the house so Sophie could see Louise's vegetable garden and then on to the livestock pens and the barn. When they got to the back fence, he stopped and faced her directly. Outside of noticing he was thinner than she remembered, Sophie had not looked closely at Christian when they arrived at the hotel that afternoon; her attention had been focused on Louise and her many questions, the children, and the people and places they had seen in town. With time now to study his features, she noted that his face was much more lined and careworn than she remembered. He looked weary and sad, and on the verge of tears.

"I am sorry, Sophie. So very, very sorry," he said, his voice breaking. Turning away from her, he buried his face in his hands, leaned on the fence, and wept.

Sophie was stunned by the depth of his emotion. The only men she had ever seen weep were her father, when he threw the first handful of dirt onto her sister Catharine's coffin at the cemetery, and Friedrich, after Marie Louise's burial at sea on the voyage to America. Both were well enough known to her that she could have hugged and comforted them without reproach. The same was not true of Christian. Though family, they were casual acquaintances at best, and what little history they did share was marked by unpleasantness.

Several minutes passed before he wiped his eyes with the back of his hand and turned to face her once again. "I have regretted my decision to leave New Orleans every minute of every day since I got your letter telling me of Friedrich's death. The fact that I failed you and Friedrich so miserably has weighed heavily on me, causing me countless sleepless nights. I should have answered your letter much sooner than I did. Indeed, the very day I received it, I should have written back to you instead of letting almost a year to go by. The truth is, I was too guilt-ridden to pick up my pen. I have wounded you deeply and added to your grief, I know. But I hope someday you can find it in your heart to forgive me."

Tears again welled up in Christian's eyes and spilled down his cheeks; this time he made no attempt to hide them. Unsure what to say or do in the face of his raw emotion—and struggling with her own—Sophie was silent for several moments, searching for an appropriate response.

How do I honor Christian's pain and receive his apology, while at the same time being truthful about my own feelings?

Weighing her words carefully, she spoke. "It was extremely difficult for me to deal with things in New Orleans on my own. Everything I loved was disappearing before my eyes, and I was desperate for help. I admit, at the time, I was enraged with you for abandoning us when we needed you most. And I found it hurtful that when you did respond to my letter, you offered no apology." A look of shame crossed Christian's face; he shook his head and looked away. Sophie paused and placed a reassuring hand on his shoulder. "I have since come to understand *why* you made the decision you did. Friedrich and my children meant the world to me, and their welfare always came first. Had I been in your position, I would likely have done the same thing. You were not being selfish; you simply did what you deemed best for your family under incredibly difficult circumstances. Guilt and recriminations will not bring my family back, nor will they help either one of us heal; stop torturing yourself over this."

"Oh, Sophie," he whispered, bowing his head in relief before once again looking her in the eye. "I do not deserve such kindness, but I am grateful. And I have been extremely busy. That is the truth, not simply an excuse for not writing sooner. Friedrich and I had planned to work the land together. As it is, it is almost more than I can handle on my own. I cannot help wondering how different things could have been if I had made another choice that day in New Orleans."

"I know, Christian. I have wondered the same thing about many of the decisions Friedrich and I made as well. But we cannot undo what has already come to pass. The only thing we can do is choose how we move forward from here. You have worked hard, and it shows; the farmstead is beautiful, and the crops are growing well. I know Friedrich Wilhelm and Heinrich Christian help you as they are able now, but they are growing up quickly. In no time at all they will be big enough to work alongside you every day; then you will have all the help you need. I appreciate you welcoming me to your home, and I am looking forward to meeting the rest of the family, but you do not need to feel totally responsible for my welfare. If I could stay with you until I am able to find employment, that will be more than sufficient, and I will help Louise in taking care of the house and the garden in the meantime. I do not mean to be either a leech, or to serve as your penance. There is no need."

"You are beyond gracious, Sophie. Although the tone of your letters was cordial, I was not certain what to expect when you arrived. Had you still been angry with me for leaving, I would not have been surprised, nor would I have blamed you. You had every right to hate me for that. It was a cowardly thing to do, and I am still shamed by it. I am thankful you have allowed me another opportunity to help, and I promise you I will. You are welcome to stay for as long as necessary, and Louise and I will do everything we can to assist you in making a life here. In the meantime, you will be our honored guest." He glanced up at the western sky, then offered Sophie his arm. "We should get back to the house. I am sure Louise and the girls will have supper ready by now."

Christian led the way past the barn and back up the lane to the back door. They were greeted by the scent of baking biscuits and the sizzle of potatoes frying in bacon fat. There was a platter of ham on the table, along with a salad of dandelion and beet greens.

Sophie took one step inside the back door and stopped. "It smells heavenly, Louise!" she exclaimed, inhaling appreciatively. "Like home."

They gathered around the rustic wooden table, hand-built by Christian, she was sure. Sophie sat on Christian's right, with their two daughters next to her. Louise was at the foot of the table, and little Friedrich and Heinrich were on the other side of the table on Christian's left. After a few moments of silent prayer, the dishes were passed and supper was served. When they were finished, the girls cleared the plates. Sophie helped Louise serve dessert, a delicious rhubarb pie—sweet and tart at the same time. Christian and the boys went outside while Sophie and Louise lingered at the table for a few moments.

"The pie was delectable, Louise. When I was a very little girl, I remember my grandmother once serving a rhubarb cake for Easter dinner, but I have never had rhubarb pie."

"I would be happy to give you the recipe. The plants grow well here. They come up early in the spring, but you can harvest the stalks all summer long. I can show you what they look like; there is a row of them along the east side of the garden. There are some things you need to be mindful of: Do not use the leaves. They look very much like kale, collards, and chard, but rhubarb leaves are poisonous. And unlike peaches, apples, and cherries, rhubarb is very, very tart. It takes a good deal of sugar for a pie."

"I am sure it takes great skill as well, but you have perfected the proportions," Sophie said. "It was wonderful." Louise smiled, grateful for the compliment. "Now," Sophie said, rising from the table, "let me help you with the dishes."

Johanna and Anna cleared the pie plates and forks from the table, then Louise sent them off to play. She wanted to know more about what living in New Orleans was like and was particularly interested in hearing about Sophie's work in Monsieur Philippe's tobacco shop. She plied Sophie with questions while she washed the dishes and handed them to Sophie to dry.

"How in the world did you figure out enough about tobacco to get employment in a tobacconist's shop, Sophie? I know nothing about anything like that and doubt I could ever learn!"

"I am sure you would be able to learn if you needed to, Louise. I knew a bit about tobacco before we made the trip to America. My sister Mina's husband is a cigar maker; his family has had tobacco shops for decades. And someone on Friedrich's side of the family—although I am embarrassed to say I do not remember who now—made cigars as well. Friedrich and Heinrich often talked about cigars and tobacco when we visited with one another. Being able to recall bits of their conversations helped me secure the job and made it easier to pick up the rest of the details necessary for running the shop. It did not turn out to be as difficult as I was afraid it was going to be. What was most challenging was becoming fluent in the local dialects and various languages people spoke in New Orleans. Those took some time to learn, but I finally mastered them well enough to be able to converse with customers in the shop and get them the items they wanted."

"Gracious me, Sophie!" Louise exclaimed, her eyes widening in amazement. "Just the thought of everything you have done and learned astounds me. And Monsieur Delaroche! What was he like? I want to know all about him!"

Sophie described Monsieur Philippe in general terms of nationality and appearance, and talked a great deal about his kindness and patience as she learned the various tasks involved at the tobacco shop. She kept the rest of the story—how handsome he was in his finely tailored suits and silk shirts, how his blue eyes danced when he spoke to her, how long and how diligently he had pursued her—to herself. *The less said about Philippe, the better.*

Even without those details, Louise was enthralled, and hung on Sophie's every word. "It all sounds so glamorous and exciting!" Louise said wistfully. "My life is positively dull in comparison."

"It was exciting, unlike anything I have ever experienced," Sophie admitted, stacking the plates on the table as she dried them. "Yet despite its unique beauty and charm, New Orleans was a painful and lonely place for me. My most vivid memories of my time there are of losing Friedrich and Sophie Elise. Having to work to support myself, I had no time to make friends. In fact, the only people I knew were my employers, and my next-door neighbors at the rooming house, the Mullers. You may think it 'dull,' Louise, but your life seems far preferable to me."

"I do have much to be grateful for, that is true," Louise admitted, wiping out the iron skillet she had used to fry the potatoes and hanging it on a hook above the fireplace. "I appreciate you helping with the dishes, Sophie, and entertaining all my questions. Forgive me if they prompted painful memories for you. I did not mean to make you feel sad."

"There is no need to apologize, Louise," Sophie said, putting the last stack of plates on the cupboard shelf.

"Oh, but there is." Louise placed her hand lightly on Sophie's forearm. "It is my fault you were left to take care of Friedrich and Sophie Elise on your own."

"Your fault? I do not understand."

"I was jealous of you, Sophie."

Sophie's eyes widened in surprise, and she listened in stunned silence as Louise continued her unsought—and completely unexpected—confession.

"You are so beautiful, so talented and creative. Your needlework is unparalleled. Your children were adorable—always well-behaved and immaculately dressed. Even in grief, you were such a loving and patient mother. I envied you and every single thing about your seemingly perfect life. I was in a state of panic that night on the *John Schmidt* after you came and asked for Christian's help. Simple and plain as I am, I could not bear the thought of spending the rest of my life in your shadow. So, I asked—no, I *demanded*—that we leave New Orleans as soon as the ship docked. I am sorry, Sophie. It was selfish and petty of me, and after the way things turned out, I will regret it to my dying day."

That was why they did not travel with us to Bremen, why she refused my invitations to spend time together on the ship, and why she did not speak to me on our wedding day, Sophie realized. *It all makes sense now.* Humbled by the amount of courage it took for Louise to admit how she truly felt, Sophie was reminded of her own anger, resentments, and ill will.

"I am grateful for your honesty, and you are more than forgiven," Sophie said, drawing Louise toward her in an embrace. "But," she said, stepping back and looking Louise in the eye, "I owe you an apology as well. Consumed with myself and what mattered to me, I made assumptions about you without bothering to get to know you and with no consideration for your circumstances and feelings. That was wrong of me, Louise, and I am sorry."

"Oh, Sophie!" Grateful tears welled up in Louise's eyes. "You are kinder than I dared hope. I cannot tell you what a relief it is to be able to talk this over with you face-to-face; it had become quite burdensome to me. And you are forgiven as well. Now we can truly be family to one another." She wrapped Sophie in a quick hug. "Why don't we join Christian on the porch? It is a lovely evening."

They sat in silence, watching the children play against the backdrop of the western sky where brilliant reds, golds, and oranges faded to dusky mauve and finally to inky black. The moon rose in the cloudless night sky while the stars winked and danced overhead. Fireflies blanketed the yard and the fields in twinkling golden light. To Sophie, used to seeing much smaller slices of the night sky from her rooming house window, the views were breathtaking, filling her with both profound joy and deep sadness. Imagining what Friedrich and her girls would have thought of that perfect summer evening left her fighting back tears. Thankfully, Louise got up just then and called the children to get ready for bed, leaving Sophie and Christian on the porch.

"I understand why you said in your letter that the Illinois prairie suits you, Christian," Sophie murmured. "This is beautiful."

"Friedrich would have loved it here," he said, his own voice husky with emotion. "I am sorry he did not get the chance to see it."

"Hmmm. I wonder. Do you ever miss anything about the life you had before? You were a shoemaker just like Friedrich. An artisan; a craftsman. Are there days when you miss taking that vision in your head and bringing it to life with your hands and some pieces of leather?"

"No. Why do you ask?"

"Friedrich missed it. There was no outlet for his creativity at the livery stable. He was dying on the inside before we ever left Rheda—long before the illness and malaise that seized him on the ship caused his body to waste away and took his life. Knowing that, I wonder whether he would have found farming fulfilling after all. He was smitten with the thought of being in charge of his own destiny—of having the freedom to make his own choices—but would that have been enough to satisfy his artist's soul? I am not sure. But I, too, am sorry he did not have a chance to find out."

"I am still creating," Christian insisted, a defensive edge to his voice. "Just on a larger scale; building a life—and my farm—from the bare earth with my own two hands."

"Ah. I had not thought of it that way, but yes, you are. Please, forgive me if my words were too forward. I in no way meant them as criticism; I was simply thinking out loud. Friedrich's dying wish was for me to 'find somewhere to be happy.' I am doing my best to honor his desire, and while I have some ideas about what that might look like, I do not know everything it will entail and have no idea if it will be possible in the end. I still have far more questions than I have answers. But this feels closer to being some-place I can call home than New Orleans ever did. I am glad I came, Christian." She rose from her chair. "If you will excuse me, I believe I will go for a walk before retiring. Thank you again for welcoming me back into your life and into your home. It is no small thing, I know."

"It is the least we can do, Sophie, and we are very glad you are here."

She strolled down the lane, savoring the cool evening air and marveling at how far and how much she could see in the silvery moonlight. By the time she returned to the house, Louise had rejoined Christian on the porch. Sophie bade them goodnight and went inside. Tiptoeing quietly past the children who were now sleeping on the floor in the front room, she made her way to the other end of the house—to the room the children normally shared—which Christian and Louise had graciously given her to sleep in. She had hoped the walk down the lane would quiet her thoughts, but her mind was still buzzing with all the things she'd seen that day, her conversations with Christian and Louise, the stunning evening views from the front porch and, as always, thoughts of Friedrich.

Oh, my sweet prince! How I wish you and the girls could have been here to see everything. It is a beautiful place, Friedrich. The land seems fertile and productive; the crops and Louise's garden are growing well, and sitting on the porch in the calm, quiet evening spoke great peace to my soul. I wonder what it would have been like for us to live here. I know Sophie Elise and Marie Louise would have loved having wide open spaces to play in and cousins to play with. But what about you? Would working in the fields and tending livestock truly have suited you, as it seems to suit Christian? And what about me? Could I have loved it here if you did not?

How I wish you were here!

Chapter Twenty

Out on the front porch, Christian and Louise spoke quietly with one another. "What do you think? How is she, really?" Louise asked.

"Better than I had hoped. I was afraid she would be bitter and resentful over the fact that we left New Orleans immediately instead of staying and helping them get settled—so bitter and resentful she would either refuse to have anything to do with us or use the opportunity to see us only to register her displeasure. I apologized profusely when I had the chance to speak to her privately, of course. She was most gracious, and seems to bear me no ill will, although she admitted that she was angry at the time, for which I cannot blame her. Had I known what was going to happen, I would have stayed, Louise, you know that. But I had no idea that Friedrich and Sophie Elise would be dead within the week."

"None of us could have imagined how things were going to turn out. Had we known, we would all have said and done things differently," Louise reminded him. "I apologized as well for my part in all of this. Do not fret about it anymore, dear one. If Sophie is willing to forgive and not find fault with you, there is no point in you continuing to find fault with yourself. Put it behind you." She reached for his hand and held it between hers.

"You are right, of course. And I think I can now that we have spoken and cleared the air. I am hopeful the change of scenery and having family around her once again will help heal her broken heart. Yet I have more than a little concern. She hides it well, but her grief is still deep and raw. And seeing us—and the children—reminds her of it constantly. I can sense a great deal of apprehension about the future in her as well. I promised her that she could stay as long as necessary to get settled, and that we would do our best to help her find employment. I hope that will be possible, and I hope you do not mind."

"No, I do not mind. She worked at a tobacconist's shop in New Orleans, so she has sales experience," Louise said, "and she is an extremely skilled seamstress, so it should not be difficult for her to find work. We will do everything we can to help her, and things will work out. You will see." He stood up. "Now come, my sweet. Let us get some rest."

They went into the house, and once settled in bed, Christian slept deeply for the first time in many months.

In her room, Sophie dozed and dreamed of Friedrich. They were back in Rheda, and it was their wedding day. But as she walked down the aisle and arrived at the altar, Friedrich's features melted away and she found herself standing at the altar with someone else—but who? The face was indistinct and nothing about the person looked in any way familiar. Startled by the mysterious image, she jolted awake. *I wonder what this means,* she thought. *Too bad Mina is not here. She would be able to help me figure it all out. Now that I am here, I will write to her and ask her. I need to let her know that I arrived in Havana safely and am staying with Christian and Louise anyway.*

Sophie's day was completely different from what she had been used to in New Orleans. She helped Louise cook breakfast, do the dishes, and straighten the kitchen, then they went outside to work in the garden. There were green beans and the last of the lettuces, spinach, and radishes to harvest. When those rows were cleaned out and hoed, Louise planted another crop of green beans. She checked the sweet corn and pronounced that in two weeks it should be ready, provided they could keep the raccoons from scouring the patch before the corn was ripe enough to eat. There would soon be ripe tomatoes as well. Seeing the bounty of Louise's garden prompted fond memories for Sophie of her mother's vegetable garden and the lush flower border lining the walkway in front of her childhood home. Sophie had always dreamed of the day when she would have a yard of her own in which to grow vegetables and flowers; they left Rheda before she had a chance to fulfill that dream.

When they were finished with all the garden tasks, Louise sent Johanna and Anna to gather eggs from the chicken house. She and Sophie took the produce into the house and began preparing it for their midday meal. Sophie and the girls snapped the green beans while Louise washed the lettuce and radishes and made a salad that would be served later with a warm bacon and vinegar dressing. When the beans were ready, they were placed in a pot with bacon and onions, then covered with water and set over the fire to cook.

While Sophie and Louise and Johanna and Anna tended the garden and prepared lunch, Christian and the boys were busy feeding the livestock, checking the fences, and looking at the crops growing out in the field. He had forty acres of wheat that would be ready to harvest soon.

"Explain to me again how everyone we are going to visit is connected to Friedrich," Sophie asked Christian as they ate the midday meal. "It has been so long since I saw any of them or heard stories. I have quite forgotten."

"Most are cousins, like Friedrich and I were. Not all of them lived near us in Rheda, so there may be names you have not heard and some families you do not remember. Do not worry, Sophie. Ask as many questions as you need to. Louise and I will do our best to help you keep straight which people belong in which families."

After washing up the lunch dishes and straightening the kitchen, they set out. It was more difficult for Sophie to remember names and keep family lines straight than she had expected; all of the boys were named Christian, Friedrich, or Heinrich, and everyone was raven-haired and blue-eyed with the same features Friedrich had. *Remember the tobacco shop, Sophie. Pay close attention, repeat things to yourself at every opportunity, and you will soon be able to remember who belongs to whom. And do as Christian says: keep asking questions. The more times you hear the explanation, the easier it will be for you to remember.* While she and Christian and Louise visited with their peers (with Sophie working hard to call people by name in order to keep from slighting or insulting anyone), the children ran around the yard with abandon, enjoying the chance to romp with their cousins. While the families saw one another often, it was still a treat for the children to be able to play with others their own age. And everyone appreciated the break from farm work.

After an hour or so of visiting, the adults gathered around the table in the kitchen and were served a delicious cake layered with currant jelly and whipped cream with coffee to drink while the children were treated to milk and cookies as they continued to play in the yard. After enjoying the cake, Sophie was given a walking tour of the farm, followed by more visiting. Some of Friedrich's family members had come through the port of New Orleans just as Friedrich and Sophie and Christian and Louise had; others had arrived in Baltimore or New York and made their way west to Illinois through Pennsylvania and Ohio, or through the Great Lakes.

Just like Louise, they were intensely curious about Sophie's life in New Orleans as a widow alone. The women were full of questions about Marie Louise's death and wanted to know all about both Madame DuVall and Monsieur Philippe. The older members of the family wanted to know the details of Friedrich's illness and death and where he was buried. Sophie was glad she had agreed to let the undertaker contact Pastor Buehler; it was very important to Friedrich's family to know that he and Sophie Elise had proper funeral services after hearing about Marie Louise's burial at sea. She was surprised—and grateful—to be able to recount those stories without becoming overwhelmed with emotion. There was so much to tell and so many questions to answer, it was nearing suppertime when they finally bade everyone goodbye and returned to Christian and Louise's to do evening chores.

After a light supper, they once again settled on the porch while the children played in the yard. After a few moments of thought, Christian spoke. "Tomorrow is Sunday, Sophie. I was wondering if you were inclined to attend church."

"I had not thought about it, Christian. With Friedrich so sick when we arrived, we had no chance to find a church, and after he and Sophie Elise's passing, I was so busy working that I just did not have the time or the energy to make the effort. I did notice two different houses of worship when I was exploring the area around the hotel the day I arrived. Is there a particular congregation you regularly attend?"

"We are members of the Lutheran Church. Most of the German citizens of Havana attend there, although there are some who attend the Methodist Episcopal Church and a few who are Catholic. If you would like to join us, you would be most welcome."

"Thank you, Christian. I think it might be good. Worship is always appropriate, and having the chance to meet people will help me get settled and may even help in my search for employment. What time will we need to leave?"

"Worship is at ten o'clock, so we will need to be in the wagon and on our way by nine. I am hopeful that is not too early."

"Not at all. May I ask, do the rest of the family members attend the Lutheran Church as well? Might I see them again tomorrow?"

"Many of them do. There are occasions when things happen with the livestock or crops on the farm and their attention is required there instead of at worship, but we see most of them regularly each Sunday."

"Thank you, Christian. I shall look forward to seeing everyone again at church then. If you will excuse me, I need to go unpack a suitable dress for tomorrow."

Sophie went to her room and looked through her trunk. She pulled out the gray cotton dress with the lace at the neck and sleeves, and located a hat and gloves. She wanted to be properly dressed, but since this was another brand-new place filled with people and customs she did not know, she wasn't sure what being "properly dressed" looked like here. She hoped the gray dress would not be either too formal or too plain. *I should probably just ask Louise,* she thought to herself, *but part of me hates being so dependent. I will be glad when I have learned enough about the people and the customs here to make my own way in the world again.*

Had she allowed herself to continue that line of thought, she would have also had to admit that there was part of her that was not interested in attending church in the least. After Friedrich and Sophie Elise died, she became used to spending time alone. Retreating to her rooms at the boardinghouse on Sunday was a lovely respite from dealing with the public all week at the tobacco shop.

As part of Christian and Louise's household now, she had had to reacquaint herself with the constant chatter and activity of a house filled with children. The hustle and bustle constantly reminded her of the beautiful girls she no longer had, as well as the loss of her beloved younger siblings Catharine and Friedrich Georg, and the memories were excruciatingly painful. It would have been preferable for Christian and Louise to have left her at home alone so she could grieve privately.

Instead of going back out to the porch after she found suitable clothing, Sophie stayed in her room. After washing her face and brushing her hair, she got out paper and a pencil and wrote to Mina.

16 June 1855

Beloved Mina,

I hope this finds you well. I am safely in Illinois, and the trip north from New Orleans by riverboat was quite pleasant. I am, at the present time, staying with Christian and Louise. I have had a chance to speak extensively with them, and the conversations have been good ones. They deeply regret leaving us in New Orleans, and both have offered me their sincerest apologies. I have apologized to them as well. You were right about Louise, Mina. She does not hate me. I understand her better now, and I think we will get along well.

I have been here just a very short time, but I find this place welcoming and hospitable. There is a rugged, natural beauty to the landscape, and the people seem hard-working and courteous. Many are from the same region we lived in.

You must keep thinking about coming, Mina. I think you would like it here. Besides, I miss you, and there is so much I want to tell you—like the dream I had last night. I was in Rheda, walking down the aisle to marry Friedrich, but when I got to the altar, it was not him; just a faceless someone. I have no idea what this means. Write back immediately and tell me!

In the meantime, know that I love you.

Your adoring sister,

Sophie

When she finished the letter to Mina, she once again read through Friedrich's journal. It could, at times, still reduce her to tears, but especially here, in another strange place, she found it comforting to read his words. She lingered for several moments on the last letter he had written. He had closed it by saying,

Take Sophie Elise and find somewhere to be happy. Find joy; find love.

I will always love you, Sophie. Goodbye and God-speed to you, wherever you may go, whatever you may do . . .

Your prince,

Friedrich

I am trying, sweet prince, she told herself. *I am trying as hard as I can.*

Chapter Twenty-One

Several of the family members Sophie had met the previous day attended the worship service that morning. She greeted them warmly, and then took her seat in the pew with Christian and Louise and the children. Many of the townspeople, particularly the wives of the local businessmen, were dressed much the same way Sophie was. Most of the farmers and their wives were dressed much more simply.

Sophie was concerned that she would spend the entire morning answering the same kinds of questions she had been peppered with yesterday when she met the family for the first time. It had been difficult enough to keep repeating the details of her husband's and children's deaths to family members who had legitimate reasons for wanting to know. She was not at all sure what, or how much, to say to people she had never met before and had no connection to at present.

Louise must have sensed her tension. As she introduced Sophie to their friends and fellow congregants, Louise was careful to explain that Sophie had recently come from New Orleans following the unexpected deaths of her husband and daughters, so Sophie didn't have to address it herself. Much to her relief, once they heard that she was recently bereaved, the ladies respectfully refrained from asking any questions about her previous experiences or her clothing.

As she sat listening to the prelude, she tried to remember exactly when it was that she had last attended church. The simple funeral services Pastor Buehler had performed for Friedrich and Sophie Elise were the last time she had heard a pastor preach, but Sophie wasn't sure they truly counted. Those were not regular Sunday morning services of divine worship, nor had they been held at the church. It may have been as long ago as the Easter before they left for America. So much had happened in such a short time she could not recall for certain.

She found the service pleasant enough, although the pastor was a bit hard to follow at times. The real highlight for her was the singing. Many of the hymns were familiar to her, and it was comforting to hear the words of the liturgy and the songs in her native tongue.

After church, they again visited briefly with the extended family members who were in attendance and then made their way back to the farm. Louise sent Christian and the boys out to kill and gut a chicken, which she then put on to cook in a pot of water. When the chicken was tender, Sophie picked the meat from the bones while Louise mixed up some spaetzli. She put the broth back over the fire, and when it was boiling again, she cut the spaetzli in. When it was nearly done, Sophie added the cooked chicken to the pot. Within a few minutes, the chicken was piping hot and ready to eat; with the rest of the green beans and salad from the garden, they had a delicious Sunday dinner.

Monday dawned bright and sunny. Christian and the boys fed all the livestock and milked the cow while Louise and Sophie cooked breakfast. After scrambled eggs and coffee, with milk for the children, they set about their tasks for the day. Sophie and Louise did the dishes and cleaned up the kitchen, then set a large pot of water on the fire to heat up. Monday was laundry day for Louise. She was once again full of questions as she and Sophie scrubbed the clothes on the washboard, rinsed them in clean water, then hung them on the clothesline to dry.

"You have only been here a few days, I know, but I am curious, Sophie. What do you think of life here so far?"

"It's very different from New Orleans," Sophie said, "but what I have seen appeals to me."

"It does my heart good to hear that," Louise said, her eyes shining. "What have you enjoyed the most?"

"The climate, for one thing. I can be outside without feeling like I am wrapped in a hot blanket!" Sophie said with a chuckle. "And being among family makes me feel very much at home. What about you, Louise? Has it been difficult to get settled?"

"The first few months were hard," Louise admitted. "There was so much to do in such a short time. Thankfully, with family here to help us, we got the house built and the barn raised before the first snow."

"Were you able to plant crops too?"

"We planted some vegetables in the garden, along with one small field of corn. And thankfully, the first frost was late last year, so we had tomatoes until almost November, and plenty of winter squash and potatoes to keep us through the winter. Christian built the livestock pens and the chicken house this spring, and planted wheat and corn."

"What you have accomplished in just a year is amazing, Louise. I am in awe. And you and Christian seem truly happy here. I am glad for you."

After their midday meal, they brought the dry clothes in off the line. Louise busied herself with the ironing; Sophie did the mending that needed to be done, and Johanna and Anna sorted the socks into pairs and folded the clothes that did not need to be ironed.

Christian and the boys were busy cleaning the soiled straw out of the barn and replacing it with fresh bales. Christian then went over the saddles and tack and made some minor repairs on the wagon. After he had the saddles and tack in order, he got the saddle soap and put the boys to work cleaning the saddles and reins.

At the end of the week, as was their custom, Christian and Louise made plans to drive into Havana to get supplies, mail several letters, check to see if there were any letters for them, and this week, to make the rounds of some of the local businesses to see if there might be employment opportunities for Sophie. They ate their midday meal early, and when the dishes were done and the kitchen tidied, they all piled into the wagon and headed for town.

Christian let Louise, Sophie, and the girls out of the wagon on the corner Main and Plum streets, where most of the shops were located, then he and the boys went on to the lumberyard. Starting at the dressmaker's shop, Louise and Sophie made the rounds of all of the likely businesses on that block and the next one: the tailor shop, the shoemaker, and the milliner. As they made their way back up the block, Christian and the boys came back in the wagon.

"How did things go, Sophie?" he asked.

"None of the shops have any openings at present, but I will keep looking. And Christian," she added, "I appreciate your efforts to help me."

"I know you are anxious to get on with your life. I am happy to do what I can, and as you say, we will continue to look."

Turning to Louise, he asked, "What do you think? Should we go to the general store next?"

"Yes, Christian, that would be good." Louise slipped a piece of paper out of her dress pocket. "There is quite a list of things we need."

After introducing Sophie and asking several questions about the stock of fabric and foodstuffs, Louise gave her list to the proprietor. Before long, there were stacks of things on the counter to be loaded into the wagon: a bolt of fabric for shirts and aprons, one of calico for dresses, and one of ticking for pillows, as well as thread, lamp oil, candles, flour, sugar, oatmeal, coffee beans, and a new crock for the kitchen. While Louise and Sophie went out to oversee the loading of their purchases into the wagon, Christian talked briefly with the store owner.

"How is business, Mr. Swing? Going well?"

"Not bad, Mr. Rieple, not bad at all."

"Do you have plenty of help these days, or could you use more?"

"At the moment, I have plenty of help. That could change at any point in time, of course. There is still a lot of land to settle west of here, and it is not uncommon for people in these parts to decide to take their chances moving west and homesteading like they did in the late thirties and forties when everyone was headed to Oregon or California. There have been several families who have left for Kansas and Nebraska just this year. Why do you ask? I know you and your boys are busy with the farm."

"We are, Mr. Swing, quite busy. It is my cousin's wife I am inquiring for. We made the voyage to your fair land from Prussia together last year, but unfortunately my cousin and his wife lost one of their daughters on the trip over, and then within the week after their arrival, my cousin and the other daughter succumbed to cholera in New Orleans. His widow has come to Havana and is staying with us while she looks for employment and gets settled. She is an expert seamstress and was also employed as a sales associate in a tobacconist's shop in New Orleans for several months before she arrived here last week."

"I am sorry to hear that such tragic circumstances have befallen your family, Mr. Rieple. As I said, I have plenty of help at the moment. You have already inquired at the dressmaker and the tailor shops, I take it?"

"We have. Not to worry, Mr. Swing. We will keep checking. I have no doubt something will turn up. Thank you for your time. I appreciate it very much. I will see you next time we are in town."

"Goodbye, Mr. Rieple. I hope things go well for you, and for your cousin's wife. If I have an opening, or if I hear of any, I will be sure and send word to you."

"Thank you again, Mr. Swing. Good day to you." Christian headed out of the general store and back to the wagon. Everything was loaded and ready for the trip home.

"Is that everything on your list, Louise?" Christian inquired.

"Yes, my dear; that is everything. If you have gotten everything that you needed, I think we are ready to return home."

"We will stop at the post office and then be on our way back to the farm."

They traveled west down Main Street toward the ferry and pulled up in front of the post office. Christian tied up the horses and went inside. As he walked in, he was greeted by a farmer he had met soon after his arrival last year. They were not close neighbors—Barney Weimber lived several miles north and east of town in Quiver Township and Christian's farm was south of town in Havana Township—nor did they attend the same church, but they had run into each other so often when they made their weekly trips to town, they had become good friends. There was a standing offer between them to help one another any time it was needed.

"Hello, Christian!" Barney said, grasping his hand in a firm handshake.

"Hello, yourself, Barney!" Christian responded warmly, slapping Barney on the back. "Good to see you. What are you up to today?"

"We needed more nails for the fence we are working on. My brother is at the lumberyard now. I stopped to mail a letter to our sisters and brother back home in Osnabruck before we head back to the farm. How about you?"

"We needed supplies from the general store and had a few other errands as well. Do you remember me telling you about the tragedy that befell the cousin who was traveling with us to America?"

"Of course. He died almost immediately after the ship arrived in New Orleans, you said." Barney shook his head sadly. "You were quite upset when you heard about it."

"Yes; it was a horrible thing. Their two children were lost as well. After working for a while at one of the tobacconist's shops in The French Quarter, his widow has come to Havana. She is staying with us while she looks for employment and gets settled. She and Louise were making the rounds of the shops to see if there were any openings for her. Let me post these letters, and on our way out, I would be happy to introduce you."

"Thank you, Christian. It would be my pleasure to make her acquaintance," Barney said, nodding slightly.

Barney was the second of his family to make the trip to America, arriving in 1850. He spent a few years working in the coal mines of Pennsylvania before making his way to Illinois, where his older brother Franz and his family had already settled.

Able to secure employment at one of the local grain elevators when he arrived, Barney later began tenant farming. His younger brother Rudolph had joined him in 1854. They had come from Osnabruck, in Lower Saxony, where times were just as difficult and uncertain as they had been for Friedrich and Sophie in Rheda. Just like Friedrich, Barney was searching for a better opportunity. And like Friedrich and Sophie, he had little when he arrived.

Opportunity was abundant here, and Barney had taken full advantage of it. He had steadily improved his life, expanding his knowledge and skills as well as his income in the years since his arrival. But thoughts of those considerable accomplishments inevitably led to other less pleasant musings. While things were good here (much better than they had been in Lower Saxony), and he was enjoying the challenge of making his own way in life, on his own terms, he had to admit that it was a lonely existence. He longed for someone to share that life with. He had spent most of the five years he had been in America on his own. His older brother Franz lived on the opposite side of the county to the east with his wife and children, and Rudolph had just arrived last year; the rest of his siblings remained in Osnabruck. While it was good to have his brothers here, what Barney wanted most of all was a wife to share his days and children to fill his home with the sounds of laughter and play. He wanted the same kind of life his brother Franz was blessed with.

Awakening early that morning, Barney had begun the day with tea and toast, then went out to do the chores.

As was his custom, he paused briefly on the back step and surveyed the farmstead.

He loved the spaciousness of this place. There was room—and opportunity—there to grow, in his own time, and his own way, without some king or prince or emperor dictating every detail of his existence. And it was beautiful country, productive and with ample resources. It was a blessing—indeed, a sacred trust—to work the land in cooperation with the Creator, and he was grateful.

While they waited for Christian to return, Louise and Sophie chatted about the styles of clothing they had seen in the various dressmakers' and tailors' shops, and the selection of fabric at the general store.

Johanna leaned forward and whispered in Louise's ear.

"Of course, Johanna," Louise replied, smiling in Sophie's direction. "Go ahead and ask."

"Cousin Sophie," Johanna said shyly, "Mama says you are the best sewing person ever. Could you make me a really pretty dress with the material we got today?"

"Me, too!" Anna begged. "Make one for me, too!"

"I would love to make dresses for you," Sophie laughed, patting each of the girls on the head. "When we get back home, I will get out my measuring tape and measure you so your dresses fit perfectly."

"Ooooh, thank you, cousin Sophie!" Johanna cried, happily throwing her arms around Sophie and hugging her tightly.

"Wheeee!" Anna squealed in excitement, throwing her hands in the air. "I get a new dress, too!"

"Can you reach the calico and hand it to me, please, Johanna?" Louise asked.

"Yes, Mama."

As Louise scooted over to take the bolt of fabric from Johanna, she noticed something on the seat. "Oh, dear," she said worriedly. "The letter you wrote to Mina fell out of Christian's pocket. Pardon me," she said, rising to climb past Sophie and out of the wagon. "I will take this inside and see that it gets mailed."

"Let me take it, Louise," Sophie offered, reaching for the letter. "I need to stretch my legs anyway. I am more used to standing and walking than I am sitting."

As Sophie walked into the post office, she heard Christian recounting her story to Barney and offering to introduce them. She paused a short distance away and waited until Christian finished speaking, then approached.

"I am sorry to interrupt your conversation, Christian, but Louise noticed this letter lying on the seat of the wagon," she said, handing him the letter.

"Oh, thank you, Sophie. Since you are here, allow me to introduce you to a friend of mine. This is Barney Weimber. He and his younger brother Rudolph are originally from Osnabruck. They farm north and east of town on the other side of Topeka."

Sophie studied Barney while Christian made his introduction. Despite being dressed in work clothes, Barney was neat and clean in appearance. He had a full head of sandy blond hair, and there was warmth and kindness in his clear, blue eyes.

"It is my pleasure to meet you, Madame Rieple," Barney said, removing his hat and bowing respectfully. "I am deeply sorry for your loss. I hope your time here will be pleasant."

"Thank you, Mr. Weimber, both for your condolences and your well wishes," Sophie answered. "I am pleased to make your acquaintance as well and have found the Illinois prairie to be very much to my liking so far."

While Sophie and Barney spoke, Christian mailed the letter, then they all walked outside.

As they approached the wagon, Barney offered Sophie his hand. "Here, Madame Rieple. Please, allow me to assist you." He helped her into the wagon, then greeted Louise. "It is a pleasure to see you again, Louise. Your children are delightful." Barney winked at the children, then pulled a small paper bag out of his pocket and offered pieces of penny candy to each of them. The children squealed with delight, then young Friedrich turned and asked Louise if it was permissible for them to eat their candy right then.

"Yes, you may, Friedrich. But first, thank Mr. Weimber properly."

Friedrich turned to Barney, smiling from ear to ear, and said most earnestly, "Thank you very much for the candy, Mr. Weimber. It was most kind of you."

"You are quite welcome, young Friedrich," Barney said with a smile, patting him on the shoulder. "Ah, here is my brother now."

Rudolph stopped the wagon and greeted the Rieples and was introduced to Sophie. "It is my pleasure to meet you, madame," he said, removing his hat respectfully.

"Well, little brother," Barney said, climbing into the wagon, "We should be on our way. We must get that fence finished before the horses arrive. It was good to see you and the family, Christian." Turning to Sophie, he once again bowed and tipped his hat. "And, once again, it was my pleasure to meet you, Madame Rieple. I hope to see you again soon."

"Thank you, Mr. Weimber," Sophie said. "I hope the rest of your day is pleasant."

Chapter Twenty-Two

The Weimber brothers headed east out of town, riding in silence. Barney was lost in thought. *She said she hoped the rest of my day was pleasant. Now that I have met her, it most assuredly will be. She is the most beautiful creature I have ever seen. That platinum hair and those blue eyes are stunning. It is sorrowful in the extreme that this poor woman has had so many tragedies befall her in such a short time. It is a wonder her spirit has not been completely crushed under so much grief. Once she becomes known in the area, there will be a long line of men beating down the door at the Rieple farm hoping for a chance to court her, I am sure. Of course, recently bereaved, she may not be interested in seeing anyone. But nothing would please me more than to get to know the widow Rieple better. Much, much better.*

They were nearly back to their farmstead when Rudolph finally spoke. "Are you thinking what I'm thinking, Barney?"

"That depends, Rudy. What are you thinking?"

"I am thinking that Madame Rieple is one of the most beautiful women I have ever seen."

"She is extraordinarily beautiful," Barney agreed.

"And I was also thinking, Barney, that she would make you a very fetching bride."

"Me? What about you? Since you commented on her beauty you must be interested in her, too."

"I am not ready for marriage," Rudolph insisted. "I have only been here a year; I would like to have a few more seasons of income—and maybe even a farm of my own—before I consider courting and marrying."

"You are sure?"

"I am. I know how much you long to marry and have a family, Barney. It is written all over your face. You dote on other people's children as if they were your own. I want you to be happy. Madame Rieple may be the woman to make you so. If I were you, I would do my best to get to know her better."

"I intend to."

"We could turn the wagon around and go now," Rudolph suggested, elbowing Barney playfully.

"The Rieples have a full afternoon of work planned. You heard Christian talking about it at the post office. I do not think it would make a very good impression for me to show up and start asking questions when he has so many things he needs to get done. No, I will let things happen in their own time; if it is meant to be, it will be. You and I have much to do as well. That fence is not going to finish itself. We had best get out there and get to work."

On the Rieple farm, Louise and Sophie put away the supplies from the general store and started making plans for the evening meal while Johanna and Anna sat in the corner near the hearth playing with their dolls. Since they had picked up sugar when they were in town, Louise decided to make a rhubarb pie for dessert. "Can you start the pie crust, Sophie? I will go out and cut some rhubarb."

Louise had intended to make the pie all along, but right now she also wanted an excuse to talk to Christian when Sophie wasn't within earshot. He and the boys were working in the barn when she walked up. She sent Friedrich and Carl out to get a drink of water and play for a few moments. As soon as they headed for the well, she turned to Christian, her eyes dancing merrily and a sly smile on her face.

"What do you think, Christian?" she asked, giggling. "Might Barney be interested in calling on Sophie? And if he is, do you think she would see him?"

"Louise!" Christian exclaimed in surprise, dropping the set of reins he was putting away. "That is none of our business. It is not our place to play matchmaker." He picked the reins up off the floor and hung them where they belonged, then turned back to Louise. "I have no issue with Barney seeing Sophie," he said, reaching for a bucket of oats and dumping it into the feed trough before continuing. "But this is between the two of them, and theirs are the only opinions that matter. Not ours."

"If Sophie is smart, she will see him," Louise pronounced with certainty. "And I think they will make a charming couple!"

"Louise!" Christian shook his head in exasperation. "If they can find happiness together, I think it would be a fine thing. Sophie has had more than her share of tragedy in life and I want things to go well for her, but we need to mind our own business and let things develop as they will."

"Well," Louise said, crossing her arms across her chest and smiling smugly, "do not be surprised when you see Barney driving up the lane one day soon."

"We shall see. You may well be right." Christian caught Louise's hand as she turned to leave, pulled her close, and kissed her cheek. "I hope, if that is how things turn out, that they are as happy as we are."

Sophie had the pie crust rolled out and placed in the pan and had the rest of the ingredients for the pie filling ready and waiting when Louise returned with the rhubarb. They chopped the rhubarb together, then Louise mixed up the rest of the filling ingredients, assembled the pie, and put it in to bake.

"Is there anything else we need to do right now, Louise?" Sophie asked.

"Nothing else but cook supper, and that won't take long."

"Then we have time to take measurements for dresses," she said, smiling in Johanna and Anna's direction. "Come with me, girls!" she said, motioning for them to follow her.

With big grins on their faces, Johanna and Anna jumped up from the hearth, leaving their dolls behind. Johanna slipped her hand in Sophie's and walked alongside her while Anna trailed behind gaily clapping her hands.

Sophie got out the tapestry pouch that held her sewing supplies. "Johanna, can you please get out my tape measure while I get a sheet of paper to write the measurements on?" she asked. "Be very careful when you reach into the pouch. The needles and scissors are sharp."

Johanna carefully picked up the measuring tape and handed it to Sophie.

"Thank you. Now, stand very still and hold your arms out." She carefully took and recorded Johanna's measurements, then Anna's.

"Very good!" she said encouragingly, rolling up the tape measure and putting back in the pouch. "I have all the information I need to begin making your dresses. Shall we go see if Mama needs help getting supper ready now?"

As they walked back toward the kitchen, Johanna ran over to the hearth where she and Anna had been playing. "Cousin Sophie," she said, grabbing her doll and holding it up, "can you make a dress for my dolly, too? One that looks just like mine?"

"Of course." Sophie smiled indulgently. "I would be happy to make a dress for your dolly. And one for yours, too," she promised Anna. Sophie leaned forward and motioned the girls to come closer, as if she had some tantalizing secret to share that was for their ears alone. "I have made dresses for dolls before," she confided.

"You have?" Anna whispered, wide-eyed with wonder.

"Yes," Sophie said. "My little girl—your cousin Sophie Elise—had a doll, and I made dresses for her. I still have the doll in my trunk. I can show her to you tomorrow. Right now, we need to help get supper ready."

Amid natural beauty and surrounded by people who had known and loved Friedrich and loved and cared for her, Sophie was becoming more comfortable with each passing day. Telling stories and sharing memories of Friedrich and her darling girls—bearing witness to their lives—was, in its own way, healing. There were still sad times; she could still be surprised by tears, but more often than not these days, the memories that surfaced were fond ones of happy times prompted by some pleasant occurrence in her daily round, like Johanna's request for a dress for her doll.

After breakfast the next morning, as promised, Sophie showed Sophie Elise's doll to Johanna and Anna, then she and Louise got the bolt of calico cloth, laid it out on the kitchen table, and cut out dresses for the girls and their dolls.

They spent the afternoon as they had the week before, visiting the home of another of the Rieple families that lived nearby. On the wagon ride home, they talked about their plans for the next day.

"We are planning on church as usual, Sophie," Louise said. "But we thought we might stay in town for a while instead of coming straight home, if that is agreeable."

"Of course," Sophie assured her.

"We will pack a picnic lunch and go down to the waterfront and eat after worship. The Methodist Episcopal Church is having an ice cream social in the afternoon. When we are finished eating, we can go up there and have dessert."

"That sounds lovely," Sophie agreed, "and it will give me another chance to meet and get acquainted with people. That is so thoughtful of you, Louise. Thank you."

Sunday's weather was glorious—high blue skies, bright sun, and a delightful breeze coming off the river. That combined with worship—during which they sang some of her favorite hymns—a delicious lunch, and a lovely hour watching boats going up and down the river put Sophie in a lighthearted mood.

The ice cream social was a popular event, and the crowd was large. They stood in line for several minutes to get their ice cream. Several of the Rieples and other families from the church were there, and Sophie enjoyed visiting with them while she waited. As she approached the serving table, she noticed the Weimber brothers, busily cranking ice cream churns. After picking up her dish of ice cream, she lingered for several moments trying to choose between the vast array of cakes and fruit pies covering the dessert table, finally deciding on a slice of cherry pie. Looking up to see where Louise had chosen to sit, her eyes met Barney's for a brief moment. They exchanged smiles but did not speak.

Making her way to the table, she sat down next to Louise and the girls and began to eat, savoring the combination of the creamy, sweet frozen custard, crisp flaky crust, and tart pie cherries. "Oh, Louise!" she sighed contentedly. "This has been a wonderful day."

"I'm so glad you are enjoying yourself, Sophie," Louise said. "Ah, you got the cherry pie. How was it? Sometimes it is hard to get just the right amount of sugar."

Before Sophie could respond, young Friedrich jumped up and ran over to Louise. "Can we have more ice cream, Mama?"

"Not right now. You and your brother and sisters can go play if you like. I see some of your cousins over there," Louise said, pointing to a grassy area on the south side of the church where several other children were playing. "Off you go. We will see about more ice cream in a bit," she promised.

Sophie watched the children scamper off to play, then turned to Louise. "The pie was perfect. There was a subtle flavor I am not used to tasting in cherry pie. It might have been cinnamon, but I am not sure. I would love to have the recipe."

"I can ask who made it," Louise offered, rising from her seat. "I need to see if there will be enough ice cream for the boys to have another dish anyway."

"And I want to take a look at those ice cream churns," Christian added, getting up and following Louise to the serving area.

Mesmerized by the sound of children at play, the hum of happy conversation, and the pleasant clink of spoons on earthenware, Sophie leaned back in her chair. Leisurely sipping her lemonade, she marveled at how relaxed and at home she felt.

I could put down roots here; truly live. I want a family of my own more than anything, but even if I never married and had children again, I have people to whom I feel like I belong, and a place where there is meaningful, productive work to do. I may never find employment in any of the shops. That does not matter. I can be of help to Louise. She has so much to do, another pair of hands would be a godsend. And I have nieces and nephews I can pour my love and care into. Her pleasant reverie was interrupted by the sound of someone saying her name. Turning to see who was speaking, she saw Barney Weimber, a dish of ice cream in each hand.

"Madame Rieple. It is a pleasure to see you again. Do you mind if I join you?"

"Not at all, Mr. Weimber," Sophie said, pulling the chair next to her out from the table. "Please, sit down."

Barney placed the ice cream on the table and settled himself in his chair. "Are you enjoying the afternoon?" he inquired.

"I am having a wonderful time," Sophie said, smiling warmly. "I noticed you were helping make the ice cream. It was delicious."

"I cannot take any credit for *making* the ice cream." Barney laughed. "The women of the church were in charge of that. All I did was turn the crank on the churn."

"Well, it turned out beautifully."

"I am glad you enjoyed it. You might like this as well," he said, sliding one of the bowls in front of her. "One of the ladies had an abundance of strawberries in her garden and added them to the custard she prepared."

Sophie took a bite of the fruity mixture, then sighed with pleasure. "It is heavenly. Thank you for sharing it with me. You are most kind."

Before she had a chance to say anything else, Friedrich, Carl, and the girls came running up. "Hello, Mr. Weimber. Where are Mama and Papa, cousin Sophie?" Friedrich asked. "Did Mama see if we could have more ice cream?"

"Mama and Papa are right here," Sophie said, as Louise and Christian came walking back to the table.

"Mama! Mama!" Friedrich called, breathless with excitement. "Did you ask? Can we have more ice cream?"

"I have some right here," Barney said, his eyes twinkling, "and I would be happy to share with you."

"Oh, no, Barney!" Louise protested. "We saw you back there working. You need a chance to sit down and enjoy some ice cream as well."

"It is my pleasure, Louise, truly," he insisted, scooting the bowl of ice cream across the table.

"Sit back down then, boys," Louise instructed. When they were settled to her satisfaction, she slid the bowl between them and handed Carl the spoon. "Do you have anything to say to Mr. Weimber?" she asked Friedrich, nudging him with her elbow.

"Thank you, sir," Friedrich said solemnly.

"Thank you!" Carl mumbled through a mouthful of ice cream.

"And Johanna and Anna can share mine," Sophie said, noticing the longing looks on the girls' faces.

While the children eagerly gobbled up the strawberry ice cream, Christian plied Barney with questions about ice cream churns—where one could be purchased, how much rock salt was needed, and how long the process took.

"Thank you again for giving your ice cream to the children, Barney," he said, eyeing the now-empty dishes. "I hope you and Rudolph get that fence finished this week. It will be a while before the wheat is ready to harvest. If you need help, the boys and I can come over."

"I would be most grateful for the help if you can spare the time, Christian," Barney said with relief.

"Then we will see you tomorrow morning. Are you ready, Louise? We should get back to the farm so the boys and I can get evening chores done in good time."

"Yes," Louise agreed. "It is time we were on our way. Goodbye, Barney. It was good to see you."

"Goodbye, Louise," Barney said, then turned to Sophie. "It was a pleasure to see you, Madame Rieple, and I hope to see you again soon. I believe I still owe you a bowl of ice cream." He bowed slightly and left before Sophie could respond.

Sophie was silent on the ride back to the farm. *It is odd. When I am in Mr. Weimber's company, I do not notice the reticence I usually feel around people I am not well acquainted with—none of the reservations I experienced in Monsieur Delaroche's presence. He has strong, capable hands, as I saw this afternoon. He is obviously no stranger to hard work, yet does not seem in any way to be a hard man. There is an air of openness and generosity about him; he is courteous and respectful, and there is warmth and kindness in his eyes. I would like to know more about him. Were he to express an interest in calling on me, I would accept.*

"Would you like me to go check the chicken house to see if there are any eggs, Louise?" Sophie asked when they arrived back home.

"Yes, of course. By all means."

Sophie took her time gathering the eggs, this time thoughts of Friedrich filling her mind. *You wanted me to* be happy, sweet prince. To "go somewhere and find joy." For a long time, I did not believe that was possible. I despaired of ever finding happiness again. But since I have made peace with Christian and Louise—and met Mr. Weimber—that possibility is before me, within my grasp. I got a tiny taste of it sitting there in the church yard, and it was as sweet as that strawberry ice cream. Yet even as I look forward to embracing life here, I am suddenly filled with doubts. Indeed, the more I think about Mr. Weimber, the more uncertain I become. After losing you and our beautiful baby girls so unexpectedly, there is a part of me that is afraid to get my hopes up—terrified to even try—for fear they will be dashed yet again.

From what I have seen, Mr. Weimber is a thoughtful and generous man; many things about him remind me of you. After watching him go out of his way to be kind to Christian and Louise's children and recalling the courtesy and respect he showed me when he helped me into the wagon last Friday at the post office, my sense is that he would make a good husband and father. But that is just my sense; I do not know him well enough to be certain of any of those things. He sought out my company this afternoon. Does that mean he has a genuine interest in getting to know me? Or did he do so out of obligation because he and Christian are friends? Worse yet, was it only because he feels sorry for me? Would he—will anyone—ever want me, a heartbroken widow who has already birthed and buried another man's *children? Earlier this afternoon, I was sure of everything. Now, once again, I am sure of nothing.*

Sophie hoped Louise had not noticed how long she had been gone. To her relief, nothing was mentioned when she finally walked back into the house. She set the basket of eggs on the table, then asked, "Is there anything else I can help you with, Louise?"

"Nothing else but cooking supper, Sophie. Anna and Johanna can set the table." After all the sweet treats at the ice cream social, Louise was planning a light meal of scrambled eggs, salad, and toast. "When Christian and the boys come in, I'll start scrambling the eggs and you can toast some bread over the fire and butter it."

While they waited, Sophie and Louise started pinning the pieces of the girls' dresses so Sophie could sew them together. An hour or so later, Christian and the boys came in and washed up for supper. He talked and played with the children while Louise and Sophie finished making supper. They gathered at the table, observed a few moments of silent prayer, then Louise filled and passed plates. When they were finished, she and Sophie and the girls cleared the table while the boys and Christian went back outside.

Chapter Twenty-Three

The next morning, after chores and breakfast, Christian and the boys, Friedrich and Carl, loaded the wagon with the tools they would need for fencing and headed for the Weimber farm. "We will be back in time for supper," Christian called, as the wagon rumbled slowly down the lane.

Barney and Rudolph were already at work laying out slats for the fence when Christian and the boys arrived. "Hello, Weimbers!" Christian greeted them.

"Hello!" Barney answered with a smile and a wave. "It is good to see you, Christian. I appreciate the help."

"I am glad to do it, Barney. You never hesitate to come when I need help," Christian said, reaching into the back of the wagon. "I brought my hammer and an extra bucket."

"Good." Barney nodded. "Rudolph and little Friedrich can work at positioning the slats, you and I can hammer, and Carl can hand us nails. With all of us working, we will be done in no time."

While they worked, Barney and Christian compared notes on how their crops were doing, when the next cutting of hay might be ready, and the other projects they wanted to complete during the summer.

"We weren't able to get a root cellar dug last fall," Christian said, "and we need a place to store vegetables through the winter. If I could, I would like to get that done right away, before I get busy with wheat harvest, haying, and corn harvest."

"If we get the fence done today, we will have some extra time this week. I could help you dig the root cellar," Barney offered. "Rudy can handle everything that needs to be done here."

"That would be most helpful, Barney. Thank you."

They worked through the morning, with one short break midmorning for water and another at noon to eat, and by midafternoon—just as Barney predicted—the fence was finished. "Many thanks, Christian," he said with a grateful sigh. "This would have taken us most of the week working alone. I will be over first thing tomorrow to help you with that root cellar. You can count on it."

"I will see you then, Barney. Come along, boys," Christian called to Friedrich and Carl. "Time to head back home."

While Christian and the boys helped the Weimbers build fence, Sophie and Louise did the dishes, then started the laundry. Johanna and Anna played with their dolls, helped bring clothes in from the clothesline, and put things away as Sophie and Louise got them mended, ironed, and folded. When the laundry was done, Sophie went back to work on constructing the girls' dresses while Louise and the girls checked the hen house for eggs and did some weeding in the garden. They were just finishing up the last row when they saw the wagon come up the lane.

"Papa!" Johanna and Anna shrieked, jumping up and down and waving as Christian pulled up.

"You are back in good time." Louise beamed at him. "How did things go?"

"The fence is all finished, and Barney is coming tomorrow to help me dig out the root cellar."

"Oh, glory be!" Louise exclaimed, clasping her hands to her chest in gratitude. "I am so glad to hear that."

They remained at the table long after supper was over that evening. Louise and Christian had an extended conversation about the size and location of the root cellar. When that was finally settled, Louise and Sophie spent a considerable amount of time discussing what to cook for the midday meal the next day, since Barney would be there to help.

"Someone will need to make sure the men have plenty of water throughout the day, too," Louise remarked, looking pointedly in Sophie's direction. "Digging in the summer is hot work."

Sophie ignored Louise's comment—and her look—and rose from the table. "If you will excuse me, Louise, now that we have dinner planned, I think I will retire early," she said. "We have a very busy day tomorrow, and I want to be well rested." She went to her room, but before lying down to sleep, she picked up Friedrich's journal and leafed through his letters, lingering over the last one he wrote and rereading it several times.

Just as they were finishing breakfast the next morning, Barney arrived. He and Christian and the boys immediately began work on the root cellar while Sophie and Louise did the dishes, then began preparing for the midday meal. A chicken was butchered and plucked and set to stew, then Louise sent Sophie out to the garden for rhubarb and a head of cabbage. After washing the produce carefully at the well, she brought it inside. While Louise made the pie, Sophie shredded the cabbage into a large crock and finely chopped a small onion. Carefully following Louise's recipe, she mixed up a tangy vinegar and sugar dressing, poured it over the vegetables in the bowl, and set the slaw aside.

Leaving Louise to tend the chicken and keep an eye on the pie as it baked, Sophie got out her sewing basket and continued working on the girls' dresses. A silent debate raged within her as she sewed, her thoughts alternating with each stitch. *Do I dare take a chance on crafting a life of my own and finding love again?* She slipped the needle through the calico fabric and pulled it back out. *Or do I not?*

Life as it is now, while not perfect, is comfortable and safe—a blessing and balm to my battered soul after all the loss and pain I have endured. Yet even though I am welcome here, I cannot help but wonder how much deeper and richer my existence would be if I had a home and family of my own. It is all I ever wanted.

And yet . . . after everything I have been through, it seems foolish to even consider walking away from safety and security for a possibility that may never be. There are no guarantees. Were I to open my heart again, I could be hurt and rejected. Even if I did find love, I am painfully aware that that alone does not ensure a lifetime of happiness. Tragedy could strike, yet again, and at any moment.

What is at the root of all this uncertainty and hesitation? She considered that question for several minutes. *I have tiptoed around it, called it many names, but the truth is, I am afraid. Afraid of what might be—and what might not.*

But I will never know for certain what can be unless I try.

Reaching the end of the seam, Sophie anchored and clipped the thread, put the dress back in her sewing basket, and walked over to the table. "How are things coming, Louise? Is there anything you need help with right now?"

"Everything is going well," Louise said, testing the simmering chicken with a fork. "The pie is cooling, and the chicken is nearly ready to take off the bone. After that is done, the only thing left to do is mix up the dumplings."

"Then I will go out and get water for the men," Sophie said. "I am sure they are getting thirsty by now." Gathering the water bucket and dipper, she went out to the well, filled the bucket, then took it around to the northeast corner of the house where Christian and Barney were busy digging and the boys were hauling buckets of dirt away as they were filled.

"Are you ready for a break?" she asked. "I brought you some water." She held out the bucket and offered the dipper to Barney.

"Thank you," he said gratefully. He took several swallows of the clear, cold water, then passed the dipper to Christian so he and the boys could get drinks.

"That was just what we needed, Sophie," Christian said. "Many thanks."

"You are quite welcome. We will call you when dinner is ready."

Wednesday and Thursday of that week were exactly like Tuesday. Each morning Barney would arrive just after breakfast, and he and Christian and Friedrich and Carl would spend the day working on the root cellar. Louise and Sophie made sure they were well fed. Dinner table conversation flowed easily between Barney, Christian, Louise, and the children, and between seeing him interact with the family and having the opportunity to watch him work over the course of several days, Sophie learned much about who Barney was. She was grateful to see that her first impressions about him—his kindness and generosity, his courtesy and respect, his attention to detail, and his love of children— were affirmed again and again.

Late Thursday afternoon, the men finished work on the interior of the root cellar. Christian came to the back door and called for Louise to come out and take a look.

"Go ahead, Louise," Sophie said. "While you do that, I will get water for Barney and the boys." She got the bucket and dipper and went out to the well as they walked up. The boys hastily gulped dippers of water, dumped one over their heads to cool off, then raced off to the barn to start evening chores.

"It was kind of you to spend so much of your time helping Christian this week," Sophie said, filling the bucket again. "It was no small thing, and he and Louise are deeply grateful."

"It was my pleasure," Barney replied, pulling a bandana out of his back pocket and wiping his face.

Sophie handed him a dipper of water, noticing as she did so that the front pocket of his shirt was torn. While she was debating about offering to mend it, Christian and Louise came back around the house.

"Well, Louise?" Sophie asked. "What do you think?"

"It looks good," Louise pronounced, turning to Barney. "Thank you for your help, Barney. You were a godsend."

"My pleasure," Barney replied. "Many thanks to you and Madame Rieple for keeping me so well fed," he continued, looking over and catching Sophie's eye. "Everything was delicious." Sophie nodded in acknowledgment but didn't speak.

"I should be on my way soon," Barney said, tucking his bandana into his back pocket. "But if you can spare a moment, Christian, I would like a word with you."

"Of course," Christian replied. "We can talk on our way to the barn."

When they were out of earshot, Barney turned to Christian and spoke. "I hope you do not consider this too forward, Christian. I know that I met Madame Rieple only recently, but I am most interested in getting to know her better. Since she is residing with you, I wanted to let you know of my intention to call on her. You are a good friend, and I do not want to bring any kind of criticism or reproach to your family. If you have objections, of course, I will honor them, but I am hoping that is not the case."

"I understand, Barney. I appreciate you telling me, although it was not necessary. You have a good reputation in the area as a hard worker and a kind and conscientious fellow citizen. And you are a good friend to me. I can think of no one I would rather have call on Sophie. I hope things work out for both of you."

A relieved grin broke across Barney's face. "I am so glad to hear that, Christian. Thank you. If you do not mind, I may drive out tomorrow evening."

"Come anytime, Barney. You are always welcome here," Christian assured him.

"I will be on my way then," Barney said, shaking Christian's hand. "I will see you tomorrow."

"Thank you again for your help, Barney," Christian replied. "And I wish you all the best."

That night, Sophie once again dreamed of being at the altar with the faceless man. She jolted awake, her thoughts turning first to Friedrich, then to Barney. She idly twisted her wedding ring as she pondered what this might mean. Unable to go back to sleep, she lit the lamp, got paper and pencil from her dresser, and wrote to Mina.

29 June 1855

Dearest, dearest Mina,

I know I just wrote you, and it will be weeks before that letter arrives, but I have to tell you this.

I had that wedding dream again! I still do not know exactly what it means, but something else has happened in the meantime, and I have some thoughts.

I was introduced to a gentleman—a good friend of Christian's—last Friday at the post office. His name is Bernhardt Weimber, but Christian and Louise call him Barney. In appearance, he is the exact opposite of Friedrich: sandy blond rather than raven-haired, and much taller. But in other ways, the two of them are very much alike. I sense in Barney that same quiet strength that was at the core of Friedrich's personality. He seems to be just as steadfast and down to earth, and from what I can tell, values the same things: family and relationships. I have seen him several times over the past week, and each time he goes out of his way to be kind both to Christian and Louise's children, and to me. We have only just met, but my first impression is that he is the kind of man who would make a wonderful husband and father.

In the last letter he wrote to me, Friedrich said, "Take Sophie Elise and find somewhere to be happy. Find joy; find love." So now I am wondering, Mina. Could Barney be that faceless someone I keep seeing in these wedding dreams? Might Friedrich have sent him?

Write back the minute you receive this letter, Mina, and tell me what you think! And please, keep making plans to come. I know you are busy with baby Marie, and I do not want to cause undue hardship for her or for you, but I so miss having you to confide in. I need you, Mina. Come soon!

Your adoring sister,

Sophie

Sophie addressed Mina's letter, got dressed, and went to the kitchen and started the coffee. Christian, Louise, and the children were up shortly afterward. "Good morning, Christian. Good morning, Louise," Sophie greeted them. "The coffee is almost done."

"Thank you, Sophie," Louise said as she bustled about getting breakfast ready. While they ate, they talked about their plans for the day, which included their customary Friday trip to town.

"The boys and I will need to stop at the lumberyard," Christian said. "We need nails and hinges for the root cellar door."

"And I need to stop at the post office," Sophie added. "I have a letter to mail to Mina."

Before Louise could comment, there was a knock at the door. When Christian answered, his cousin Heinrich was there, holding a large crock. "Evelina sent me over," he said, handing the crock to Christian. "We had a huge crop of cherries this year and could not use them all. Not wanting them to go to waste, she said to bring some to you. She thought perhaps you could use them, since you do not have any fruit trees planted yet."

"We would love to have them! I will make a cherry pudding," Louise exclaimed, reaching for one of her crocks. "Here, pour them into this bowl, Heinrich, and you can take hers back home. And please, give her my thanks!"

When Heinrich was on his way, Christian and the boys went out to do morning chores and check the wheat. Louise and Sophie pitted the cherries, and then Louise assembled and baked the cherry pudding. Sophie continued working on Johanna and Anna's dresses.

After their midday meal, they went to town as they had planned, making all their usual stops as well as going by the post office so Sophie could get Mina's letter in the mail. When they got back home, Sophie and Louise put away their purchases and started supper while Christian unloaded the wagon and did evening chores.

"What do you think, Christian?" Louise asked when they finished eating. "Would you like your dessert now, or would you rather wait a bit?"

"Waiting for a bit is fine with me, Louise. If you and Sophie want to go ahead and serve the children, I believe I will go outside for a while." He winked at Louise, then went out onto the porch. Louise and Sophie served the children their cherry pudding, then sent them out to play.

"If you like, I can help you do the dishes and clean up the kitchen now, Louise. All that will be left for later will be our plates and forks."

"That would be fine, Sophie. We will get this all taken care of, and then we can enjoy the rest of the evening." Louise's eyes were twinkling, and there was a faint smile tugging at her lips. Sophie could have sworn she heard Louise humming under her breath as she worked.

When the dishes were done and the kitchen was straightened, they took off their aprons and joined Christian on the porch. It was another beautiful summer evening with a slight breeze and bands of wispy, feathery clouds in the west that promised a spectacular sunset. They talked about the trip to town and about how soon it would be appropriate for Sophie to go back and inquire of the storekeepers about employment while they watched the children play hide and seek. After a half hour or so, Louise shooed the children inside to get bathed and ready for bed.

As Sophie and Christian continued conversing, a cloud of dust in the northeast caught her attention. As the dust cloud got closer, she saw a wagon approach, slow down, and turn into the farm. When the wagon stopped, Sophie was pleasantly surprised to see Barney Weimber climb down, tie up the horses, and walk up to the porch.

"Good evening, Christian," Barney nodded to Christian, then turned his attention to Sophie. "Good evening, Madame Rieple. I was wondering if I might have a few words with you."

Sophie's heart skipped a beat. She never expected Barney to ask to speak to her; she assumed he was there to see Christian. "Of course, Mr. Weimber," she said after a moment's hesitation, smiling warmly. "I would be delighted to visit with you."

"Please, call me Barney. And if you do not mind, may I use your first name as well?"

"You may, Barney," she said, scooting over to make room on the step. "Please, sit down and make yourself comfortable."

"Actually, the sunset promises to be quite stunning; perhaps we could take a stroll down the lane and talk while we enjoy the view."

"As you wish. It is a beautiful scene."

As they walked, Barney talked about the rest of his family, their life back in Osnabruck, and his trip to America. He told Sophie about the farm he was working with his younger brother Rudolph, and about his older brother Franz and his family, who lived on the eastern edge of the county. He described how much he loved living and working in America but also spoke with candor about how lonely he'd been. "And you, Sophie, tell me more about you. I know the events surrounding your arrival in America were most unfortunate. I am so sorry."

Sophie felt none of the reticence or guardedness around Barney she had experienced around Philippe Delaroche. Instead, conversing with him was like talking to an old friend. She told him about her parents and siblings—especially her sister Mina—about Friedrich, about the horror of losing Marie Louise on the voyage to America, and how that horror had increased exponentially with Friedrich's and Sophie Elise's deaths the week they arrived in New Orleans. Tears welled in her eyes as she recounted those experiences, but she felt no need to hide them. She described in general terms her experiences working in the tobacco shop and her decision to leave and make her way to Havana. She, too, talked at length and with candor about how she wished for a home and family of her own once again.

"I find you beautiful, delightful, capable, and sincere, and those are just my first impressions, Sophie. I would like nothing better than to become better acquainted with you."

Sophie's heart fluttered with excitement. "Thank you for your kind words, Barney. I was most favorably impressed with you when I met you. I found it particularly comforting to see your kindness to Christian and Louise's children. I would like to get to know you better as well."

"With your permission, then, Sophie, I would like to call on you regularly, if you have no objections."

"I have no objections at all, Barney," she said, the barest hint of belonging settling in her soul. "You may call on me anytime."

They stopped at the end of the lane and stood for several moments taking in the view of the western sky. It was awash with vivid red-orange and yellow splashes of color highlighting swaths of deep purple rooster-tail clouds. After several moments of drinking in the spectacular beauty, Barney spoke.

"It will be dark in just a few moments, Sophie. We should make our way back to the house. May I?" Barney asked, offering his arm.

"Of course." Sophie offered Barney a dazzling smile and wrapped her left hand around his arm.

When they got to the house, Christian greeted them and invited Barney inside. "Louise made a delicious cherry pudding today. Please, come in and join us for dessert."

"With pleasure, Christian," Barney said. "Thank you for your hospitality."

Louise and Sophie busied themselves serving dessert and coffee while Barney and Christian chatted about the prospects for the wheat crop, which would soon be ready to harvest. When they were finished, Barney stood to leave. "Thank you again, Louise. The cherry pudding was delicious. And thank you to you as well, Christian. I have thoroughly enjoyed the evening, but now I need to get back home."

"Let me see you out," Sophie said, smiling at Barney as she rose from her chair.

"I had a most enjoyable evening, Sophie," Barney said as they walked out the back door. "I look forward to seeing you soon. It would be my honor to escort you to the Independence Day festivities next Thursday," Barney continued, a roguish smile on his face. "I believe then I will be able to offer you that dish of ice cream I owe you."

"It has been a most enjoyable evening for me as well, Barney. I will look forward—with great delight—both to seeing you again and to the ice cream." Sophie laughed. "I do have one request, though, on your return."

"If it is within my power, I will do it," Barney assured her.

"I noticed the pocket was torn on the shirt you were wearing on Thursday. Bring it with you next week, and I will mend it for you."

"You are beyond kind, Sophie. I will see you next Thursday, with the shirt."

"It is my pleasure. Please take care on your way back to your home, Barney."

"I shall, Sophie. Until Thursday." Barney nodded, then climbed into the wagon and made his way home.

They passed the remaining summer months spending as much time in one another's company as possible, attending all manner of social events together. When they were not in town at a gathering, Barney could be found at Christian and Louise's, he and Sophie on the porch or strolling the lane, deep in conversation. At the end of August, he formally asked for her hand in marriage, and plans were made for an October wedding.

31 August 1855

Dearest Mina,

I cannot begin to tell you how wonderful the past few weeks have been. Barney has been calling, and we have gotten to know one another well. He is a good man, and I am rejoicing in my good fortune of meeting him.

And tonight—oh, Mina, I'm so excited I can hardly hold onto my pen!—tonight he asked me to marry him! And I said yes!! But I was so torn! Part of me wanted to rush home immediately so I could write and tell you, but the other part of me wanted to stay in Barney's arms forever and never leave his side.

We will marry in October, and the only thing that could make me any happier than I am at this very moment would be for you to be here for the wedding. I know from what you said in your last letter traveling right now is impossible for you, and that breaks my heart, but at the same time, I am so happy and so much in love I cannot wait to become Barney's wife. You understand, I'm sure! You know me—and my impatience—better than anyone.

I will write again soon and tell you all about the wedding. Please promise me you will keep making plans to come and will be in America as soon as possible!

Your adoring and deliriously happy sister,

Sophie

On 16 October 1855, a glorious fall Tuesday, Barney and Sophie were joined in holy matrimony. It seemed all creation was rejoicing with them. The spectacular oranges, reds, and yellows of the fall leaves added to the festive nature of the day.

No one gave Sophie away; Barney met her at the front door of Louise and Christian's home, and they walked together to the hearth where they exchanged vows and rings in front of a small group of immediate family. For her wedding dress, Sophie chose the blue watered silk gown she had worn for her sister Mina's wedding. It seemed appropriate to wear a dress that held so many joyous memories on a day when her own dreams were coming true. And as was always the case when she had on that dress, Sophie looked—and felt—beautiful. Louise, Johanna, and Anna stood alongside Sophie, the girls clad in the beautiful new calico dresses Sophie had made for them that summer. Barney's brothers, Franz and Rudolph, stood with him as his witnesses.

Following the ceremony, Louise served a sumptuous luncheon. There was roast pork, baked potatoes, the last of the fresh tomatoes from the garden, sliced carrots, boiled and served with a butter and brown sugar glaze, and baskets piled high with freshly baked biscuits. Golden brown apple pie, served with a choice of sharp cheddar cheese or whipped cream, completed the meal. A variety of beverages were available to toast the bride and groom: beer, cider, milk, and coffee.

Chapter Twenty-Four

Barney and Sophie's relief at finding and falling in love with one another was palpable. For Barney, this was the culmination of everything he had wished for his entire life: a chance to make his own way in the world in the new land America, a beautiful wife to share his days with, and the prospect of a loving home filled with happy children.

For Sophie, it felt, quite literally, like resurrection: a new life rising from the ashes of the tragedy and death that had defined her former existence. While she was aware, and had been since that Mardi Gras encounter with Monsieur Philippe, of how achingly lonely her life was and how much she missed the deep conversations and companionship she had with Friedrich and the girls, she had not realized the extent to which those absences had colored her existence until Barney came into her life. The grim resolution that had kept her putting one foot in front of the other and never looking back faded.

And much to Barney's delight, their home did, in fact, quickly fill with children. Albert arrived just thirteen months after their marriage, in 1856. Charles was born two years later, in November of 1858. This was a particularly celebratory month for Sophie. Not only did she and Barney welcome another healthy baby into the world, she received word two weeks later that Mina and her family had arrived in New Orleans and would soon be on their way north.

From that moment until the afternoon when she finally wrapped her arms around her beloved sister once again, eager anticipation marked Sophie's days. She rose each morning wondering where Mina and Heinrich and the children might be on that particular day, how the trip was going, and how soon they might arrive. As she went about her own household tasks, she relished the thought of helping Mina unpack and get settled in her new home. As she sat in her rocking chair nursing baby Charles, she plotted and planned all the things she and Mina would once again be able to do together.

While she cooked breakfast one mid-December morning, Sophie talked at length about how quickly they could get to Peoria, where Mina's husband planned to open a cigar shop and where they would live.

"But are you sufficiently recovered enough to travel, Sophie?" Barney asked with concern. "Charles is just a few weeks old."

"There were no complications with Charles's birth," she reminded him. "And he is not a fussy baby—unless he is hungry. We have been apart so long; nothing is going to keep me from seeing my sister as soon as it is humanly possible."

"I understand how important this is to you and how eager you are to see your sister again. I also know how important you are to me, and I do not want anything to jeopardize your health and well-being."

"I know, my sweet." Sophie smiled and kissed Barney's cheek as she placed a platter of scrambled eggs and sausages on the table. "But do not worry. I am well, and the trip will be no problem for me to manage."

To her great delight, within a week, Sophie was rushing up the sidewalk to Mina's home in Peoria's First Ward and flinging herself into Mina's arms.

"Oh, my beloved Mina!" Sophie buried her head in Mina's shoulder, both laughing and crying with joy. "I have missed you so much!"

"I know, Sophie," Mina said, her own tears flowing freely. "I am sorry it took so long, but do not worry. I am here now."

"Yes. And you must promise me you will never leave!" Sophie said, hugging Mina even tighter.

"I will always be here for you, Sophie," Mina assured her. "Now, come in and let me show you the house."

While Heinrich and Barney toured the first floor and discussed Heinrich's plans for the cigar shop, Mina led Sophie and the children upstairs to their residence. Sophie introduced Albert to his cousins Maria and Carl and left them playing quietly in the parlor. With baby Charles sleeping in her arms, she and Mina walked from room to room, talking nonstop about anything and everything.

Now that Mina was here, Sophie was not sure life could be any better, but her joy—and Barney's—increased two years later with the birth of their only daughter Elizabeth Louise.

Life was full. Sophie had a bustling household of three small children to care for, and as the tenant on a large farm, Barney was busy from sunup to sundown every day. There were crops to plant, harvest, and market, livestock to tend, fences and machinery to repair, and bookkeeping and production records to maintain. Always diligent and efficient, Sophie made sure her household tasks were completed in as timely a manner as possible each day so that she was available to help Barney whenever necessary. The children learned from an early age how to tend the yard and garden, gather eggs, and help with the stabling and feeding of the livestock. They loved nothing better than to ride the horses with Papa when he was out working in the field.

With Barney's attention to detail, his desire to get ahead, and his strong German work ethic had come financial success, and there was no doubt Barney and Sophie loved farm life, but after their daughter's birth in the fall of 1860, he began growing restless. The one thing he did *not* like about the life they currently enjoyed was the fact that the land he worked so hard to make a living from was not under his ownership and direct control. He had an excellent relationship with the family he served as a tenant, but he had always dreamed of owning a farm of his own, and having children just increased that desire. Especially now that he had sons, it was important to him that there be something tangible to pass on to them when he and Sophie were gone. He said nothing to Sophie at the time, but when harvest was complete that winter and the daily workload wasn't quite as intense, he began looking around the county every time he had occasion to leave the farm to see if any parcels of land were available for purchase.

One such trip took him to the opposite side of Mason County from where he and Sophie lived. He had heard his older brother Franz talk about how different the soil was on the far eastern side of the county: dark, fertile, and loamy, perfect for field corn, soybeans, and wheat; not the pale, light soils around Havana better suited for vegetables and melons. It sounded good to Barney; so good he wanted to see it for himself. Telling Sophie only that he was going to Franz's, he made his way east to the farm his brother owned in Sherman Township. After visiting briefly with Franz's wife Wilhelmina, the brothers set out for the eastern edge of the county to look around.

Once you left Havana and headed away from the stretch of the Illinois River that formed the western border of Mason County, the land flattened out considerably. There were some hilly areas here and there, but nothing like the high river bluff the town of Havana sat on. Although the topography was slightly different, the soil on Franz's farm was virtually the same type as the soil near Topeka where Barney farmed. But as they continued east, things changed markedly in a very short distance. He had thought perhaps Franz had exaggerated just a bit about the land on this side of the county—it did not seem possible that it could be that different from the land Barney and Rudolph farmed—but Barney now saw for himself how accurate Franz's description was.

Anywhere there was bare dirt, it was black and rich, not the light sandy soil Barney was accustomed to. The ground cover was of a completely different variety and much taller than what lined the roads and fencerows on the western side of the county. Barney was used to seeing things like spiderwort, porcupine grass, dwarf dandelions in various colors, and the ever-present prickly pear cactus. Once you crossed from the sand prairie that covers most of Mason County to the heavy soils on the eastern edge, those plants gave way to lush prairie grasses: foxtail, brome, sedges, fescues, Johnson grass, and big and little Bluestem. Fields of corn, bean, and wheat stubble stretched out in every direction, interspersed with pastures, orchards, and

well-ordered farmsteads surrounded by protective wind-
breaks of pine, oak, elm, maple, and hedge. The sheer
volume of stalks and stubble remaining in the fields indicated that the previous growing season had produced a bumper
crop. The change was stunning, and Barney marveled to
himself as they rode along, imagining what this side of the
county must look like in the spring when the wildflowers
were all in bloom, in the summer when growing crops filled
the fields, and in the fall when the timber was a riot of red,
yellow, and orange. He thought wistfully of Sophie, hoping
that one day soon she would be able to see it for herself,
from her very own front porch.

As they traveled, Franz noted the family names associated with each of the farmsteads they passed. Continuing
east across Prairie Creek into Logan County, they looked
around briefly before turning back toward Franz and
Wilhelmina's home.

"This is amazing country, Franz," Barney said. "I love
the look of this land, and if any of it comes up for sale, I am
definitely interested in buying. If you happen to hear that
there are parcels available, you will let me know, won't you?"

"I will, Barney. There are people moving in and out
of the area all the time, and with the way the country has
continued to expand to the west, I do not think that will
change any time soon. I will keep my eyes and ears open."

"Thank you, brother! This has been a most enjoyable afternoon. Give Wilhelmina and the children my best; I will be looking forward to hearing from you soon."

"My pleasure, Barney. Give our best to Sophie and the little ones. I will let you know if I hear anything about land sales."

Barney turned toward home. The sun was slanting lower and lower in the western sky, and soon everything would be wrapped in shadow. He quickened his pace, hoping to arrive home before it became completely dark; Sophie would be worried if he were not back by then. As he rode, he mulled whether or not to discuss with her the real reason for making the trip to Franz's that afternoon. It was not his practice to keep things from her; since they shared the workload for maintaining the farm and the household, he was of the opinion that they should share the decision-making as well. But he was also fiercely protective of the woman he loved as much as life itself, and the last thing he wanted to do was cause her undue worry and concern.

The news out of the east these days, and even in their own state, was filled with political unrest and angry rhetoric. The issue of slavery was threatening to tear the country apart, with some so passionate they vowed to defend their point of view with their own blood, if necessary. As much as he hated to admit it, war looked more and more likely all the time. Barney had no idea exactly what that would mean for them, living in a free state, but he'd seen and heard enough to know firsthand that everybody suffered during wars, and there would likely be hard times ahead. This may be the worst time to purchase land. And yet, he could not stop thinking about how much it would mean to him to finally own a farm of his own. Just as the sun slipped below the western horizon, he pulled into the lane. He poked his head in the back door and greeted Sophie.

"I am home, my sweet. I need to take care of the horse and wagon, and then I will be in for supper."

"I am so glad you are back, Barney!" Sophie sighed with relief. "Everything will be ready by the time you get back inside."

Barney left the delicious aromas wafting from the kitchen and led the horse to the barn. He removed the mare's harness, brushed her down, then blanketed and fed her. He checked the rest of the stock, then made his way back to the house. After hanging up his coat on one of the pegs at the back door and washing his face and hands, he took his place at the head of the table while Sophie brought bowls and platters of food. There was a plump, golden-brown chicken on a bed of roasted potatoes and carrots, fried green tomatoes from the last of the garden, freshly baked bread, and apple strudel for dessert.

Sophie filled Barney's plate and served him, then filled plates for the boys and settled them in their seats. After filling her own plate, she turned her attention to her husband.

"So, Barney, tell me about your afternoon. How are Franz and Wilhelmina and the children? All well, I hope. And how were the crops on that side of the county? I hope Franz had a good year."

"It is amazing, Sophie. The farther east you go, the richer the land becomes. From everything I saw, it was a very good year indeed for the farmers on that side of the county. One of these days, I will have to take you over there to see it. Franz and Wilhelmina are well, as are the children. They send their best. We should make plans to visit soon. The children would enjoy playing together." Franz and Wilhelmina had a large family; there were already seven cousins for Albert and Charles to play with.

"I am glad to hear they are well. It would be interesting to see what things are like on the other side of the county, and I always enjoy visiting with Wilhelmina. You are right; we should visit soon."

While Sophie cleared the table, did the dishes, and straightened the kitchen, Barney settled himself in the parlor with the children. With baby Elizabeth nestled in the crook of his arm and Albert and Charles sitting on either side of him on the settee, he adjusted the oil lamp and began reading. Both he and Sophie believed that learning and education were of utmost importance, and regaling their children with stories and tales—especially those from other times and other lands—had become a regular part of their family life. Just as she had done with Sophie Elise and Marie Louise, Sophie often told fairy tales from her childhood in Prussia. The story Barney was reading that evening was from Nathaniel Hawthorne's *Tanglewood Tales*, a favorite of Albert's. When she was done in the kitchen, Sophie joined them, taking the baby and settling herself in the rocker. She enjoyed hearing Barney read the stories every bit as much as the boys did. When the tale ended, they set about readying the children for bed, Sophie taking Elizabeth to change her diaper and Barney helping the boys get dressed in their nightclothes and turning down their beds.

"Run and tell Mama and your sister goodnight, and then it is off to bed for you two!" he laughed.

"Goodnight, Mama; goodnight, Lizzie," Albert dutifully replied.

"Night, Mommy! Night, Wizzie!" Charles echoed, as only exuberant two-year-olds can. Sophie had begun using the nickname "Lizzie" for her baby girl because she thought it would be easier for the boys to pronounce than "Elizabeth Louise." Unfortunately, even that proved to be a challenge to enunciate for Charles, but the nickname stuck.

"Goodnight, my sweet boys," she said, kissing each one of them on the cheek. "Go with Papa now, and he will tuck you in. Mama will see you in the morning."

As the boys raced off to bed, she turned her attention to Elizabeth Louise. She never tired of the vision of her beautiful babies snuggled at her breast, the cooing sounds they made, or the physical sensations that coursed through her as she nursed them. She loved feeling their soft baby skin next to her own, and if it was close to feeding time, often just hearing her babies cry or picking them up caused her breasts to tingle and throb in the most exquisitely pleasurable way. The act of nursing itself left Sophie with a level of satisfaction and fulfillment that she could not put into words. She settled into the rocker and unbuttoned her dress, carefully positioning her daughter at a comfortable angle. She leaned her head back and closed her eyes, sighing contentedly as she felt the sweet pull of Lizzie's mouth rhythmically tugging on her nipple. As she rocked, she idly stroked Lizzie's tiny, perfectly formed hands and smoothed her hair. *Does every woman feel this way?* she wondered. *Or am I just one of the lucky ones?*

Looking up, she saw Barney standing in the doorway, a tender look of love on his face and tears shining in his clear blue eyes.

"You are the most beautiful creature in the world, Sophie," he whispered. "At times I find it difficult to believe that you are mine. I cannot tell you what a vision of loveliness it is to see you in that chair cradling our beautiful baby girl in your arms!"

"Oh, Barney, my sweet! You are too kind. But I love you for saying so, and I must admit that it fills me with joy to care for our babies. Lizzie will be asleep soon, and then you and I can talk more about your day and what you saw as you traveled back and forth to Franz's."

Barney settled himself on the settee with a book while Sophie finished feeding the baby and tucked her into her bassinet. She checked on the boys, then rejoined Barney in the parlor. She was torn between wanting to bury her face in his chest and feel his strong arms around her and the desire to look into his eyes and study his facial expressions as they conversed.

Barney was torn as well. He'd been debating for most of the day how much he should tell her about his trips around the county, not sure which was more important: keeping her involved in all of the decisions that affected their lives together or keeping her from worry. In the end, bewitched by her beauty and caught up in how very much he loved her, he told her everything. The real reason for the trip to Franz's that afternoon, and all the thoughts and feelings behind it.

"I know you want to know all about my trip to see Franz and Wilhelmina this afternoon, Sophie, and I apologize if you wind up feeling I misled you, but I must confess I did not drive over there just to visit. I did converse with them, in fact Franz and I spent the entire afternoon talking together, but seeing them was not the point of the trip. The real reason was to look at the farmland on the other side of the county. And I went particularly looking to see if any of it happened to be for sale. I was not sure how much to tell you, or when, but you may as well know the whole story. Since harvest, every time I have had occasion to travel anywhere, I have taken time to look around hoping to find a farm to buy. I am tired of not being the one to make the decisions about the land I work so hard to make productive.

"You have given me beautiful babies, Sophie—sons!—and I want to be able to pass the land I tend so carefully on to them. But I am also aware of the growing unrest in the country these days and how damaging a war would be to the economy and our livelihood. I became well acquainted with that in Osnabruck, and I know you lived through the same thing in Rheda. Illinois is a free state, so perhaps there would be no fighting here, but there is no way to be sure of that. Nor is there any reason to assume we would escape the other negative effects of war should one happen to start. This may not be the best time to risk buying land. In fact, it may be the very worst time to do so. Part of me did not want to tell you what I was considering for fear it would cause you no end of worry and concern, but you are the entire world to me, Sophie, and I cannot keep anything from you."

"Ah, Barney!" She could see the love in his eyes, as well as the concern. She stroked his face, hoping to ease his furrowed brow. "You have always put my welfare and that of the children first, and I know you would never allow anything to cause us harm if it were within your power to prevent it. I appreciate you wanting to spare me from worry, and I do not think ill of you for not mentioning the real reason for traveling to Franz's, but you were right to tell me. I saw enough of what war can do to the countryside and those who live in it when I was growing up, and I have experienced more than my share of personal tragedy and loss since I left the continent and made the journey to America. I know you want only the best for us, and are working for that, but I also know that we do not always get to choose every event on the path our lives take. We can, however, choose how we navigate that path. Above all else, I have learned that even in the face of tragedy and in its aftermath, life goes on. I love you, Barney, and I trust you. If you are asking my permission to purchase a farm, you have it, and whatever befalls us, we will face together."

"I am so fortunate to have found you, Sophie!" Barney grasped her hands in each of his and covered them with kisses. "You have enriched my life beyond measure. I cannot tell you how much joy your understanding and devotion bring to my heart and life. Franz promised to let me know if there was any land for sale on that side of the county. With any luck, we will find something soon."

They talked on into the evening about hopes and dreams, finances and priorities, the families they came from, and the family they shared.

"You mentioned visiting Franz and Wilhelmina soon so the children could play, Barney. I agree; that is something we should do. But Christmas is coming as well; we should start making plans to celebrate the holiday. Now that Christian and Louise have moved to Sangamon County, there are just you, Franz, and Rudolph on your side, and Mina and I on my side. We should see if it would be possible to share Christmas dinner together."

Mina! It always warmed Sophie's heart to think of her sister and (outside of Barney) her closest confidant. She recalled their last face-to-face conversation the night before she and Friedrich left Rheda. Sophie was an emotional wreck that evening, reduced to tears over the prospect of leaving the one person in her life she could tell absolutely anything. Mina had suggested at the time that if things were in fact good in America, she and Heinrich might make the trip as well. In the fall of 1858, they boarded the ship *Ernestine* with their daughter Marie and son Wilhelm Carl, arriving in New Orleans in November. They made their way north to Peoria, where Heinrich found a location on South Washington Street just a few blocks from the RheinPfalz Hotel that could both serve as their home and accommodate his cigar business. Sophie and Barney had made the forty-five-mile trip north to Peoria to help them get settled, with Sophie and Mina unpacking and getting the residence in order while Barney helped Heinrich ready the cigar shop. Reunited at last, it was a glorious Christmas that year! Filled with happy memories of that day and joyful anticipation of this year's celebration, Sophie could not wait for Christmas to come.

Barney wrapped his arms around her and held her close, stroking and kissing her hair. "That is a wonderful idea, my sweet. I know you are anxious to see your sister again. I will inquire of Franz and Rudolph; you write to Mina and see if they can bring the children and come down from Peoria on Christmas Eve. It will be good to see everyone, and I know the children will enjoy having a house full of playmates."

The Christmas celebration was everything she had hoped for and more. Sophie cooked and baked for days. On Christmas Eve morning, after finishing chores, Barney trekked out to the timber north of the house and found a small thickly-branched evergreen and cut it down. He fashioned a wooden stand for it and brought it in the house shortly before everyone arrived. The children busied themselves decorating it with strings of popcorn, colorful pheasant feathers the boys had found, and bits of ribbon and lace from Sophie's sewing basket. There were sweets and treats at every turn, conversations buzzed in every room, and the air was filled with music and the laughter of frolicking children. After dinner, each child received a stocking stuffed with apples, nuts, and a pair of warm hand-knit woolen gloves. For Sophie, it was the best day of the year.

Chapter Twenty-Five

After their joyous holiday celebration, Barney and Sophie began 1861 full of optimism and hope, but that soon gave way to grave concern. Following the election of Abraham Lincoln as president in November of 1860 came a cascade of secessions from the Union by southern states, which continued throughout the following spring. Rumors of Civil War became louder by the day, tensions continued to escalate, and the fighting began in earnest with the attack on Fort Sumter in Charleston, South Carolina, in the early morning hours of April 12. While there was insistence on both sides that the conflict would be short-lived, Barney was not convinced. His own experience back in Saxony had taught him that it was easy enough to start a war—one misplaced or ill-spoken comment was often all it took—but much more difficult to end one.

Against a backdrop of uncertainty, yet committed to securing a tangible inheritance for their children's future, Barney and Sophie continued searching for a farm. Newspapers were scoured weekly, both for news of the war and advertisements of land for sale. A few parcels sold near where they were living, but Barney had his heart set on owning some of the rich, black land on the eastern edge of the county, so they waited, hoping against hope they would find land, and that making such a significant purchase at this particular point in time would not be a colossal mistake.

Late that fall, Franz sent word that there was an eighty-acre farmstead for sale in Logan County, just across the county line from where he and Barney had looked at land the previous year. On a gray and bitterly cold December day, Barney and Sophie drove to Franz and Wilhelmina's. They had graciously agreed to keep an eye on the children while Barney and Sophie toured the farm and talked with the seller. Pleased at what they'd found, they negotiated a price and planned to finalize the sale just after the first of the year.

Life in the early days of 1862 turned out to be doubly joyful. Not only did they now have a farm of their own, Sophie soon discovered she was pregnant again. But trying to get ready for the move with three very active children (and a fourth on the way) was exhausting for her. It took a herculean effort by all of them—including Franz and

Wilhelmina, Rudolph, and Mina and Heinrich—to get packed up and moved in time for Barney to begin spring planting.

By March of 1862, they were at home in Prairie Creek Township in Logan County, Illinois. After getting the crops in, Barney set about getting the rest of the farmstead in order while Sophie organized the house, planted her vegetable garden, and crafted blankets, gowns, and diapers for the baby.

Mina returned in August a few days after baby Henry was born, with Marie and Wilhelm Carl in tow. Up until then, every day had been a blur of activity; there was always more to do than Sophie could get done, and with all the extra tasks involved in establishing their own farm plus the upcoming arrival of a new baby, each new day brought an avalanche of activity. But now, with the household running smoothly under Mina's watchful eye, Sophie had the opportunity to get some much-needed rest. She adored her children and reveled in motherhood, and yet now, without the endless round of household tasks and the constant demands of caring for her three older children to occupy her mind, instead of the joyful contentment she'd experienced when her other children were newborns, she found herself uncharacteristically consumed with worry about the future of her family, and the future of the country. Just a few months earlier, the war department had issued orders for a military census for all men between the ages of eighteen and forty-five in order to supply soldiers for the Union army, and with battles raging from Arizona to Virginia, her concern that Barney would be called to serve mounted with each passing day.

Gathering up baby Henry for his afternoon feeding, Sophie settled herself and her newborn son in the rocker. The possibility of losing Barney and concerns over the future of her growing family weighed heavily on her mind, which in turn led to thoughts of her mother.

Ah, Mama! I am so worried these days. Is this what it was like for you when we were all little ones at home? Did you fear daily for your family's future as I do? I do not remember ever seeing you overcome with worry, but you had to have been more than a little concerned. Papa was too old to join the army by then, but I am sure you must have worried about the boys. Just like I am worried for mine. When the war started last April, everyone insisted it would all be over soon—in a matter of weeks, or a few months at most. Yet here it is more than a year later, and the fighting just keeps dragging on with no end in sight. How many more years can this go on? And will there be anything left of the country when the battles finally stop?

I try not to dwell on it, Mama, but I cannot help myself. I do not know what I will do if Barney must leave and join the army. How will I manage taking care of the farm and my babies on my own? And what will I do if he goes off to fight in this war and does not come back home? I have already lost one family; I do not want to go through that ever again. I know I should not worry so. I have survived tragedy before; I likely will again. But I do not even want to think of a world without Barney. And the longer the fighting goes on, the more afraid I am of how very hard times might get.

There had been battles in Missouri—just one state away. *Could we see fighting here too? And if we do, will that or the blockade make it impossible to market our crops? How will we pay for the farm then? This place is Eden for Barney. All he ever wanted, the fulfillment of a lifetime of hopes and dreams. I do not think he could bear it if we lost the farm.* She had seen that before, too. She had watched Friedrich become crushed under the weight of the decisions he made and the circumstances that resulted from those decisions. Sophie did not think she could face that again either. *I know what you would tell me. You would tell me to choose life, and remind me that somehow, some way, everything will be all right. Your fierce optimism defined your existence, and everyone who knew you saw it. But it is, oh, so hard to choose life when the future looks so frightening!*

Tears streamed down Sophie's face, splashing on baby Henry's perfectly formed hands as he nursed.

"Sophie! What is wrong? Is something the matter with the baby?" Mina said, hurrying through the door to Sophie.

"No, Mina," Sophie sighed. "I am sorry if my tears frightened you. Henry is fine. I let my thoughts wander, and I should not have. But these times are so uncertain! I do not think I could stand it if something happened to

Barney, and I do not think he could stand it if we wound up losing the farm because of the war. I must work harder to be like Mama and not worry so much."

"You know what she would tell you if she were here: 'Everything will be all right, Sophie. Somehow, some way, everything will be all right.'"

"I know, Mina. And I was able to embrace that after I lost Marie Louise, but it gets harder each time. After losing Friedrich and Sophie Elise, I was not sure I would ever find joy again. But I have my life back now. I have a husband who adores me; we have four beautiful children, and a farm of our own. I cannot bear the thought of losing it all again. I will try my best not to worry, I promise. And you must promise as well: do not breathe a word of this to Barney. He is working so hard to get the farm established. I do not want him distracted with worries about my well-being or thinking that I am unhappy."

"I promise, Sophie. I will not say a word. Here, dry your eyes. I will take baby Henry and get him settled in his cradle, and then you and I will talk about happier things."

"Oh, Mina! I am so fortunate you are here! I do not deserve such love, but I am so grateful to have it."

Busy raising their family and improving their farmstead, time passed quickly for Sophie and Barney. The Civil War ground on and casualty lists became longer and longer, but to Sophie's great relief, Barney had not been called for service. Her concern did not disappear completely; at forty-three, he was still within the age range of the draft, but she was not as consumed with worry as she had been earlier. They filled their days with housework, farm tasks, and the rearing of their children. Stories were read or told each evening, and special care was taken to ensure that Albert's school work was in order for the next day. Sophie did her best to mark each day with optimism and hope, to choose life in every circumstance, and to live and work for the future. It was not always easy, and the next two years proved to be the most challenging yet.

Eighteen sixty-five should have been a year of joy and celebration. In early spring, Sophie and Barney were blessed with yet another beautiful baby boy, Friedrich Bernhard, known to everyone as simply "Fred." And after four long years, hundreds of thousands of lives lost, and a depth of physical and emotional devastation that defied description, the Civil War finally ended. Although the last Confederate General would not formally surrender until June 2, 1865, it was clear after the fall of Richmond and General Robert E. Lee's surrender at Appomattox in April that the conflict would soon be over. Yet the country remained in turmoil and grief, still deeply divided, and still reeling from the assassination of President Lincoln on April 14, 1865.

The economic and political uncertainty continued to nag at Sophie, despite her determination to choose life and not give in to despair. Yet that was not what concerned her most these days. What had her nearly frantic with worry was the fact that she was once again facing the specter of an ailing child. Until they contracted cholera, both Sophie Elise and Marie Louise had been healthy, robust children. The same was true for Albert, Charles, Elizabeth Louise, and Henry. They had occasional colds, bouts of fever, or stomach upsets, but always recovered quickly.

Baby Fred had seemed well enough the first few days after his birth, but that soon changed, and by the end of his first month of life, it was clear he was not growing as quickly as her other babies had. He fussed often, had difficulty eating and sleeping, and spent most of each day in a malaise that Sophie did not understand and could find no solution for.

She was consumed with thoughts from the past, reliving over and over again those dark days of her sister Catharine's illness and death, the death, just sixteen months later, of baby brother Friedrich Georg, and the loss of the beloved daughters she and Friedrich had cherished so. The thought of baby Fred enduring the same fate was becoming more than she could bear. Barney and the other children did everything they could to help; regular trips were made to Mason City to see the local physician, Dr. Walker, a skilled diagnostician and surgeon, and yet no remedy undertaken brought relief for very long, either for baby Fred or for Sophie.

After another fruitless trip to see Dr. Walker, Barney stabled the horses and came into the house to find Sophie standing by Fred's bed, tearful and shaking. "I am so, so sorry," he said, pulling her close. "It is agonizing to watch our baby boy suffer so. And I know the anguish is doubly difficult for you because you have been through this before and never wanted to see it again. I wish we could find something that would help. I know you are heartbroken. It is breaking my heart as well."

Sophie buried her face in Barney's chest and sobbed. She tried not to cry in front of the children—she vividly remembered how distressing it was to her to see her mother weep over Catharine and Friedrich Georg—but as Fred continued to suffer, her mental and physical exhaustion deepened, and her grief was closer and closer to the surface. Her only saving grace was the fact that while she was once again suffering a mother's worst nightmare, this time she was not alone. Her weeping finally subsided, and Sophie found herself calmer than she had felt in days.

"Ah, Barney! I love you so much, and I do not know what I would do without you. You have done everything you can to take care of Fred, and of me. I know you are just as worried and heartbroken as I am. I am so grateful you are here with me. We will just have to keep doing the best we can to take care of our baby boy and see what happens."

So passed the days. The economic and political climate gradually improved as the months went by, and with Barney's hard work and the help of Sophie and the children, the farm did well, but Fred did not. After a round of spring colds from which the other children recovered without incident,

Fred was stricken with pneumonia, and breathed his last in Sophie's arms in March of 1867, just days before his second birthday.

While not unexpected, Fred's death was as emotionally devastating to Sophie as the previous losses she'd endured. Even though, for many reasons, they had not regularly attended worship and were not at that time regular attenders of any of the local congregations, she was adamant a proper church funeral be held for young Fred. At the same time, she found herself apprehensive about what the pastor would say when he came to their home to meet with them. The German Methodist Episcopal church in their neighborhood had formally organized mere weeks before Fred's death. While most of their neighbors worshipped there, with Fred to care for, Sophie and Barney had not been able to attend and had not yet met the pastor. Even more concerning to Sophie were flashbacks of the platitudes and clichés she found so distasteful when Catharine died.

I do not want to hear about Original Sin, or God's plan. What kind of God plans to inflict suffering without end on innocent little ones and snatch them away from their parents when they are but mere infants? I do not want to hear that my baby boy is in a "better place" when he should still be here with me. I do not want to hear that things "happen for a reason." I said it when Catharine died, and I still mean every word of it: I cannot think of a single good reason for something like this to happen to anyone. And I most assuredly do not want to be told that I should be thankful because Fred is "not suffering anymore." He should never have suffered like he did in the first place.

As the hour of the pastor's visit approached, she tidied the parlor and set out cups and plates. Steeling herself for the worst, she prayed she would be able to hold her tongue and be more gracious to this man of God than she had been to Pastor Schilling.

In the end, she needn't have worried. Pastor Koeneke was the very soul of compassion. The service was planned around the great love and grace God offers all human creatures, particularly those who are weak and suffering. While there were assurances that Fred was now a child of the Resurrection, safely at home with God, there were no platitudes, clichés, or trite explanations, just words of faith and hope from God's Holy Word. And rather than placating or sidestepping Sophie and Barney's very real grief, great pains were taken to acknowledge the deep sorrow they bore, while assuring them that God wept with them, and sought their comfort.

The entire community turned out to mourn little Fred, filling the one-room schoolhouse in which the church held worship despite the fact that it was a glorious spring day and by all rights, the men should have been out sowing oats and preparing to plant corn. When the service was over and Fred's small body had been carefully laid to rest, Sophie thanked Pastor Koeneke.

"You have been most kind and gracious, pastor. Your words were honest, and yet also comforting. It has been a long time since I regularly attended church, and I was not sure I would ever do so again, but I think perhaps I could worship in the congregation you are serving."

"I am honored to be of service, Mrs. Weimber. And God would be greatly glorified and pleased by your attendance at worship. I look forward to seeing you and your family soon. Sunday Worship begins at nine a.m."

True to her word, Sophie and her family came to worship the very next Sunday, and soon publicly professed faith in Christ and became members of the church. Her faith had come full circle, and she was able, once again, to lay down the burdens of worry and concern she had carried for so many months and live life joyfully and with hope.

She and Barney watched with joy as their remaining children grew to adulthood and became productive citizens in the community. Before her death in November of 1896, Sophie was blessed to be present for the marriages of her sons Albert and Charles and her daughter Elizabeth Louise, and to welcome eight grandchildren into the world. Her son Henry did not marry, instead seeing to the care of Sophie and Barney and the management of the farm they had built over the years, which had grown to two hundred and forty acres.

Epilogue

harlotte Sophia Weimber's earthly sojourn ended in November of 1896, her baptism completed in her death. As her obituary noted, at the point of her conversion, she "immediately united with the German Methodist Episcopal Church in this place and remained an honored member until her death. Sister Weimber was an unassuming, thoughtful, conscientious Christian, and was always faithful in attendance on the means of grace and faithful in the relations of wife and mother and as a follower of Christ . . . She was held in highest esteem by all who knew her and was always ready for any and every good work . . ."

All of those things are true, Barney mused, as he sat, alone, in his chair in the parlor the evening of the funeral, after everyone had gone home. *But there was—there is—so much more to her, and to our life together.*

I understand now—at a level I previously had no comprehension of—the depth of her grief when she lost her beloved Friedrich. I have now experienced that type of devastating loss myself.

There are no words that can contain that sorrow, no words that can accurately describe that pain, except to say that the light has gone out of my life.

I will be forever grateful she was willing to take a chance on finding love once again when she met me, and that we had so many happy years together. The tragedies she endured were so painful; she could easily have resolved to never put herself in that position again. She could have looked at me—unmarried, at age thirty-four—and surmised I must have some deep and abiding character flaw that made others keep their distance, and chosen to avoid me as well.

She did not. She welcomed me into her heart, showered me with affection and care, and made mine a life richer and more blessed than I could ever have imagined. I despaired often, when I first settled here, of finding someone to share my life with. And yet, as her mother Margarethe forever insisted, somehow, some way, things did indeed turn out all right for us.

I also have deep gratitude for the beautiful family we were blessed with. Our children—our grace and glory—learned the value of industry and hard work from me, and resilience, determination, and trust in the face of adversity from Sophie. I also see in each one of them—in various ways—glimpses of her intelligence and her stunning creativity.

From the old country to the new, from nothing to everything, we have been blessed with grace upon grace.

Rest in peace, sweet Sophie.

Author's Afterword

ophie is a work of fiction. While real people, places, and historical events are referenced, they are woven into a tale that is my own creation, along with people, events, and conversations that are purely fictional.

The inspiration for this book, however, is rooted in reality, in the life of my late husband's great-great-grandmother.

She was born in Prussia in 1824 and married in 1851. In 1854, she and her family sailed to America. She lost one child on the voyage, and shortly after arriving in New Orleans, her husband and remaining child died.

She arrived in the Midwest alone and grief-stricken but found love and married again in 1855. She and her second husband had five children, four of whom lived to adulthood.

Her faith, her grit, her determination, and her courage in the face of adversity live on in the lives of her descendants. Some of her material possessions survive as well, including the brass candlestick and samovar shown on the cover and referenced in chapter six. The candlestick sits on my piano, and the samovar holds a place of honor in the home of another of Sophie's great-great grandchildren.

Kathy Swaar Bio

A writer, blogger, retired pastor and adjunct professor, Kathy Swaar is the author of *Fine Lines: Walking the Labyrinth of Grief and Loss*. CEO of her family's Midwestern US farm corporation, Kathy makes her home in Central Illinois.

When not writing or tending farm business, she can be found reading, watching sports and cooking shows, digging up dead relatives—indulging her genealogy hobby—sewing, and collecting cookbooks and antique glassware.

Kathy writes in multiple genres. To find out more about her latest project and read her blog, visit her website www.kathyswaar.com. You can also connect with her on Facebook at www.facebook.com/KathySwaarAuthor and on Instagram at @kathy_swaar.